D-Day – They are coming.

Tom Zola

Panzers Push for Victory

D-DAY: THEY ARE COMING!

Tom Zola, a former sergeant in the German Army, is a military fiction writer, famous for his intense battle descriptions and realistic action scenes. In 2014, the first book of his PANZERS series was released in German, setting up an alternate history scenario in which a different German Reich tries to turn around the fortunes of war at the pinnacle of the Second World War. Zola doesn't beat around the bush; his stories involve brutal fighting, inhuman ideologies, and a military machine that overruns Europe and the whole world without mercy. He has developed a breathtaking yet shocking alternate timeline that has finally been translated into English.

Zola, born in 1988, is married and lives with his wife and two kids in Duisburg, Germany.

Berlin, German Reich, November 4th, 1943

There was a knock at the large double door leading into the office of the Reich Chancellor. Von Witzleben's adjutant, a young officer, entered. The Chancellor had almost closed his eyes. Now he kept them open with all his might to avoid dozing off in the presence of his subordinate. Von Witzleben was very exhausted.

"Herr Reichskanzler, Generalfeldmarschall Rommel has arrived and requests permission to enter," the adjutant reported.

"Send him in."

"Jawohl."

The young officer disappeared behind the door. Field Marshal Erwin Rommel, however, turned up. With swift steps, he marched towards the chancellor, his boots clacking on the floorboards. As usual, Rommel's uniform was meticulously correct and his body was tight and under tension. Rommel stopped halfway in the room and saluted snappily.

"Herr Reichskanzler, Feldmarschall Rommel reporting as ordered!" he announced loudly. Rommel was a man who attached great importance to military formalities.

Von Witzleben smiled weakly and got up from his chair. He was too tired to salute; instead he stepped out from behind his desk, walked towards Rommel and held out his hand. Finally he led Rommel over to a table, offered him a seat and ordered coffee, water and cake from his adjutant.

"Thanks for leaving so early," von Witzleben started the conversation.

"Nevertheless, I am concerned that I am going to leave the Balkan theater without having achieved anything," was the reply. "Our efforts to defend the Balkans must be further intensified, because even if the enemy has opted for Italy and France for the time being, the Balkans remains a worthwhile target. And of course, the partisans..."

"But the focus is not on Italy and not on the Balkans – neither from us nor from the enemy. We must turn our attention to France."

"True. Time is pressing and there is much to do," Rommel remarked in his Swabian dialect.

"No doubt. They'll come next spring." Von Witzleben's eyes became glassy. "My God," he whispered, "everything's on a knife edge."

Rommel nodded with a serious expression. Von Witzleben rallied and continued, "We must not let them get boots on the ground again."

Rommel vehemently agreed with this statement. Von Witzleben leaned back in his armchair before proclaiming: "I will have the commission signed and handed out today. This makes it official: You are the Commander-in-Chief France-Benelux. I congratulate you from the bottom of my heart on your new assignment. The Wehrmacht couldn't have found a better man for this assignment."

"Thank you. However, the best leader is useless without resources. But what is currently in France, with the exception of some divisions, is a catastrophe. All I have there are East-Battalions and units of old men and reservists. Erwin, I need real soldiers, if I'm going to stop this invasion!"

The troops of the Wehrmacht in Norway, Denmark and other "pacified" regions were also more thinned out these days than Hitler would ever have allowed. Under von Witzleben everything had been transferred to the Eastern Front, true to the motto: "If you defend everything, you defend nothing!" In the meantime, however, the long duration of the war was becoming apparent. There was a shortage of... just about everything, not only on the sideline theaters, but everywhere. In Italy, massive forces were needed to keep the Allies in check. And in France, the current defense forces were in a miserable state.

"Don't worry about that, my old friend," von Witzleben said. He was aware of the strait situation – and had not remained inactive. "That old daredevil von Manstein has an idea how we can release enough troops for France," he explained in a serious voice.

5

Dearest Elly,

things have changed since my last letter. Life in France is good, and our regiment is almost back on track. We have a lot of new comrades now -- also many recruits, but they are all exellently decent people. Only the new commander is... well... exhausting. But that will develop! Anyway, we enjoy the French autumn, which we face with brilliant weather. Oh, my Ellie. If only you were here. You and Gudrun! That's all I need to be happy here! I miss you very much and it hurts me that I have to be so far away. We'll have a lot to catch up on when all of this is over!

At least we'll get new tanks soon. My whole platoon will be re-equipped, and then we will finally be rid of those Panzers III, with which you won't get anywhere these days. Don't worry, then I'll be sufficiently protected, if the Yank should arrive some day! I don't know exactly which tank we'll get, the commander just grinned at my question. So it could be something big! You can imagine my men are looking forward to it like little children. Most of them are quite enthusiastic about technology and can be lured with the big equipment anyway! I, however, would leave the tank immediately, if I could go home to you! But I can't -- not yet! But look, Elly, please don't be sad. Look how well they we doing in the East lately and how much Feldmarschall von Manstein has stabilized the front. I believe Russia will soon enter into peace negotiations. Or we'll manage to convince the Americans that the real danger lies in the East after all. Either way, we're in a better position than people think.

However, I still have a big surprise for you: I can go home for three weeks, soon! December or January, more details to follow! But basically it's approved. That makes me so incredibly happy at the moment and that is my next big goal, which I can look forward to every day. Soon we will see each other again! Give Gudrun a thousand kisses from

me. And let her give you a thousand. I love you!
Your Sepp

Houlle, France, November 8th, 1943

"They can't be serious, can they?" Münster, who was promoted to the rank of Staff Sergeant, tilted his head and bit his lower lip.

"That's not a tank, that's a monstrosity."

Nitz whistled through his teeth and crossed his arms. Ludwig and Jahnke seemed to be completely aghast.

"This... this can't be true. They want to take us for a ride," Jahnke stammered.

Sergeant Gottlieb Stendal, an emigrant from South Tyrol, which one could clearly hear when he spoke, remained silent. He was one of the new guys. Lieutenant Engelmann, who frowned at the sight of the five steel monsters and was not sure what to think about them, had made Stendal his radio operator. Nitz, on the other hand, who was promoted to master sergeant, was assigned commander of the second platoon tank. Engelmann would have liked to keep him in his tank, for there was no one better, but the lieutenant had to restructure to keep the platoon ready for action: The last men of the old school who were fit for combat and had been with the platoon since Kursk were Münster, Nitz and Ludwig. Some of the crew members of Meinert's and Meyer's tanks had also survived, but they were still in the military hospital and would not return soon. After the Battle of Kursk, the subsequent defensive successes in the Belgorod area and the counter-offensive against Tula, the 16th Panzer Division had been reformed. In return, the provisionally formed Kampfgruppe Sieckenius no longer existed.

In the late summer of 1943, the 16th Panzer Division had finally been transferred to France, where the top priority was to recover its forces. Apart from a handful of experienced veterans of Russia and Africa, Meier, commander of the III Abteilung, had mostly assigned young recruits, who were still wet behind the ears, to the 9th company. Since the end of July, young soldiers, who had just finished their basic training, had been coming into the unit one by one. The required strength still hadn't been achieved – and there was a lack of high-quality material, fuel and sufficiently trained personnel. All in all, Engelmann felt very clearly how much in the entire Wehrmacht was done hastily; how scarce all resources essential to the war had become. What he saw now confirmed his fears.

"Papa, why don't you say something," Münster told Nitz and nudged the master sergeant.

"What should I say, lad?" Nitz murmured in his Leipzig dialect. "Orders are orders."

"Exactly," Engelmann muttered and turned to his men. "And that's why I'm now looking for the person in charge and will take care of these things."

The entire 1st Platoon had gathered at the edge of the forest outside the tiny village of Houlle, where the new tanks of the platoon had been put that morning. The Reichsbahn had delivered them to Caen the day before. Engelmann looked around for his soldiers. 19 men had gathered behind him, and in front of him were five tanks. Lack of personnel at every corner!

The lieutenant raised one eyebrow. He still couldn't quite believe what he was going to receive, either. In front of him were misshapen tanks, which rightfully could be described as monstrosities. The hulls were unmistakably Russian T-34 models, but on them were tiny turrets of German Panzers III with stubby, small 5-centimeter cannons. German tank skirts above the chassis completed the funny look of these iron vehicles. The Russian hulls and the rest were painted grey, while oversized white Iron Crosses should protect against their own fire. Maybe that was the reason why these things were used in the West – although of course it wasn't certain that Engelmann's unit would not return to the East.

8

And again a less capable cannon than the one of good Elfriede, Engelmann thought. He was shaken with horror when he thought of being transferred to Russia with these things.

Meanwhile, the Eastern War had become a static war of position. After the tough battles of the recent months, both sides were currently licking their wounds. The Wehrmacht was incapable of new offensives, but at the same time the forces of the Red Army were considered insufficient. No Russian attack was to be expected before the end of 1944, according to the tenor. Meanwhile Stalin had found his scapegoat for the failures of 1943: Marshal Zhukov was not in any command anymore.

Engelmann wiped away such thoughts and looked at these strange tanks once more. *We'll have to invest a lot of time in training to become familiar with these T-34-for-the-poor,* he thought. The men behind him murmured softly. They all looked at these strange panzers with big eyes. Some soldiers from a logistics unit were running around between them. After all, they had camouflaged these bastards out of T-34 and Panzer III properly. A young lieutenant, a lanky, tall guy with a dirty uniform, finally approached Engelmann.

"Oh, there' s someone already," Engelmann said, "let's go."

East of Velikiye Luki, Soviet Union, December 1st, 1943

The Russian climate was merciless. Icy gusts swept over the front section of Army Group North. No snow had yet fallen in the area around Velikiye Luki. But near Leningrad everything was already covered in white powder.

Master Sergeant Pappendorf, leader of the 2nd Platoon, had assigned a system of foxholes to Berning, which was situated in a slightly elevated position above the road leading from Velikiye Luki across the river Lovat to the East

– i.e. towards the enemy. The River Lovat was located a few kilometers behind the German front line. In front of the men of the squadron, 500 meters of no-man's-land opened up before one would stumble over a Red Army Soldier. Right now the scene remained peaceful. From time to time, harassing fires blasted across from over there, and sometimes the squadron's own men picked up a lost Russian at night who hadn't found his way back after taking a leak. Sitting around for days and weeks up in the North was a blessing for the men of the 253rd Infantry Division, who had fought a fierce mobile warfare until late summer. The sun, which could hardly shine more than a hazy glow through the thick cloud cover these days, had just set. Both sides took great care to avoid any sources of light, which is why it was so dark at the front at night that you couldn't see your own hand in front of your eyes. If snow started to fall, this would change.

Squad leader Berning had set himself up in one of the two earth bunkers that lay in his area of responbility. His bunker was located in the middle between the positions on a narrow hill, so that he had a good view of everything when visibility was adequate. A Hindenburg light – neatly covered – illuminated Berning's sleeping corner, where he made himself comfortable with blankets as best he could. The sergeant leaned against the wall and stuffed a slice of dry bread in his mouth. The rations were rather poor these days, but the paymaster promised every day that the Wehrmacht was just saving for a sumptuous Christmas meal. This had to be very sumptuous, because Christmas was still four weeks away! On the other hand, hunger had been rummaging through the bowels of Berning and his men for six days, because that was the last time they had been given something warm and nutritious to eat. Since then it had been nothing but millet soup, which, after the catering troops had dragged it through the pampas for hours on end, could actually be better described as cold water with bits and pieces; with a piece of bread, margarine, marmalade, very rarely sausage and two cigarettes per day and per man. That was at least an advantage for Berning.

Since he had remained being a non-smoker over the war so far, those two cigarettes were a valuable object of exchange. The chain smoker Rudi Bongartz - Berning's friend who was killed in action – would have suffered a lot under such conditions.

Although, Berning thought, *somehow Rudi had always managed to organize cigarettes.*

Berning was shivering – not only because thinking about Bongartz made him also think about the huge guilt he had incurred. Cold air was blowing through Berning's bunker like an icy hand. He pulled the winter coat he was wearing tighter around his neck, but the cold had taken hold of him mercilessly and gnawed at him with sharp teeth. Suddenly Berning's arms trembled violently, while his chest felt as if blocks of ice were lying on it. Right now he could imagine a thousand places where he would rather be now, but that was out of the question. For better or worse, he had to go through this war before he could continue his normal life at home. He had realized and accepted that. Sometimes he had to think about the alternatives he had to military service. Self-mutilation was not an option; Berning had already experienced that the doctors were after this. And people who tried to avoid military service in this way were often dealt with quickly. Russian war captivity was also not an option, although even former German officers encouraged defection via leaflets and loudspeaker announcements. They promised a hearty welcome and a warm meal to every deserter. What should Berning think of this? He had experienced the brutality of the Russians. Often the Soviets roamed their own villages murdering and raping after they had recaptured them. Would these barbarians really welcome their hated enemies with a warm handshake when they could not even restrain their violent nature among their own people? Berning did not know. Not everything which the Wehrmacht and the Wochenschau tried to put in his head was reality, he had well realized that. But it was difficult for him to distinguish between propaganda and reality. Nevertheless one thing he knew for sure: If Russian captivity was only nearly as cruel as one

11

had heard, then death would be better in any case.

Berning rubbed his hands, wrapped in gloves. His fingertips were already burning from the cold, as were his toes. The Wehrmacht boots were still completely unsuitable for the Russian winter. Unfortunately, this also applied to most of the German equipment. The machine guns sometimes froze up, so that the cocking handle could no longer be moved; and occasionally – when it was really cold – the belts and helmet straps became completely stiff. Then it could happen that the material simply ruptured.

Sometimes the cold was the German soldiers' greatest enemy, while the Russians were hardly noticed at all. Many were suffering from illnesses at the moment, some were hanging around in the rear echelon, having been put on sick leave by the army doctor. Senior Lance Corporal Weiss, for example, had been ordered to be the driver of the company sergeant major for a week because of a bad cold that had turned his voice into a hoarse croak.

Berning breathed out noisily. A visible cloud left his blue lips and vanished in the bunker. Then he thought of Gretel. A few warm thoughts certainly couldn't hurt now.

"Unteroffizier Berning?" The voice of one of his soldiers entered the bunker, then one of the new recruits, Private First Class Egon Reuben, stood in the entrance. Reuben was in his early thirties and was from somewhere in Northern Germany, where he ran a farm with his family in peacetime. He had the appropriate body: tall, sturdy, with strong hands and the ability to do a good job. No matter whether the work involved digging trenches or laying wire entanglements, Reuben was Berning's first choice for all craftsmanship.

"What's up?"

"The Russians have appeared on the street again."

"At Hege?"

"Jawohl." Reuben said the word very quickly, so it sounded more like "Jawoll".

"I'm coming."

Berning got up, grabbed his Karabiner 98k and stahlhelm and followed Reuben down the trench to the left. At the end

12

of the trench was Hege's MG nest, slightly ahead of the other positions. It offered the best view onto the street.

The fact that the Eastern War had been deadlocked for months was clearly evident from the trenches and holes dug in the ground. The front finally had come to a standstill after the fierce battles of Kursk, Belgorod, Orel and Tula – and the soldiers had started digging. The German system of emplacements had been extended to deep trenches, in which the German infantrymen did not have to duck to get from one foxhole to the next.

Reuben stalked ahead through the trench system, Berning followed him closely. Since everything was pitch black, they slowly groped their way along the trench wall. Then they reached Hege's emplacement, the second earth bunker of the trench system. The private crouched underneath his loophole and carefully peeked over the edge into the forefield. Next to him was the machine gun 42, which was placed on a field mount, so that even longer bursts of fire and full automatic fire could be carried out with a steady hand. Berning and Reuben entered the earth bunker and joined Hege, leaning against the bunker wall next to him.

Berning took the helmet off his head, because he did not want to reveal the sharp silhouette of a German stahlhelm under any circumstances. Now he, too, carefully glanced over the edge and out onto the forefield. Of course, he couldn't see anything except dark areas in different shades of grey that overlapped. One had to know that there was the road to Velikiye Luki right in front and next to them, which was nothing more than an unpaved, better beaten track.

At a distance of 200 meters the road made a right turn and disappeared behind thick bushes, while pine trees towered on both sides and the ground rose slightly to the right. Behind the slope and also somewhere behind the bend in the road the Soviet territory began.

"There were three men in the street again," Hege whispered while chewing on an old piece of sausage. "Four o'clock, about 250. This time in the middle of the road."

"You sure?" Berning wanted to know for sure. Hege

looked at him with an uncomprehending look.

"SURE? That's what I asked!" Berning shouted at half volume.

Hege was an experienced veteran, but if you were standing at the alarm post for hours on end, just staring into the blackness of the night, your brain would start playing tricks. Suddenly you saw figures everywhere and heard noises.

During his training, Berning once had to lie in his post for three hours after midnight and after what felt like an eternity he suddenly saw huge red beetles waddling around in front of him.

"Nah, I saw red beetles," Hege grinned. Reuben grinned too. Berning should never have told his men about this.

"This is the third time since Saturday," Hege whispered, and suddenly he was serious again.

"Mmh, yeah, that's right, the third time," Reuben repeated. The guy could be annoying at times. Berning frowned.

"I'm telling you, something's happening," Hege said in an insistent voice. "Something big, I mean. The Russians are already getting into close contact with everything here."

"They said the Ivans were down for the count," the sergeant whispered.

"You should know by now to make up your own mind instead of swallowing the news from above." Hege stared at Berning and choked down the last bit of sausage he had left in his mouth.

"That's right, you should make up your own mind," Reuben had to add, rubbing his arms against the cold. They were all freezing. Hege wore a beanie that his mother had sent him under his helmet and had thrown a blanket over himself, but such improvisations were of little use: A soldier in Russia had to reckon with the fact that he was freezing from October to March; that he was shivering, that at some point his limbs were aching from the constant shivering, and that his fingers and toes were burning because they were most exposed to the cold. The only constant hope was to avoid getting frostbite, which happened faster than

14

expected. Above all, the dangerous thing about frostbite was that it started with a terribly pleasant warmth and one had the feeling that the affected body parts were near a crackling fireplace. Once the terrible burning began and the affected areas were already blue or black, while the skin was swelling and tightening, it was usually too late. Then only the bone saw helped.

"Maybe they're out to steal posts again," the sergeant thought. The Russians had already managed twice in the last few weeks to enter the German front line at night and kidnap one of the guards. Nobody knew how they did it.

"Wretched swines," Berning finally said, after thinking for a moment. "I'm fed up with these games. Hege, give the street a good harassing fire. Them brothers should realize that there's nothing to get here. And then shoot harassing fire at irregular intervals every few hours. Pass this on to your relief."

"Harassing fire, understood."

Addressing the private first class, Berning ordered: "And you go up to the platoon command post and report to Pappe."

Then Berning left the earth bunker while the machine gun behind him fired three short bursts into the darkness.

*

Berning squatted in his bunker again and gnawed at a thin slice of brown bread. Afterwards he wanted to try to get some sleep. He thought about wandering from foxhole to foxhole again, to see if his men were okay – to show presence in general as their squad leader.

On the other hand, he had just found a position in his coat and between his blankets that protected him somewhat from the cold.

Why even get up? Nothing would happen today anyway.

Suddenly Master Sergeant Pappendorf stood half crouched in the entrance of the earth bunker. Berning startled; he straightened up as much as the low bunker ceiling allowed. In the field he didn't need to salute, but he

15

had certain reflexes that told him to stand up straight and take a stance whenever his platoon leader was nearby. And Pappendorf obviously liked that.

"Unteroffizier Berning!" Pappendorf whispered surprisingly clearly.

"Jawohl, Herr Feldwebel?"

"Commander's order: Patrol! You're in charge."

Berning's eyes grew large.

"Take two men. Leave all your equipment here; in short, anything that might rattle. Just the gun and magazines. One hand grenade per man! And turn in your pay books! Marching distance: About two kilometers. The commander wants to know: strength and armament of the enemy forces behind the bend in the road. So stalk up to their posts and keep listening for at least two hours. From the 3rd Platoon, a private will immediately report to you who understands a bit of this damn Slav language. Take him with you and have him listen to everything you can pick up. Then back. No sloppiness, Unteroffizier. Get your heels in the dirt, you've got about 12 hours of darkness from now on. Get back here before they get light to fire at you. You are of no use to me dead! You've got five minutes to give your preliminary instructions to your men, then we're going up to the commander for the issue of orders. Make sure you have your notepad and pencil handy."

"Jawohl, Herr Feldwebel! Patrol over two kilometers with the aim of recon enemy strength and type of armament. Two men plus myself plus language expert from 3rd Platoon. Just weapons and magazines. I'll give the preliminary instructions now, then to the commander for issue of orders."

"Very well, let's go!"

*

Shortly before midnight Berning and three soldiers entered the no-man's-land between near Hege's machine gun nest. He had informed his neighboring squads and platoons about the plan beforehand, so that they would not

16

get the idea of firing at figures in their forefield. Moreover, in the darkness, even at the shortest distances, it could quickly happen that one got off track. Then it was of particular importance that the neighbors were informed about the patrol; namely when you suddenly appeared directly in front of their guns. Meanwhile Pappendorf had issued a new password for the whole move: Winter Joy. *Haha.*

Berning lay flat on his stomach and slowly pushed himself over the edge of the trench onto the gently descending slope leading down to the road. In fact, the eleven hours remaining until sunrise were not much time for the task ahead of them. They couldn't just march through to the Russian emplacements, but had to crawl the barely 500 meters through no-man's-land and be extremely careful, because parts of it were mined and contaminated with booby traps. Berning roughly knew the positions of the deadly surprises and moreover he had sketched out the corresponding map from the commander, but what use was a piece of paper in the deepest night?

Berning crawled ahead, behind him his soldiers followed: one comrade from the 3rd Platoon, a private named Michels, then Private First Class Barth as well as Reuben. Michels was fresh out of training and was still a greenhorn, but he graduated from high school and was the only one in the company with some Russian language skills.

Centimeter by centimeter Berning felt his way with his fingers over the rock-hard frozen forest ground and dragged his body along. He had put his rifle around his neck and had stuffed the pockets of his coat with bullets. The soldiers had also left their helmets in their foxholes in order to hear better – and because the silhouette of a German steel helmet was simply unmistakable.

Berning's fingers groped forward. On the right there was a trunk of a thick tree, but on the left everything seemed clear. So he turned his upper body to the left and pulled himself past the tree. Every few meters he stopped and remained in absolute silence, as he did now. The first thing he heard was the scraping noises of his comrades dragging their bodies across the ground behind him before they realized that they should stop. After that absolute silence dominated the scene. The wind whistled softly across the slope and made a branch crackle in the treetops. Sometimes withered leaves crackled. Otherwise Berning could hear absolutely nothing. So on we go! Sweat moistened Berning's hair, and his breathing went faster and faster. It was exhausting to move forward at this pace, but it would be much worse to lie down in front of the Russian positions: When the bodies came to rest again and the soldiers remained motionless, then the wet sweated bodies would be torture for them. It was always like that in winter: As long as you were moving, you wanted to stop and rest. But as soon as you came to rest, you would like to do push-ups all the time to keep warm somehow. The constant hunger did not make it easier.

Finally Berning's fingers felt a fine wire stretched just above the ground. Immediately the sergeant felt a bit hotter as his pulse went up his throat. Mine! Berning gave his rear man a weak kick against the shoulder; they had agreed this as a sign that a mine had been found. Berning knew the terrain by day and roughly knew where the mines were. He had intentionally chosen a route where he shouldn't get any nasty surprises. Now he thought about which of the mines he had found. Anyway, he must have already lost his path by now. Berning pulled off the glove of his right hand with his teeth, and followed the wire very carefully. The terrible cold immediately took hold of his fingertips, but at the moment he had more urgent concerns. Slowly Berning moved his fingers along the wire. He finally found an egg-shaped grenade that was connected to it. It was jammed between two thick sticks. They had placed such a construction in only one place, right in front of his own bunker! Berning sighed and wished he could just cancel this patrol. Apparently they had been moving parallel to their own positions for the last 30 minutes instead of in the direction of the enemy. Everything up to here had been in vain! Half an hour of work for nothing!

Shit! The sergeant thought and wished he could get away

18

from here. But it didn't help at all, so he groped his way back along the wire. He fervently hoped that his men hadn't noticed this faux pas on his part, but simply crept after him blindly. *They'll think I'm a good-for-nothing after all,* he was worried.

After two hours of crawling they had reached the road. Berning's breathing was rapid, sweat flooded his body. He could feel his uniform all wet under his coat. Curses against the war and everyone who had anything to do with it filled his thoughts.

Berning sighed, then he stretched out his arms and felt for the road. The ground was plain, the road should not have any obstacles. Berning had told his men in advance that they would continue to crawl across the road, but at a higher speed, because he didn't want to stay there too long. Maybe the road was being watched by Russian eyes. Berning heard the men behind him reaching his boots. They groaned softly, the only other sound to be heard was the scraping of the boots and uniforms. Certainly they all had the same aches and pains as their squad leader himself: Berning's hands were already completely numbed from crawling and on his arms bruises had formed everywhere, which became unpleasantly noticeable with every inch he moved. However it didn't help. Pappendorf certainly wouldn't have much understanding for Berning canceling his patrol because of bruises on his limbs. So he had to move on. He sighed, then kicked back twice, the agreed signal for: "Road ahead!".

Now move! Berning had to motivate himself. He then crawled across the road as fast as he could. His men followed him closely. In no time at all he had reached the other side of the road, but he advanced a few more meters and finally stopped when his fingertips felt a tree. From this point on it went slightly uphill – and somewhere behind the hilltop, about 40 meters ahead, the Russians' emplacements would be. Maybe they had taken a reverse slope position, or maybe Berning had to go quite a bit further. He knew a Russian trench system that was located a good 200 meters away from the top on another hill, but it didn't have to be

19

their front line. Perhaps the enemy also had single forward observation posts. The Russians finally had no rival in concealed entrenchments. From this point on, Berning and his soldiers had to be really careful in any case. Everywhere someone could be lying in ambush. And time was running out for them.

The minutes Sergeant Berning was waiting for his men seemed like eternities. He felt his body begin to chill. The salty water on his back soaking through his shirt became very cold and created a disgusting feeling. Suddenly Berning began to tremble.

Shit! He cursed in his mind. Abruptly Michels slapped against Berning's boot, which meant that the entire patrol had reached the other side of the road. They could move on!

Berning struggled painstakingly up the slope. Now he moved even slower and tried to make even less noise. Relieved, he noticed that his comrades behind him were also very quiet. He could hardly hear them, which was a good sign after all. It took another three quarters of an hour until the squad arrived at the top of the slope. Berning searched meticulously every inch in front of him with his fingers, before he pulled himself further forward. There could not only be hidden charges and mines of the enemy lurking, but also dud bombs and other dangerous things that had been left behind after the last battles in this area.

Finally Berning was on his stomach on the top of the hill, to his left the thick trunk of a fallen tree. Private Michels crawled forward to Berning and lay panting to his right. Sweat poured down Berning's face, his breath was racing.

"We listen for five minutes," Berning whispered to Michels who nodded and passed the order to the rear by kicking three times. The sergeant wanted to listen into the terrain once before he threw himself further into the unknown.

A minute passed.

"I wonder where the Russian positions are exactly. What do you think?" Michels suddenly asked.

"Eavesdropping means keeping your mouth shut," Berning hissed, but suddenly his eyes grew very large.

20

Michels froze and held his breath. There was movement in the forefield! Berning recognized black shapes that were shifting. Suddenly the sergeant felt as if his own breathing was louder than anything else. He could no longer concentrate on the sounds around him. The next moment his eyes grew even larger. There was not only movement somewhere in the forefield, there was something moving right in front of them! Berning saw the outline of a Russian bowl helmet with a head underneath, moving once across from left to right – just one meter away! Berning's heartbeat stuck in his throat and cut off his air. Heat flooded his head. A Soviet trench opened up right in front of him and there was a Red Army soldier staggering through it!

Thoughts were running through Berning's mind. *How is this possible?* That was the leading question in his head. *How could we have overlooked the fact that the Russians had dug a trench right under our nose?*

But there was no time to answer these questions. The Soviet soldier didn't seem to have noticed the German patrol and kept stumbling along the trench. With every step he took, he was moving away from Berning and his men. Only when Berning heard nothing more of his boots, which were slowly and regularly touching the ground, he dared to exhale. His relief was clearly audible. Suddenly he heard voices from the right; a language Berning didn't understand. The sergeant nudged Michels, who nodded eagerly. Then he lowered his head and concentrated on the voices. Berning could clearly hear two men speaking to each other rather quietly, but still clearly perceptibly. Michels took his time. 30 seconds passed.

"What do they say?" Berning finally asked in the quietest possible way in which audible sounds were nevertheless produced. Tension lay like a blanket over the patrol.

"I don't know," Michels returned.

"I thought you knew the language?"

"Do you know how many languages are spoken within the Soviet Union? It could be Armenian or Ukrainian or Kyrgyz or God knows what."

"Bastards! Can't they agree on one peasant language?"

Berning got angry. Had the whole effort been for nothing?

Suddenly the voices on the right fell silent, followed by a few moments of quietness. Then a foreign voice sounded with a tense, questioning undertone. This voice was definitely louder and had a completely different melody than the ones before.

"That is Russian," Michels breathed and turned into a lying pillar of salt.

"What did he say?" Berning demanded to know. Michels took his time for a few seconds, then he answered: "He said: 'I think I heard something'." Now Berning also stiffened. He could see nothing, no moving areas – nothing at all. There was also nothing to be heard. Seconds went by. Moments became eternities. Terrified, he stared into the darkness. Then a Russian voice was heard again.

"They've got us!" Michels uttered and suddenly got up. Next thing Berning heard was a bang. Rifle shots roared through the night, Russian voices screamed. Berning jumped up and yelled, "Go, go, go, get back!" He pulled out the hand grenade he was carrying, pulled the pin and threw the explosive device roughly to where the two non-Russians had just been talking. His men already rushed down the slope, back to the German front line. Russian bullets chased after them. Projectiles hit tree trunks and caused wood splinters to crack off. A Russian machine gun rattled. But the enemy did not know where to fire. So they just pointed their guns into the gloom.

Berning also ran off and chased after his men. "Come on, down the slope and back to us!" he shouted, while his grenade exploded behind him. There was a flash of lightning in the darkness, then a shrill scream cut through the night. Apparently, Berning's grenade had hit something. The Germans ran on and reached the road. The Russian fire ploughed up the whole landscape. Tracer bullets hissed around like glowing arrows and there were flashes of light everywhere. Now, the Soviets shot flares up into the air, which lit up the terrain for seconds. Berning and his patrol threw themselves on the ground in the glaring light and remained motionless. The Russian gunners were probably looking for German steel helmets, but there were none. When darkness returned, the Germans immediately pulled themselves up, while Russian bullets roamed through the night like glowing threads. The German side remained quiet. Apparently the comrades remembered that they had a patrol in the area in front.

Berning saw nothing. Sometimes running, sometimes crawling, sometimes walking – always with his hands protecting his face – he made his way back. He heard the hasty steps of his men, he even heard their loud, fearful gasps at times. Unexpectedly there was a loud bang right beside him. Then a scream. The sergeant threw himself on the ground, but forced himself back on his feet immediately. Barth was screaming like a banshee. Berning jumped to the right and was already with him. Barth had run into one of their own mines, now laying on the ground with a torn up leg.

"Oh, boy!" Berning said. He didn't know where the rest of his patrol was. In front of him, he heard someone shouting, "Winter! WINTER!" like an idiot, then at some point another voice replied, "Joy!"

An inner feeling of discomfort gave Berning a sharp stab in the stomach. He threw himself beside the wounded, meanwhile the Russian projectiles rushed over his head so that he could feel their hot breath. Once more Berning wanted to get away from here. For a second he had to close his eyes to get his emotions, which materialized as a pressing feeling against his eyes, under control. Next to him Barth screamed constantly.

Pull yourself together! Franz ordered himself. *Your comrades expect that you do your duty! Pappendorf expects that!* He spoke to himself as if to a stranger, then his eyes opened. He had no time for that shit! Berning swallowed the tears and grabbed Barth by the shoulders. Half ducked, he dragged the private first class with him. He prayed that he wouldn't run into a mine as well, but he didn't have time to search the path carefully. So press on regardless!

Behind him the Russian fire was diminishing, while Berning pulled the screaming Barth over the edge into a trench. The sergeant had not only made it back to the German line, he had even returned to the emplacements of his own squad. Immediately he ordered two of his men to take Barth to the casualty assembly. It did not look good for the boy: Both legs were covered in blood and the right foot was practically gone.

When the soldiers had left with the wounded, Berning let himself sink to the ground and leaned against the wall of the trench. Over there, the Russian fire fizzled out. Berning breathed quickly and uncontrollably. Adrenaline had taken over his body and replaced hunger and cold. Slowly, very slowly he calmed down. His breathing slowed down again and his pulse stopped racing. Berning lowered his head backwards and hit the wall of the trench. Small lumps of dirt rolled into his coat. He closed his eyes, although that was unnecessary; because everything still was pitch black. After some time a short moment of joy came over him; joy that he was still alive. But this was quickly replaced by anger. Berning gritted his teeth and clenched his hands into fists.

Why the hell did the commander have to order this patrol? Rage ruled his thoughts. It was an irrepressible fury at the realization that he and his comrades were just used as cannon fodder.

Who does he think he is? Does he think he has to be a big shot just because he wears a tin tie? Berning shook all over. He wanted to scream. *And Pappendorf! Why does this ox allow his men to be sent on such a suicide mission? Why does this bastard even seem to have a perverse delight in getting us blown away like this?* Berning slammed his fist against the wall of the trench. *All of them are inhuman pigs! And because of them, Barth might die!* But then suddenly a completely different thought crossed his mind...

"Unteroffizier Berning!" Pappendorf's barking interrupted his train of thought. The sergeant looked up with a tired expression on his face. He realized that Pappendorf was standing right in front of him. Berning could only see his outlines, but the upright posture and the arms crossed behind his back were unmistakable.

"Why am I not getting a report from you about what happened to the patrol? Why are you dozing around here?"

Berning was terribly tired, at the end of his rope. He felt too weak to get up and even too weak to answer. The sweat on his body also cooled down; it started to make him feel uncomfortable. Then, however, he got back to his train of thought, which Pappendorf had just interrupted: It wasn't the commander or Pappendorf who was to blame. Yes, actually – Berning had to admit to himself – they were just doing their job and were actually quite good at it. The real blame for Berning's miserable situation, yes, the blame for the whole war and for everything that was terrible, was to be found with the Russians, he suddenly thought. New and unexpected evil thoughts rose in Berning's mind.

Those inhuman, despicable wild bastards! Those barbarians! A deep wrath of a whole new league flooded his mind, flooding it with hatred and thoughts of violence. *Cursed scum with their miserable Bolshevism! Why did they have to threaten us with their false ideology? After all, they wanted this war and they brought it upon Germany! We were just defending ourselves. The safety of the German Reich is also defended on the Moskva! And now I have to sit here in the cold and mud, just because these sons of bitches know nothing but violence and destruction!* Berning was boiling inside. He was raging. And he liked it. *Those barbarians,* he ranted, *those Slavs! Damn Slavs!*

Berning stood up and duly reported.

Houlle, France, December 3rd, 1943

"Shh! Be quiet, you fool!" Münster hissed at the young Private First Class Birk. He froze immediately in his movement, because he had just cracked a few branches with his boots.

"Don't talk rubbish, Hans, and move on!" Ludwig said,

stalking behind them through the bushes. Stendal was last, who, as usual, spared any comment.

Münster cautiously approached the end of the scrub, behind which a slightly hilly clear area opened up. The tank driver stopped and gestured to his comrades with a hand signal to stop as well.

"Shh," he said again, then, "They're right over there."

"Well, come on, Birk," Ludwig said, nudging the infantryman whose unit happened to be in Houlle that day.

Münster and Ludwig had immediately chosen Birk as *their* man after the arrival of his unit and had approached him. After all, the dogfaces had real rifles and the tank men only had pistols, sometimes also machine guns.

Birk positioned himself next to Münster, carefully peering through the fine branches and leaves of the shrubs to the meadow in front of them. In fact, the whole area was crowded with rabbits. That would be a feast. Birk aimed.

"Come on!" Münster whispered.

"Now let him be," Ludwig ranted immediately. Birk shot. The bang echoed over the landscape of the Pas-de-Calais, the department where the city of Calais was located. The bullet flew towards the floppy ears, but it missed. It stirred up the earth and threw up grass, while the rabbits were startled and scurried around like mad.

"Great!" Münster spat out. "You couldn't hit a barn door if you were standing in front of it!"

Birk repeated his weapon while defending himself: "They are much too small and fast. And shooting was never my strong suit."

"Well, you've come to the wrong place then."

"Here? In France?"

"No, in the Wehrmacht." Münster laughed, but Birk didn't find that funny. He made an offended face and looked out into the meadow. The rabbits had calmed down and were now happily bouncing around again.

"May I?" Stendal's high voice with the Tyrolean accent came out of the background and surprised everyone so much that they just turned around. Birk nodded as he handed him the gun. Stendal stalked a step forward, pulled his field cap back into his neck, aimed and fired. Score! A rabbit's head burst while the pressure of the projectile threw the body up into the air. Again the animals ran in confusion, but Stendal did not wait until they calmed down again. He repeated the rifle and immediately took aim at a jumping hare.

Three more shots rang out. A total of three roast rabbits lay in the meadow afterwards. Four shots, three hits. Not bad!

"Natural talent!" Münster was pleased.

"Give me another five," Stendal demanded. Birk made a disapproving face.

"I can't do that. My Unteroffizier will kill me if I waste all my ammo on rabbits!"

"Then he'll get one too," Münster played down the remark; Ludwig nodded. "Now hand over the ammunition. You're hungry, too, aren't you?"

Birk exhaled theatrically, but he reached into his ammunition bag and conjured up another clip. Ludwig immediately whipped it out of his hand and handed it to Stendal. He reloaded, fired five times. Four more roast rabbits lay in the grass. Münster and Ludwig laughed, then they all patted each other on the shoulders for the feast that awaited them. Birk grinned too.

"Man, where did you learn to shoot that well?" Ludwig asked on the way back. They were carrying seven bleeding hare carcasses.

"My father's a hunter."

They all nodded their heads.

*

Slowly evening fell and with it the light disappeared. This day had been a relatively warm one, the temperatures stayed just above ten degrees. Engelmann sat, leaning against a tree, between the tanks of his platoon. Directly in front of him stood his tank, christened "Quasimodo" by his crew, which Ludwig had painted on the barrel in white letters. Branches and leaves as well as the lush treetops

27

protected the tanks from curious eyes from the air. This was important, because these days Allied aircraft could be seen more and more often in French airspace. It was sad, but reality: The sky above the Reich and the countries it occupied belonged to the enemy. Even in Russia, an enemy air superiority was slowly emerging. Engelmann shoved a piece of chocolate between his teeth and wrinkled his nose.

While the daylight was fading and it smelled of damp grass, the first lights were turned on over in the village of Houlle, which consisted of several hundred buildings. A headquarters company had taken up residence there overnight. The tank men of the 3rd Division stayed outside the village. With the agreement of a local farmer, Engelmann's platoon had moved into an old barn, about one kilometer west of the village and thus very close to the tanks, where, after weeks of residence, they had made themselves quite at home. The last months since their arrival in France had been very quiet compared to the war in the East. Occasional assignment of a new area of responsibility, maintenance work and training characterized the everyday life of the regiment's soldiers. France seemed to the lieutenant as if it were on another planet, so different was life in the West from that in the East. Engelmann still could not believe that after years of fighting and the constant danger of life he was allowed to have it pretty cushy on the so-called Western Front. In France, life was reasonably safe; the sun was shining, the men could play football on the beach, and wine and food were available in abundance. Here in the Pas-de-Calais, the birthdays of comrades were suddenly celebrated again, there were trips to Paris or to Vichy, and in the evening, they sat together with a beer and a slice of sausage. Life in France was so easygoing that Engelmann was sometimes even afraid that he would not enjoy it enough. After all, peace would be over sometime, Engelmann knew that, and he knew that it was for the best. At the moment the enemy was hiding on the other side of the Channel and was therefore out of reach for the Wehrmacht. But sooner or later there had to be a battle, otherwise this war would last forever. And the battle could only take place on French soil, and in fact only here in the area around Calais, at the narrowest point of the English Channel. Everyone knew that the invasion was imminent, and many – including Engelmann – even longed for it. If the Reich were to fend off what is probably the most gigantic and costly military undertaking of all time, it would break the Americans' will to fight, Engelmann was certain of that. Then the USA would be ready to sit down at the negotiating table. On its own, Britain might defend its island, but it could not win the war. So even Churchill would have to sit down at the negotiating table at some point. Engelmann nodded happily at such thoughts. Moreover, one should not forget that the Americans were dealing with the Japanese on their own doorstep. The lieutenant regarded the Empire of the Rising Sun as being superior to the USA in the long run, as long as the United States were so arrogant thinking they could fight two major wars at the same time. At some point America would therefore withdraw from the European theater of war to concentrate on Japan… at the latest after a failed invasion in France.

Meanwhile, in the East, there was a standstill, the fronts continued to hold. But as long as the sword of Damocles of the Allied invasion hovered over the Wehrmacht in the West, the situation was fragile. So the earlier the battle took place, the better! If the Western powers would agree to peace first, Germany could turn all war efforts against Russia. In this case the chance of an early draw would be maintained. Perhaps the Soviets had also enough of the war? And perhaps even the English and Americans would finally realize that the real enemy of the free world was to be found in the East?

Amis, come to France, Engelmann mused, and raised the book, he was holding in his hands, threateningly into the air, *the sooner the better!* He was certainly not keen on further fighting, but he had to survive this one battle at least. Suddenly Engelmann noticed that he had continued to read his book, but had been so distracted by his own thoughts that he could not recite at all what the last passages were about. He grasped the page stained with dried blood and turned it back. On the outside cover was the title of the book: "The World Set Free". Engelmann finally found a passage he could remember and continued reading:

"I do not believe that any of us felt as if we were part of a defeated army, nor did we feel that the war was a determining factor for us. We rather felt that it was an enormous natural catastrophe. The atomic bombs had reduced international problems to utter insignificance. When we were not dealing with our immediate needs, we talked about the possibility of stopping the use of these terrible explosives before the world was completely destroyed."[1]

Engelmann stopped reading again, because not far from him there was suddenly a loud laughter. He looked over to the dugouts of the 2nd Platoon of his company, where Captain Stollwerk stood together with the new platoon leader, Master Sergeant Kranz. Stollwerk patted the master sergeant on the shoulder, grinned, and left. Kranz, a grumpy man of tall physique, stayed behind and wiped his chin with his hand.

So no further reading, Engelmann thought. The light was also slowly fading. The lieutenant closed the book and stood up. Perhaps it was a good opportunity to get to know the platoon leader of the 2nd Platoon of his company a little better. After all, Engelmann liked to know who he was dealing with. Leisurely the lieutenant strolled over to Kranz, who at that moment was tapping his hand against the steel of one of his Panzer III.

"Guten Abend."

"Oh, guten Abend, Herr Leutnant." Kranz smiled invitingly. His dialect unmistakably identified him as someone from the Cologne area.

"Well? Old acquaintances?" Engelmann pointed to the leaving Stollwerk.

---

[1] From: The World Set Free, H. G. Wells, Paul Zsolnay Verlag, own translation from German

"Yes, indeed. We used to serve in the same unit. Went to Poland together." Kranz nodded. "The Wehrmacht is a village."

Engelmann's face, on the other hand, had become darker and darker with every word of the master sergeant. The lieutenant had distanced himself from Stollwerk as best he could since he had revealed his extreme opinions to him. Stollwerk was a very good soldier and leader, no question; but personally he and Engelmann were not on the same wavelength. In general, the lieutenant immediately developed some resentment towards former members of the Waffen SS -- as well as towards Kranz.

"Is something wrong?" the master sergeant asked, trying to read Engelmann's face.

"You were with Stollwerk in the SS?" The lieutenant's question had a sharp undertone, without him intending it.

"Yes. In Poland and in Russia. I already knew him as Scharführer."

"He's come a long way..."

"Have you anything against soldiers of the Order?" Kranz asked directly, and looked at the lieutenant.

"No, that's all right."

"But it sounds different. You know, every now and then I meet comrades who don't like us. They think the SS was a rival organization to the Wehrmacht, but that's wrong. We were brothers in arms -- and we fought together."

Engelmann whistled through his teeth. "Fighting? Running into enemy fire with a roar of cheer is more like it. I'm sorry, but what I experienced in France with the Waffen SS beggars description. Except for fanaticism and false elitism, there was nothing."

Kranz tilted his head to the side. "Then you never saw us in Russia."

"No."

"All right. The early days were difficult. We made mistakes in France. But we learned from them and became more and more powerful. Before von Witzleben came to power, there were many soldiers in the Wehrmacht who were happy when the Waffen SS fought on their flank.

Several times we got you out."

"No wonder. You were consistently favored in the allocation of materials."

"These are rumors, Leutnant, due to a sudden bias against former comrades."

"These are not rumors. Before the French campaign, Hitler ordered all SS units to be motorized. And who was left behind? The army! We lacked vehicles everywhere!"

"I can't say anything about that."

"It's true."

"Yet we fight the same enemy. Now even in the same army. So we should support each other instead of being enemies. We all serve the same purpose."

"Well, are we?"

Kranz blinked at Engelmann confused. The lieutenant swallowed his anger and explained calmly: "You were there, in Poland. Were you also there when the SS burned down whole villages – including the inhabitants? Or were you also accidentally not there, or on holiday or anywhere else, like everyone else who is asked about it? In any case, the Wehrmacht leadership had made it clear at the time what they thought of such practices."

"No, I was there."

Engelmann had not expected this answer.

"The Hauptmann and I served in the Wachsturmbann Eimann. Ever heard of Sturmbannführer Eimann?"

Engelmann shook his head.

"The man is a bastard. In any case, back then in Wielka Piaśnica we shot hundreds of people and buried them in the forest. Poles, but also Germans, clergy, handicapped people. Jews. We shot them, and Polish prisoners had to bury them."

Kranz looked at Engelmann with flickering eyes. The lieutenant found no hate in it, only the courage to realize and express his own guilt.

"Did you shoot?"

"Yes, I did."

Engelmann nodded slightly.

"But I want to tell you," Kranz continued in a strong voice, "not everyone in the SS was like that. We saw ourselves primarily as an elite unit – we had the claim to form the fighting elite of the Reich. We were soldiers! We mercilessly killed anyone who dared to raise his weapon against the Reich."

"And if there were some without weapons, it wasn't so bad, huh?"

"You're looking down on us from a bloody high horse. The Wehrmacht has also shot civilians, burned villages."

"I did no such thing."

Both stared at each other for a moment, then Engelmann's features softened: "But you are right. A lot of crap has happened in this war. Let him who is free from sin cast the first stone, heh?" He smiled weakly. "I'm sorry I snapped at you like that. The Waffen SS is just a weak point of mine at the moment."

"You should also remember that even in the SS, not everyone was a volunteer, the next time you attack an old comrade."

"You were not voluntary in the SS?"

"No, I was." Kranz showed his teeth. Gold gleamed from his upper jaw. "But some people weren't."

"Like I said, I didn't mean to snap at you. There are decent guys everywhere – and less decent guys..."

"It's okay, Leutnant." They shook hands. Kranz had a powerful handshake.

"Now, if you'll excuse me, Herr Leutnant, I must get back to my men."

"Yeah, I guess, I may as well see what the boys are up to."

The two men separated. Lieutenant Engelmann slowly walked across the meadow back to the barn where his platoon was based. Confused thoughts were at work in his head. He passed the tanks of the other platoons of his company, all of them Panzer III. The tanks of the other companies were all of type IV – but some of the still had the short barrel. Finally, after years of armored warfare, the Panzer IV outnumbered its mercilessly outdated predecessor, the type III. Only Engelmann was unlucky again, even though only half of Quasimodo was a Panzer

III. Von Witzleben, in cooperation with Guderian, had decided that the Panzer III and some other antiquated models should still not be withdrawn from service, but "used up" instead. The motto was: Better an old tank than no tank at all.

When Engelmann approached the barn, it was already dark. The wind carried various sounds to his ear. Laughter and loud conversations were in the air. Engelmann also heard the crackling of flames, and he smelled fire.

I don't believe it! He thought to himself and ran off. If his platoon was involved, he'd give his men hell! Engelmann turned the corner of the barn and found a whole bunch of soldiers gathered around a big bonfire, over which they prepared meat. Wine bottles were emptied, cigarettes glowed, bread and sausage from the Wehrmacht rations disappeared in roaring mouths. Engelmann recognized at once that almost the entire platoon was present, as well as some infantrymen whom he did not know. He didn't care that some of the men had taken off their field blouses and generally looked like higgledy-piggledy. What was insane, however, was the gigantic fire that gave every enemy pilot in the sky a perfect target.

"Herr Leutnant!" Münster's agitated voice came from the crowd. "Come and join us."

Engelmann saw his driver in the crowd: He stood there, topless, with a field cap on his head, a cigarette butt in his mouth and a bottle of wine in his hand.

Great! Engelmann thought. *Mine stand out even from the worst wretched swine! And if Rosenkamp hears about it, he'll give me stupid lectures again!*

Captain Rosenkamp, the new leader of the 9th company, attached more importance to outward appearances than to anything else. Engelmann already had his problems with this officer, who was a completely different kind of man than Engelmann. So he couldn't afford to get into a fight with Rosenkamp over such trifles of his men. The lieutenant snorted accordingly, especially since his boys knew better. But they hadn't done that for nothing! The lieutenant's eyes narrowed. He marched off and walked straight towards the celebrating soldiers. He'd give them a good chewing out! Münster seemed to interpret the face of his superior correctly, for suddenly his cheerfulness vanished. He reached for his head to turn his field cap around.

Engelmann had almost got to the fire over which the hare meat was sizzling. Suddenly a very special smell rose into his nose: a little sweetish, a little bitter-biting through the stench of fire. It was the smell of burnt meat. Engelmann stopped. Everything was spinning in his head. He lost his footing and fell to his knees. The next moment his lunch shot out of his throat as half-digested pulp. He spat into the grass until he only spat stomach acid. His intestines spun, his eyes narrowed to a black and white tunnel.

"Herr Leutnant!" Engelmann heard Ludwig shouting, then everything went dark around him and he tilted to the side.

West of Velikiye Luki, Soviet Union, January 5th, 1944

The AOK had made the best possible Christmas present to the soldiers of the 253rd Infantry Division by removing them from the front line shortly before Christmas Eve and transferring them to an assembly area West of Velikiye Luki. West usually meant: away from the Russians. In the new assembly area the men had been able to celebrate Christmas in its entirety, and there was indeed a large extra ration of food: With vodka, bread, ham, potatoes, coffee and other groceries that were rarely seen on the Eastern front, they had certainly celebrated a lavish feast. One staff sergeant of the 1st Reconnaissance Squadron had even organized a Christmas tree including decorations.

Now the holidays were over and the new year had begun. Von Manstein's plan, which should free forces for the West, was about to get executed these days. The field marshal's idea was brilliant, but also dangerous, nonetheless the Germans had to do something, if they did not want to be completely without a chance against the already superior Allies in the West. Under strictest secrecy, the units transferred to the rear, began to carry out special work before being further transferred to France. This time the participation of Russian prisoners of war in the work was not an option; the risk of revealing von Manstein's agenda would have been too high. And if the Soviets got scent of the matter, the entire Eastern Front would be in danger. For this reason, the Wehrmacht soldiers had to lend a hand themselves.

*

Berning was pissed. He felt exploited in his work force. He had enlisted as a soldier, not a carpenter! But now he was asked to cobble together some wooden tanks. Under the supervision of an army engineer sergeant, who gave help and instructions, each squad of the squadron had to build up a wooden tank similar to the Panzer IV. The soldiers were located outside the town near a forest on a larger meadow. Hundreds of Germans worked here, while Renault trucks brought wood, tools and nails, paint and metal barrels. The whole division had plunged into work; even the squad leaders were not exempt from this by order of the commander, much to the displeasure of Pappendorf.

Why can't we be part of the security forces? Sergeant Berning asked himself in his mind, while he was putting two boards together with nails. This construction was to become the upper part of the tank hull. Besides him, his soldiers worked on the rear part of the hull as well as on the turret. Meanwhile landsers of the 1st group rolled up barrels to three bundles at the edge of the forest. The barrels would be painted and then serve as "wheels". Everything was to be worked out precisely and in every detail so that not only enemy air reconnaissance but also curious eyes on the ground would believe the dummies to be real. However, as long as the construction was going on, the area was strictly shielded from all civilians.

Why do we have to do this shit? Berning thought, while his hammer blows became more furious.

"Argh!" He shouted out after banging another nail in crooked. "Bloody rubbish!" He hurled the hammer away and stood up. His soldiers looked at him.

"Steady," Hege said to Berning. "It's better than the front," the machine-gunner remarked.

"Everything is shit!" Berning groaned and went to get his hammer. "I'm not a fucking carpenter. And this war sucks!" Berning stomped, holding the hammer in his fist, back to his place and snorted. He had no idea how important this seemingly not soldier related work was, because as Rommel had already taught the world, sometimes you had to be cunning and think outside the box to win. Berning also had no idea how much effort was invested in the background to make the feint perfect: Fake divisions were set up and equipped with staffs that sent out radio messages and dealt with the paperwork for imaginary units. Trucks, partly converted into dummy tanks, were used to imitate troop movements behind the front. And this game had only just begun.

The driving in of nails and the banging together of wooden slats echoed from everywhere over the place. On the left, at the 2nd Platoon, the first tank was assuming shape.

Bern, Switzerland, January 8th, 1944

Thomas and Luise liked to go for walks and let the leading restaurants in Bern cater for them. Aaron Stern was, after all, a wealthy businessman and could afford such things – which meant simply that the Abwehr could afford these things.

That day they sat in a Swiss bistro in the old town of Bern, this wonderful and impressive city. The old town was situated in the so-called Aare loop, which means that it was enclosed to the east, south and north by the river Aare, which meandered through the city like a blue ribbon. Old sandstone buildings formed the center of the old town. The typical arcades – alleys covered with stone arches – characterized the townscape. The bistro where Thomas and Luise dined for lunch also offered a view through the large windows onto an arcade alley. Snow, rain and sometimes a mixture of both were alternating that day; so the covered town areas were a blessing. Fortunately the bistro itself was heated. Luise and Thomas had taken off their coats and sat at a small table right by the window. The waiter had already served wine – a French Merlot – and soon they would get bread with butter and sausage. The Federal Council had issued a decree that no more fresh bread should be given out, and that it should be stored for at least 24 hours beforehand, but when Thomas took money from the Abwehr in sufficient quantities, fresh pastry was suddenly also available. It was the same with all other groceries, which were strictly rationed because of the war.

Once again their conversation was about Luise's father. He had not been able to travel to Switzerland for Christmas, but he would come at the end of January – as he does every year. By coincidence, Luise and her sister Stella both had their birthdays at the end of January; Luise on January 30th, Stella on January 31st. Not even the war had been able to prevent Luise's father, the British general, from coming to Switzerland every January to visit his daughters. To do so, he accepted a long and dangerous journey across the unoccupied part of France. Taylor suspected that it was not only private intentions that drove the man to Switzerland.

Thomas enjoyed blowing cigarette smoke through his teeth while listening to Luise's soothing voice. She was in a vehement struggle with herself about telling her father about her relationship with Taylor. She had been unsure for a long time, but now she was tending to do so. On the one hand, Thomas was pleased about this – for business reasons. But on the other hand...?

38

He was afraid something might go wrong and end his relationship with Luise. Thomas knew that his feelings were getting in the way of his duties... They were getting stronger and stronger, forming in his chest a dream of life, which he dared to vision more and more often.

"I'm very unsure about my dad," she explained and sipped on her wine, "sometimes my heart says yes, then no. You know, my father can be very difficult." She looked at him questioningly.

"Luise, this is your decision after all," he circumlocuted and emptied his glass.

"You know, actually, I'm thinking about something else."

"What is it?"

"It certainly wasn't always easy with my father. But I think we *modis* have sometimes made life very difficult for him. In addition, he was away a lot and we were practically raised by the nanny. It was a difficult time after Mom had died."

"I see."

"But my father is a man of honor. And he is a soldier. By the way, he told me on the phone yesterday that he'll be involved in the invasion of France."

Luise was thinking for a moment and apparently didn't even notice how Taylor's eyes grew big and he leaned forward.

For some time the German Reich had known from other sources about a planned invasion of Northern France – although no details were revealed. Luise had heard about the existence of specific plans in December – without knowing any details as well.

What was she supposed to know? She was just a typist at the consulate. Sometimes Thomas found his mission thoroughly ridiculous – but her father might be interesting... Even on the phone he seemed to talk about sensitive issues.

"I don't even know, if he's allowed to tell me something like that," she mused. "The Germans are probably listening to everything."

"I hardly think their arm will reach as far as Switzerland,"

Thomas remarked. He would have liked to grin.

"Oh, don't make a mistake. Sometimes I see my father making secrets out of the most trivial things. I'm sure he has his reasons. Anyway, he is a man of honor. And he'll be back in action in May. I hope not, but what if he is killed? Then he would never have met my possible future husband!" She gave him a playful look and a cheeky grin. Her porcelain skin glistened in the light of the bistro, a golden strand fell on her face. This sight stabbed Thomas in the heart. For a short moment he wished he could just be somewhere else.

"Maybe this is the last chance, you know? And Stella already knows you."

Yes, and the little snake is suspicious like a young fawn, Thomas added in his thoughts.

"On the other hand, with my daddy's temper, this could be a really unpleasant encounter. Oh, I just don't know," she finally sighed, grabbed her wine glass and emptied it in two gulps. They both remained silent for a moment while the waiter brought the bread. Taylor ordered another bottle of wine and water.

"So, your dad's gonna be at the invasion," he finally resumed the conversation.

Moringhem, France, January 15th, 1944

Moringhem was an even smaller village than Houlle. To avoid staying in the same assembly area all the time, the division had moved to Moringhem, only a few kilometers away, after Christmas, where they took up positions again and parked the tanks as camouflaged as possible. Lieutenant Engelmann had actually been able to spend the Christmas holidays with his family. His time at home had been both nice and painful. It was especially nice because he finally saw his family again: Elly, Gudrun, his parents, his parents-in-law and all the others. It was even nicer because he could hold his wife in his arms after all. Never before he had longed so much for affection and never before he had needed her caresses and her beautiful body so much.

It was painful to see that Bremen, his home town, had changed a lot during the year of his absence. The city center, the harbor and also some outlying districts lay in ruins, and even during his holidays there had been four air-raid alarms in the city area. Then they had hurried into the cellar every time, while Gudrun screamed terribly. But Gudrun herself had become the most painful experience for Engelmann. Not only did she not recognize him; no, she even screamed and cried as soon as she saw him. It had taken her a whole week to get used to her father again, and it wasn't until the third week that she had really laughed and been happy while playing with him. Engelmann was afraid that the little girl, who did not yet understand what was going on in the world, would resent him for leaving again and probably staying away for at least another year.

This world was cruel, especially cruel for the children who did not understand the war and for whom there was nothing else in life but playing and eating and sleeping. But sometimes this world was also cruel for the adults, especially for the fathers, who had to watch their own children becoming alienated from them.

Therefore Engelmann concentrated on his tasks as a platoon leader while he was on duty. Anything else would only make him sad. And there was enough to do these days.

Light drizzle and icy temperatures challenged the soldiers, who had work to do in the open field. Rommel didn't get tired of denouncing the weaknesses and shortcomings of the Atlantic Wall and the defense systems behind the beaches, as well as taking measures to improve the Wehrmacht's defenses in the West. The beaches along the English Channel were equipped with wooden obstacles, Czech hedgehogs and mines to make enemy landings more difficult. Bunkers were extended, trench systems were enlarged and guns were installed. Rommel used everything he could get his hands on. He had old Renault tanks of the French army buried on the beaches as fixed fire positions. Even cannons from the Great War were installed. The focus of all the work was of course on the area around Calais, where the enemy would probably land. But also the Normandy coast was prepared in this way – just in case.

The CiC France-Benelux even went so far as to forbid any military training as long as there was work to do. In this way he forced the conservative officers, who saw in Rommel only a foolhardy inventor, to let their units participate in the construction of the defense systems. From engineer to tanker to radio operator, everyone within the reach of Rommel's command had to be involved. The hinterland was not spared: Since the end of December, the Panzer Regiment 2 was already busy digging up the hard frozen French soil in order to plant the so-called "Rommel asparagus" everywhere in the fields of the canton Saint-Omer-Nord. These were long trunks of wood that rose vertically from the ground into the sky and were installed every few meters on as many open spaces as possible. They should prevent enemy air landings; or at least inflict losses on military gliders and paratroopers before the first shot was fired. Some of the stakes were sharpened at the top, others were fitted with mines. In any case, the Brits and Americans would get the shock of their lives if they came down here.

Engelmann's platoon was busy digging holes into which the engineers would then insert the stakes, in a large open area, which was enclosed on all sides by light deciduous forest. Since Engelmann did not like officers who had forgotten how to work, he joined in and struck again and again with his spade against the rock-hard ground. Münster and Stendal tried to break up the tough soil with him. But the ground was so frozen that every millimeter of earth had to be painstakingly wrested from it.

Everywhere on the open space up to the horizon, where the leafless forest began, the tank men fought with the ground. Engineers drove around in lorries and unloaded stakes and steel frames, which were to protect the part of the asparagus that was in the earth from decaying.

Only last Friday, Field Marshal Rommel, who turned out to be a real workhorse in France and the Benelux countries, had visited the regiment and held a speech in front of the troops. He had demanded the highest effort from all soldiers during the preparation for the invasion. Stendal, in particular, had been very impressed by the CiC's performance, with the result that the sergeant was talking a mile a minute about his hero Rommel ever since.

"In any case, I think Rommel's doing everything right with his strategy," the radio operator explained.

"Well, I wouldn't be too sure about that. I honestly think Rommel's getting too excited about his beaches. We must not throw our reserves from the hinterland directly onto the beach, where they are defenseless against enemy fire from ships. Not to mention the Allied strafers! If our forces are already being destroyed on the beaches, the Americans can march through to the Rhine." Engelmann thought Rommel to be a very capable officer, but had strong reservations about Rommel's tactics. He thought it wrong to move all available forces directly on the beach, because that would expose the Germans' hinterland.

After all, Field Marshal von Leeb, Commander-in-Chief of Army Group B, and many other high-ranking officers were Engelmann's opinion, but Rommel had won against all odds.

As a result, large movements of troops were currently taking place throughout France and the Benelux countries, with one destination: the coast. A single division still had to defend sections of beaches more than 50 kilometers wide. Rommel's ideas were ten kilometers per division.

"But the weakest moment of the enemy is immediately after landing, Rommel said so himself. Then the soldiers are seasick and disoriented, and then we have to throw them back," Stendal remarked in a surprisingly passionate way.

"That may be, but the effect of our tanks is fading away on the vast beaches. Either we get stuck in the sand or we get stuck in the dunes. And what should we shoot at? The

43

enemy will strike in the first wave with light landing crafts and therefore with infantry. We are the wrong people for that."

"With high explosive rounds we can also help to fight off the invasion, if we put the landing crafts under direct fire."

"You are forgetting one thing, Unteroffizier: The British with their Commonwealth buddies as well as the Americans will come across the Channel with such a tremendous material superiority that every beach around Calais will sink in the fire of their ship cannons and planes. In this respect we are powerless. I mean, when I see that the Luftwaffe has less than 400 planes in the North of France, I do not know whether to cry or laugh." Engelmann wiped the sweat from his forehead and, groaning, rammed the spade into the ground once more.

"Therefore, we have to beat them where we can use our strengths and the terrain is in our favor," the lieutenant continued. "We have to get them where their ship's artillery is no longer sufficient and their planes cannot see targets because of all the trees, namely in the hinterland."

The enemy fighters and bombers always played a decisive role in Rommel's considerations, and he had made that clear to the men, too. Rommel was one of the few German officers who had experienced first-hand what it meant when the enemy ruled the skies. He knew how quickly every German tank force crumbled to dust in the face of enemy planes.

Therefore Engelmann simply did not understand why Rommel sought the fight on the beach, where there was no protection against attacks from the air. Now Münster shook his head vehemently, but Engelmann was not sure whether the tank driver actually agreed with Rommel's strategy or whether he was just looking for opposition to his tank commander and platoon leader. Since the attack against Tula the difficult relationship between the two had not eased.

"You don't have to shake your head, Herr Feldwebel, even Feldmarschall Rommel is not infallible," Engelmann growled.

"But the material superiority of the Americans is exactly the point why we must never allow them to leave the beach. Once the Yank gets established on the coast, we'll never get him off. Then every day supplies will sail across the Channel, he will drag his planes over here and within days he will have brought a force into France against which no one can stand. Therefore, 'do not let them come ashore' is better than 'let them come'," Stendal explained. Apparently he immediately thought that he had adopted the wrong tone with the lieutenant, which is why he quickly added, "I think so".

"You can believe an old officer when he tells you something about tactics, after all, I have been trained in it," Engelmann finally joked and raised his eyebrows.

"Well, I'm thinking like Rommel," Münster murmured, who seemed to be completely obsessed with his spade.

"As you like, as long as you don't forget how to work," the lieutenant remarked and jokingly pointed to Münster's spade. The staff sergeant showed no reaction.

So the three tankers in their black uniforms continued to work in silence, while each of them followed his thoughts. Slowly the ground gave way and something like a hole was actually formed.

The threatening invasion hung like an invisible cloak over everyone; Engelmann felt this. With every day that passed, spring was getting closer and with it better weather. With every day that passed, the enemy attack became more likely. The soldiers' tension crackled noticeably in the air. The weather, the tides and German reconnaissance reports determined the conversations. One did not know exactly what the Allies were concentrating on the other side of the Channel; especially since they were also setting up dummies and dummy armies, but with every new report that came in, the eyes grew larger and so did the fears. The superior US economy, which was able to produce at full speed overseas, became noticeable through aerial reconnaissance photos and reports from agents: According to the latest information, more than 5,000 military ships gathered on the coasts of England, while in 1940 the

Germans were converting cutters and ferries in order to have enough floatable means of transport available for a possible landing in Great Britain. In England, more than two and a half million Americans, British, Canadians, New Zealanders, Indians, Australians, Poles and French were to wait for the crossing. That was twice as many soldiers as the Wehrmacht had stationed throughout France. In addition, there were over 12,000 aircraft; bombers, fighter bombers, and fighters – that was an air force the German side could dream of. In the meantime, the German Air Force was permanently overwhelmed; its fighters had to protect above all the important industrial plants in the homeland, otherwise fuel production would go down even further and German panzers could then only serve as defense turrets. It was enough to make you cry: While the Allies assembled the most modern war machines of the time, the German troops in France had only foot soldiers and second-rate rifles at their disposal. Not even significant naval forces were available. Thus, with a handful of soldiers who were poorly equipped and in many places had an average age of 40 years, Rommel was to fend off the largest and most modern armed force of all time. It was like the battle of David against Goliath. No, worse: It was like the battle of David against Goliath, with the giant attacking the poor boy with his slingshot with an armada of fighter planes and battleships.

"Perhaps they'll come earlier, Herr Leutnant. The Allies, I mean," Stendal suddenly said.

"I don't think so. The weather is too bad. With the rough sea in winter, the landing crafts will hardly make it across the Channel," the lieutenant replied.

"This is exactly why I would strike now, if I were the American commander," Stendal returned. "Because nobody expects it. I would come now and at low tide."

"They never come at low tide," Münster remarked. "Then they'd have to walk hundreds of meters of beach without cover. They'll come at high tide, and then half their boats will get tangled up in our obstacles."

Stendal nodded and continued digging. Lieutenant

Engelmann, however, turned away, for the sergeant's words had made him think. The British and the Americans were not to be underestimated. They were not only excellent fighters, but also daring warriors. If they were to come now, possibly at low tide and then also in Normandy or even in Brittany, then some on the German side would look like idiots. The Wehrmacht really had a Herculean task ahead of it. Only the fact that the enemy had to come from the water and that the German side was acting from positions that had been developed made him believe in the possibility of a German victory, but in the meantime Engelmann was again anything but optimistic. They were facing a murderous battle, yet the Lord put the lieutenant to the test enough by torturing Engelmann daily with his experiences in Russia.

West of Velikiye Luki, Soviet Union, February 10th, 1944

Master Sergeant Pappendorf didn't understand why he should lead these, in his opinion, dirty bastards through the prairie West of Velikiye Luki, and he also didn't understand why his squadron commander Balduin insisted that Pappendorf had to carry out this order personally; that is: Of course the master sergeant understood the meaning behind the order, but the whole thing was against his will.

Shoot down the Slavs and let them rot in no-man's-land, he demanded in his thoughts. But orders were orders. So Master Sergeant Pappendorf, together with Private Bailzer and Private Lenz, led a troop of 15 Russian POWs along the edge of a forest. They trudged through the snow over an open area that stretched to the horizon and there was only now and then a lonely scarecrow or a collective farm. The white powder covered everything. A cool wind breezed over the country.

47

"That is one filthy country," Pappendorf hissed and spat green slime into the snow, while his gaze was lost in the open landscape. The private beside him nodded silently.

"Fortunately, we'll soon meet Herrn Generalfeldmarschall Rommel," Pappendorf grumbled.

The march was long and the Russians were smelling intensely. Pappendorf wrinkled his nose. Despite the cold, he could still smell them. They simply disgusted him. The Russians marched silently, their heads bowed. Some of them had been in captivity for a long time. Their coats were matted, dirty and tattered. They wore different head coverings. Some were Soviet style, others civilian. They followed the private who was at the front; meanwhile Pappendorf and the private at the back made sure that none of their protégés got any stupid ideas. After all, the situation was not without danger: There were only three of them and the Russians had spades and shovels with them. Therefore the Germans kept their distance and pointed threateningly with their submachine guns at the prisoners. They could shoot the Ivans immediately, if they were to make a fuss.

The private knew the way, Pappendorf had instructed him in detail. He led the pinched and starved out Russians in a footslog for many kilometers around Velikiye Luki before turning East towards the front line. Already after half an hour the Russians began to groan and stumble. Pappendorf grinned. On purpose he had chosen the two soldiers with the strongest legs in his platoon for this mission and ordered the private to set a high speed. And he did not disappoint the master sergeant. They did not run, but Lenz trudged through the thick blanket of snow with quick steps. Already the Russians dropped behind.

"Dawai! Dawai!" Pappendorf roared, but the POWs didn't get any faster. So the master sergeant raised his weapon and fired a burst into the air. The bang of the shots echoed long after.

"Dawai! Move, you dirty slaves!" he roared. And indeed, the Russians moved on again, groaning, even if only for a short time. With fearfully contorted faces and shiny sweat on their skin, they tried with all their might to keep up.

"What's the matter with you?" Pappendorf had fun. "Had a bad breakfast this morning?" He laughed out loud. He liked it that way.

Lenz led the Russians past huge German panzers hidden all over the woods. German tankers climbed around on fighting vehicles. Panzer IV, Tiger, Panther, assault guns; the whole range of the German art of destruction was positioned around Velikiye Luki. The Russians could not know that these were only wooden dummies.

When the private turned further East according to the route and moved closer to the front, the small troop had passed wooden tanks with the strength of two regiments. Pappendorf had not failed to notice that the POWs had registered the alleged panzers with large eyes.

Good! he thought. Then he noticed that his "sheep" were already slowing down again.

"Must I make you get a move on?" he shouted at the prisoners. The Russians tried eagerly to speed up. They were afraid of the Germans, you could see that. They were especially scared of Pappendorf. But they were also at the end of their strength. Months of war captivity had turned them into skeletons with no reserves of energy left.

At some point – they were indeed close to their destination – the first one collapsed and lay motionless in the snow. Pappendorf was already there with his MP 40. The other prisoners of war stared at the German master sergeant with eyes wide open.

"Don't worry, I'll take care of the garbage for you," Pappendorf murmured, pointing the barrel of his gun at the Russian who was lying in the snow in front of him hyperventilating in a staccato.

"No, please," one of the Russians said with a heavy accent. He was one of three officers in the group. He quickly organized that his comrade was carried by the others.

"Don't think we'll slow down now, you mangy mutts!" Pappendorf said. The Russian, who had organized the transport of the comrade, helped to carry him himself, loudly urging his comrades to catch up with Private Lenz.

"What sons of bitches," Pappendorf murmured, spitting another greenish grit in the snow.

They finally reached the place where everything was arranged; a wide open space, interspersed with a few groups of trees that looked like square green boxes on a map. Right next to one of these groups of trees Private Lenz stopped. The wind blew mercilessly across the plain, banging with icy force against the battered bodies. The Germans ordered the Russians to stop, who, panting and sweating, lowered their exhausted comrade. The POWs almost collapsed themselves.

"No wonder you're losing the war," Pappendorf commented on the sight; then he pointed to the Russian officer who had revealed some knowledge of German earlier, and whistled at him like some would call a street dog. The Russian came.

"Listen, you scruffy bastard. You understand me?"

"Da." The Russian's eyes revealed his tiredness.

"German is the language used here and that means 'Jawohl, Herr Feldwebel'."

The Russian didn't answer. Pappendorf's face turned red.

"Jawohl, HERR FELDWEBEL!" he shrieked with gritted teeth. But the Russian just looked at him. His mouth remained shut. Pappendorf burst with rage from every pore. He took a swing and gave the Russian a loud slap. The blow knocked his face to the side, but the Russian immediately looked back to focus the screwed up eyes of the master sergeant. Everyone was staring at them – both the Germans and the Russians.

"Say 'Jawohl, Herr Feldwebel'," Pappendorf insisted in a threatening voice. The Russian remained silent, just stared back. Pappendorf was about to explode. The anger and hatred made his features tremble. Slowly he raised the muzzle of his submachine gun until it pointed at the Russian's stomach. The man's eyes were briefly directed at the gun, then they immediately moved back into Pappendorf's face. The Russian remained silent. He stared back with a steady gaze and clenched lips. Pappendorf was already breathing heavily and loudly.

I'm gonna kill that piece of shit! He whispered in his mind.

Only a year and a half ago it would have been no problem. Nobody would have asked for it. Many people would even have welcomed such measures.

And now suddenly everyone is doing brouhaha around the prisoners of war, as if this Slav scum had any value, Pappendorf raged in his mind, *as if these barbarians had any rights!* He snuffled his nose loudly and sucked green slime from the bottom of his throat, then he spat the snot right in the Russian's face.

There you go, peasant! He thought. But the Russian didn't move, just as if he was frozen. He stared back with a determined expression, while the slime stuck to his face.

Pappendorf pointed to his gun again with a nod of his head, but even that did not impress the Russian. Once again sheer fury chased through Pappendorf's body. He pushed the Russian aside and stomped towards the other prisoners of war, which he roughly drove apart. Then he aimed his submachine gun at the collapsed man, who was still lying motionless in the snow breathing only shallowly. Pappendorf reloaded his gun, which caused the first round to be ejected and disappear in the cool white. The reloading served as theatrical support for his intention. He crouched down next to the Russian and pressed the barrel against his cheek, his gaze directed at the Russian with the German language skills.

"Say 'Jawohl, Herr Feldwebel'!" Pappendorf ordered. Very angry glances met. Seconds passed. Everyone stared at the two opponents. No one dared to move. After everlasting seconds the Russian opened his mouth: "Jawohl, Herr Feldwebel!" he whispered with a heavy accent. Pappendorf's angry, distorted face suddenly turned into a broad grin. He stood up and lowered his weapon. "You see," he said to his two soldiers and raised his arms, "these pigs don't even have principles! They'd sell their own mother, if it gave them any advantage."

With large steps he stomped towards the Russian officer and built himself up in front of him. Then he took a map of the terrain from his pouch and spread it out on the ground.

"Here an antitank ditch must be placed," he explained to the Russian and pointed first to the ditch marked on the map and then again to the same place in the terrain. "Two meters deep, two meters wide and about 70 long – from the trees over there to the group of trees over here."

The Russian stared at Pappendorf with big eyes, while the slime still hung in his face.

"Digging?" he finally asked. "It's forbidden!"

"I don't give a damn! You'll start digging now, or this filthy piece of shit land will be your grave."

"70 meters?" The Russian was confused. "We only 15! And ground hard!"

Pappendorf kicked the Russian against his shinbone, so that the man dropped and landed in the snow.

"Start working, Slav! And hurry up! The work of 15 men must be done here today. But I only see 14 who can work!"

Reluctantly, the POWs began to drive their shovels into the snow. Some of them took off their coats and bedded the still unconscious man on them. There was nothing else they could do for him. Pappendorf called the two privates over to him, then he looked at his pocket watch.

"Listen, men! Everything's set for ten o'clock, which means we'll leave in an hour. Until then, let the Slavs do some more digging." He grinned at his men, who replied as if from one throat: "Jawohl, Herr Feldwebel." Pappendorf then turned to the groaning and working Russians: "And don't exhaust yourself too much. We must march back tonight after all!"

*

Another ten minutes and the trick would begin. Pappendorf wandered among the working Russians and stroked his submachine gun. The POWs had indeed already dug a considerable pit, struggled groaning and sweating against the frozen ground. These people disgusted Pappendorf. He felt the need to bathe immediately.

As you can see again: Slavs are made to work. They're good at it. The master sergeant grinned. *So sometimes it's good to make them work before slaughtering them!* He liked such thoughts, and for the first time he really looked into the faces of those Russians. They all had sunken cheeks and a very pale skin color. They were generally in a bad condition. In moments like these Pappendorf wished to leave this stinking, miserable Russia and return to Germany, where he could stay among educated people, among his own kind, as he always said.

Pappendorf's gaze fell on the Russian lying in the snow. His comrades had covered him with more coats, but nothing had helped: 20 minutes ago, the man had stopped breathing. The corpse was now lying there wax-pale, while a few falling snowflakes began to cover him. The officer with the German language skills had asked to be allowed to bury the man. Of course Pappendorf had refused. *If we were to dig a hole every time one of these bastards died, we would never finish here in Russia. The Slavs are dying like flies!* He thought selfishly.

The master sergeant stood in front of the dead man. His bladder was pressing, so he unbuttoned his pants and brought out his penis. Deep yellow urine hit the dead man and poured over him while Pappendorf groaned theatrically. The Russians stopped with their work, and also Bailzer and Lenz, who were repeatedly looking nervously at the prepared position back between the trees, 200 meters away, stared at their platoon leader. The behavior of the master sergeant seemed to shock even them, who both were not known as very Russian friendly. 16 pairs of eyes goggled at Pappendorf in bewilderment as he turned around and packed his genital away. Smirking, the master sergeant looked down the row of Russians, then suddenly his face became very serious.

"You bastards are supposed to work," he barked. The prisoners of war continued with unmistakable glances.

Suddenly Pappendorf's gaze caught on one of the Russians, a private. The man was lean and emaciated, but his physique indicated that he had once been tall and strong. Blond hair peeked out from under his wool cap, and blue eyes focused on the frozen ground into which he drove

53

his spade.

Oh? Pappendorf thought and tilted his head to the side, *that's not possible! Coincidences do exist!* Immediately he whistled at Private Lenz, who arrived on the double.

"Jawohl, Herr Feldwebel?"

"That one!" Pappendorf pointed to the Russian with the blond hair, who immediately noticed that they were talking about him. He kept working, but his eyes filled with fear. The officer with the German language skills was also aware of the matter.

"Get the Slav and go over to the starting position. There you wait for us."

Lenz faltered. "Herr Feldwebel, I..." he began. His dialect revealed that he was from Berlin.

"You were not ordered to Russia to think, Herr Gefreiter!" Pappendorf shouted.

"Jawohl, Herr Feldwebel." The Berlin man briefly repeated the order, then trudged towards said Russians and pulled him away from the others. He signaled the prisoner of war to move westward. He didn't understand anything. He turned to his comrades looking for help, but they looked back just as helplessly. Only when Lenz hit him in the back with the butt of the submachine gun, the blond Russian marched off with uncertain steps. They quickly moved away from the group as the snowdrift became more intense.

However, the Russian officer with the German language skills suddenly broke away from his comrades and stomped towards Pappendorf with a determined look, who had already puffed up his chest like a rooster awaiting the next confrontation.

"What doing?" the Russian asked blatantly. "What doing?" He pointed to his departing comrade.

"'What are you up to', is the right question!" Pappendorf shouted, "Doing word, predicate, object! That's how you form a German sentence, you dim-witted ape!" The master sergeant shook his head dramatically. "And most of all, every sentence that leaves your filthy mouth ends with 'Herr Feldwebel', so that we understand each other once and for all!"

"What doing? Want shoot?" The Russian, a skinny bag of bones who'd already been drained of most of his vitality during his German war captivity, planted himself up in front of Pappendorf, as good as his condition would allow. As worn out and lean as his body was, his spirit seemed unbroken and strong, and pure determination emanated his eyes. Pappendorf, however, shouted out: "HERR FELDWEBEL! UND JAWOHL! I don't want to hear anything else from you!"

"You want shoot? That forbidden!" he immediately replied.

Smack! Pappendorf's flat hand slapped loudly across the Russian's face. The slap echoed across the open space and mingled with the whistling of the wind.

"You dirty bastard, I just told you something!" the master sergeant shouted, but all he got was a look from the Russian. His eyes reflected steadfastness and honor.

"You want shoot? Da? Then stop talking and do, fascist!"

Pappendorf held his breath. *Did he just talk back?* The master sergeant couldn't believe his ears. He clasped his submachine gun tighter, while he could just see in the corner of his eye that the private had disappeared with the blond Russian in the drifting snow.

Slowly he raised his weapon, when suddenly a machine gun rattled off nearby. Immediately the Russians, Pappendorf and Bailzer threw themselves to the ground.

"Machine gun fire, take cover!" the private yelled.

Pappendorf pulled out his pocket watch and looked on the hands. He had completely forgotten the time! He indicated to his soldier that it was starting. Lying on the ground, they turned away from the Russians, who had thrown their arms over their heads to protect them. The machine gun fired long bursts of fire, the muzzle flash was just visible through the rainfall at a distance of 200 meters. Pappendorf and Bailzer quickly unloaded their weapons and loaded a new, marked magazine each. Pappendorf then began his orders: "Grenadier Bailzer, dodge firing, on my mark!"

"Jawohl, Herr Feldwebel! Dodge firing!" They both rose to

their feet and fired at the machine gun, which also continued to fire. Pappendorf and his soldier quickly ran away, increasing the distance between them and the supposed enemy. They took the same path that Lenz had already taken with the blond Russian. Firing from the hip, they emptied their magazines and disappeared.

*

The Germans were gone, just left in the face of machine gun fire. The Russians stayed behind, lying rigidly on the ground. Soon after, the machine gun stopped. Slowly the POWs, who could not make out a guard for miles around, rose. The officer with the German language skills organized his comrades, then they began to dig a grave for the dead man. Afterwards they marched off in the direction of their own troops.

*

Pappendorf and Bailzer had loaded the other magazines into their weapons again. They quickly arrived at the appointed position; a hollow in the ground, surrounded by old pines. They lowered themselves into the hole where Lenz waited with the prisoner of war as ordered.

You could see that the Russian was in mortal fear; that his emotions were running wild.

He thinks I killed his men, Pappendorf was smiling. "It's such a waste," he said at the same time. Lenz and Bailzer nodded politely.

"It would have been enough to send two or three of them."

The Russians were probably long since on their way to their own front lines. Those Germans, however, who were operating the machine gun, certainly radioed the squadron that everything had gone according to plan. By firing more blanks from other positions they would drive those Russians to the place where they had the opportunity to cross the Lovat.

Pappendorf ordered the march back.

*

The squadron had recently stopped work. The day-to-day business – cleaning weapons and maintaining material – was done. Slowly the daylight was fading, but the men could still see well with the naked eye. Berning was sitting at the squad's place.

The squadron had moved into a forest West of Velikiye Luki and pitched their tents there. Sergeant Berning felt terrible. Because of the snow everything was damp and the cold was everywhere, even in the tents. Life in the forest was miserable during the Russian winter.

Berning sat on a tree stump and stared into the snow. His pants were soaked, and watery wounds had formed on his legs. He froze bitterly and pulled his coat a little tighter. His fingers and feet ached, while the soft murmuring of his comrades filled the air. The old deciduous and coniferous trees cracked in the wind while powdered snow trickled from the branches.

"Unteroffizier Berning!" Berning jumped up immediately and grabbed his helmet and rifle.

"Here, Herr Feldwebel!" he barked, turned around and recognized Pappendorf, who was standing on the connecting path to the 3rd squad, a narrow path that the landsers had cut into the undergrowth.

"Come here!"

"Jawohl, Herr Feldwebel!" On the double, he rushed towards his platoon leader.

"Follow me!" Pappendorf commanded, turned around and left on the double as well.

Oh no, Berning moaned in his mind, while he was chasing after him.

*

Pappendorf rushed far out of the squadron's area of responsibility and finally also out of the area of the

57

battalion. Deeper and deeper they dashed into the forest. Berning gasped and groaned, but he did not dare to slow down.

In front of him the master sergeant, unimpressed by the blanket of snow and the woods, ran along at high speed, jumped over stick and stone, waded through brooks and climbed up hills. *Whew!* Stitches burned in Berning's right side. Air burst out of his mouth at a rapid pace. He moaned while his helmet slid wildly around on his head. It seemed to him as if they were far away from all their own forces – somewhere in the middle of the deepest forest. And it was getting darker and darker. He could barely see anything.

Is he gonna shoot me? Out here nobody would notice that anyway, the sergeant tried to distract himself with gallows humor. But he was a little scared. Then they arrived at a tiny clearing. Lenz and Bailzer sat there on a lying tree trunk and showed each other photos of their families.

Pappendorf broke through the undergrowth and stopped. Immediately the two soldiers recoiled, packed the pictures and jumped up.

"Get away!" Pappendorf barked.

"Jawohl, Herr Feldwebel," they said with one voice. Then they trudged away on the path across which Pappendorf and Berning had come, greeting the sergeant briefly as they passed by. He just nodded, because he had already discovered something else in the clearing: A Russian was squatting there.

The man knelt in the snow and looked down, trembling heavily. Who knows how long he had been sitting in the frosty snow like that. Pappendorf approached the prisoner of war, who slowly looked up.

Berning turned to stone.

The face of that Russian triggered fierce feelings in him… In front of him in the snow was not just any POW! Not just any Red Army soldier, like there was millions of them. An old acquaintance knelt there!

Berning would still recognize this guy out of an army of men.

This is the murderer of Rudi Bongartz! That was the only

58

thought that Berning's mind allowed at that moment. *There's his killer!*

Pappendorf looked at Berning's face. He seemed to realize, that something was going on in the sergeant... and the master sergeant seemed to like that. After endless moments, Berning's gaze detached itself from the Russian. With quivering lips and glassy eyes, he looked at Pappendorf. Asking, pleading, he stared at his platoon leader.

"We're far away from anyone, Unteroffizier," Pappendorf said calmly.

Berning looked at the Russian, who glanced at him with a tired and sad look. Apparently he did not seem to recognize the sergeant. Berning shook.

He clasped his rifle tighter until his fingers hurt. Inside him, emotions struggled with the sense of duty, his conscience with the urge to seek revenge. But the victor was already determined. Berning believed that he had a chance to get rid of the eternal feelings of guilt once and for all.

He could revenge Bongartz and get a clean slate, he thought at that moment, while his rifle suddenly felt light in his hands.

The Russian looked at him. Freezing and at the end of his strength he was flailing violently back and forth. His head vibrated like a running engine. Seconds passed.

Suddenly Berning raised his rifle and fired. The bang roared through the forest. Animals were startled. The bullet entered the Russian's chest and cut through his lungs. He tilted to the side as the snow below him turned red. But he was not dead.

His whole body trembled and twitched like a fish on dry land, without producing any sound. Determined Berning approached and raised his rifle a second time.

He placed the second bullet right in the neck of his victim, killing the prisoner. Blood and tissue stained Berning's uniform. The bullet left an ugly hole.

The sergeant looked around. It shook him serverly. He zeroed in on Pappendorf who seemed to be very satisfied.

59

Velikiye Luki, Soviet Union, February 24th, 1944

Private Rudi Bongartz lay on the ground with a dark blue face. He opened his mouth and wanted to scream, but he couldn't. He grabbed his neck with both hands. Something was strangling him. Rudi's arms and legs fidgeted and flailed around. He was like mad, and tried to breathe convulsively. But something blocked his windpipe. Berning stood beside him and was condemned to watch. He wanted to help his comrade – his friend after all – but he could not move. Berning tried to move his hands. But they hung down on him heavy as lead and did not want he wanted. Rudi was in death throes – and he lost it. The flailing of his limbs became weaker, until it finally went into a twitch. Rudi's mouth still opened and closed like a carp. But he was no longer able to suck air into his lungs. Rudi's eyes became glassy, then they focused on Berning, who startled.

I want to help you, the sergeant wanted to yell, but he couldn't get his teeth apart. It was like his mouth was taped shut. Rudi stared at him, his eyes reflected reproaches and recriminations. Berning couldn't bear the glance, but he couldn't turn his head away; yes, he couldn't even close his eyes. His whole body condemned him to watch. Slowly, very slowly Rudi was dying. The twitching of his limbs stopped. Finally the mouth closed – and did not open anymore. But the eyes remained open. Dead eyes looked at Berning and did not let go of him.

Berning startled. He wanted to scream, but he could prevent that at the last moment. He lay together with hundreds of comrades in a huge hall that had once served as a factory's material store. In the upper part of the room there were large windows on all sides of the walls, showing the darkness outside and the starry sky.

Berning was bathed in sweat. His undershirt was so wet he could have wrung it out. His hair and his neck were shiny. He was breathing fast and heavy. It took him a while to calm down, until his pulse dropped. Comrades were sleeping around him, writhing back and forth or smacking in their sleep. Somewhere, someone was moaning, barely audible. Elsewhere someone was farting. The crowded room reeked of food, urine, human evaporations and socks. Slowly Berning sank back to his cot and pulled the blanket over his body. He felt unwell and sick. Through a narrow window he could look outside, where the city lay peacefully. It was hard to believe that the war was only a few kilometers further East.

Velikiye Luki had already been suffering severe destructions. Battered industrial plants, which had survived the fighting so far, rose above the residential buildings. Most of the wooden panje huts on the outskirts of the city had been burned down to their foundations. Where once had been small town quarters made up of such huts, only the stone chimneys were left, pointing to the sky like bony fingers. Bomb craters and ruins in the city center and on the outskirts showed the destructive power of modern weapons. Where destruction had not yet happened, white and red magnificent buildings were standing. Whether town hall, church or residential building; Velikiye Luki reflected the elegance of Russian architecture.

Berning's squadron as well as two other companies of the battalion had been staying in that empty hall near the railway station for almost a week. In two days the train journey to the West would begin, thousands of kilometers across Europe... and partisan attacks were to be expected almost along the entire route.

The blisters on Berning's legs had almost healed. His wounds had become worse at first and became infected with pus. Berning was about to be sent to the military hospital – he had secretly been looking forward to it. But then they went out of the wet forest and into the city, which caused an immediate healing process to begin. It was remarkable what a few days in dry clothes could do. Nevertheless, despite all the advantages of the rear echelon, despite his generally good physical condition, Berning felt horrible.

West of Bénouville, France, April 1st, 1944

The Opel trucks rumbled leisurely across the paved road and approached their destination, the double bridges over the Caen Canal and the river Orne at Bénouville respectively Ranville. The sun had only been shining for minutes and its rays made the country glitter. The trucks drove leisurely along the road. They passed fruit trees lined up in rows, their branches forming fresh leaves that still looked like rolled up knobs.

Spring arrived inexorably and transformed the barren land into a colorful one. It wasn't really warm yet, but it wasn't as icy cold as it was in mid-March. It hadn't frozen at night for a week, and during the day the temperatures rose more and more into the double-digit range with each passing day.

The truck of the 1st squad had taken the lead of the convoy, which consisted of a total of four squads – that is, four trucks. While one of the soldiers drove and another navigated the route, the rest spent the bumpy ride on narrow benches on the loading area – the squad leader, Master Sergeant Pantelis Schneider, had also squeezed himself onto the loading area between his men. In a regular squad, the leader would certainly enjoy the privilege of sitting in the closed driver's cab rather than on the open loading area at the back. As mentioned, in a regular unit this would be the case, but this was not a regular unit.

"So, men!" Schneider shouted against the wind and the rattling of the Opel. "How does it feel to wear your own uniforms again for a change? To be under the command of a regular unit again and to do regular things? It's an amazing feeling, isn't it? Like being born again, right?" The German with Greek origins grinned broadly into the circle. His black, curly hair peeked out from under his helmet and was actually much too long for a German soldier. But someone should try to teach Schneider. The guy had a mind of his own.

"You mean, how does it feel to not violate the Hague

Land Warfare Convention for a change?" the white South African Jack Calvert shouted. He had brown, short hair and thick lips.

Like all foreign members of the "Brandenburgers", Calvert also volunteered for the Wehrmacht. Some of them were driven into this unit by a thirst for adventure, others by the hope of being allowed to live in such a modern German Reich sometime after the war. Even during Hitler's time, when racial fanaticism was on its peak, the Brandenburgers had already been a colorful mix of all nationalities. Hostility on account of skin color or origin was rare in this unit, for the members of the Brandenburgers knew of the special value that foreign soldiers had who voluntarily fought for Germany, especially for commando operations. At present, of course, men with roots in the Soviet Union were in particular demand, which is why such people filled the majority of the personnel lists of the Brandenburgers. All other nationalities were grouped into a few companies. The 2nd Company of Sonderverband 804 – Special Unit 804 – was such a mixed unit. People from all five continents served in it.

"Yes, exactly," Schneider grinned.

"Shit!" Anton Schumann, the tall Norwegian with German grandparents, complained. Schumann was always complaining, and always found a reason why everything was a mess. The redhead wiped his face with his right hand and knocked against the metal of his Sturmgewehr 44, a brand-new machine carbine with the magazine slightly bent forward. The weapon was to become the standard weapon of the infantry as soon as possible. The Karabiner 98k would then only play a secondary role as a precision weapon.

The semi-automatic Gewehr 43, on the other hand, had not been able to establish itself. The few thousand rifles produced had been issued to the troops though, and the Brandenburgers had also received a few.

"It's just as shitty as before. We are being used as cannon-fodder again for some officer's brain fart, just because the eggheads don't know what to do with us. The whole system is already fatal, that we are not led by competent people who know how to deploy us, but are hooked every time to some garden-variety division."

Schneider formed a babbling mouth with his hand while looking at the faces of the men. They grinned, but Schumann kept on chattering unperturbed: "The idiots will then employ us as quick reaction forces again, and we will have to run back and forth all day long, or they will use us as cannon-fodder immediately to spare their own boys. It just sucks." Schumann leaned over the back of the truck and spat on the road. Then he took a sip from his canteen. In addition to his military skills, Schumann was a gifted drawer. When the staff of the Brandenburger unit, which at that time only existed in regimental strength, wanted to give the commander a very special birthday present, they had made him a picture album with self-written verses. Schumann had made the really outstanding drawings for this.

"Why don't you give us a break for a minute. You talk without interruptions." Schneider grinned like a Cheshire cat.

"Then make things better at last and I'll shut up. Until then, put up with me or put me in a unit with brains." Schumann took another big sip from the canteen. Schneider shook his head, then he said, "You're acting as if you're not here voluntarily. And besides: Are you drinking cider again?"

"Somehow I've got to put up with you nitwits."

"Zo gia na s'agapo," Schneider smirked. Schumann raised his index finger threateningly. "Someday I'll learn Greek, and then you'll be surprised when I suddenly know what you keep saying to me!" Schneider laughed.

"I don't know what is the matter with you, Mannerheim," Kaspar Schütz, a small, slender boy with tiny eyes, who was born in the Reich and could shoot like a big shot, interfered.

"Mannerheim" had become a nickname for Schumann and was inspired by the Finnish military officer Carl Mannerheim. By the time Schumann's comrades had finally learned that Norway was not Finland, the name had long

64

since become established.

"We're out of Russia, so why don't you just shut up for once," Schütz said and shoved the helmet down his neck. Then he lit a cigarette and passed the pack on. Schumann shook his head and tapped against his forehead.

"Besides, now we are fighting regularly. Then we don't need those stupid aliases anymore," Schütz murmured and dragged on his cigarette.

"Why, I always liked yours," Schneider said happily.

"What? Scampi?" Schütz tapped his forehead at his squad leader. "I don't even know what that is."

"Hey! Is this about you or me?" Schumann hissed with a fury.

"It's about me, folks," Schneider proclaimed, raising his hands threateningly.

"You've just lost all your pebbles," Private First Class Fourie Moseneke, a black South African, grinned at this moment and showed his teeth. The others laughed. Moseneke was a giant, tall, slim and muscular.

As the only Black of the company he stood out from the group like a shining Christmas tree. Of course he often had problems in the Wehrmacht because of his skin color, but not within his unit. Anyone who had seen Moseneke in battle once, where the South African mutated into a raging tornado that swept everything away, would never again raise a word against this man. Moreover, Moseneke was an excellent comrade, and many of the Brandenburgers owed him their lives. There were, however, sometimes still a few problems with the German language.

"Club, that means marbles," Schneider corrected him.

"Marbles?" Moseneke frowned and scratched his chin with the muzzle of his machine carbine.

"Yeah, marbles, not pebbles."

"Okay." Moseneke was wondering. "What's the difference?"

"Well, marbles are..." Schneider stumbled and waved his hands. "Marbles are just marbles. And pebbles are different somehow. They're round, but... Golly, now help me to explain this!"

"Don't look at me like that!" Schumann raised his hands defensively. "I'm Norwegian, and I can't even speak my own language properly."

"Anyway, pebbles are on the ground. Marbles are more like... well... it's marbles, for Christ's sake!"

"Okay, jawohl." Moseneke nodded exaggeratedly. "Anyway, you've lost your marbles," he proclaimed. "France is a beautiful country! And here we are! Better than the cold in Russia!"

"And the chicks! Did you see those chicks over in Lyon?" Schütz raved. "Beauties!" he added and began to daydream.

"Yeah, too bad for you they don't jump into bed with kids, huh?" Schneider grinned.

"Fuck you!"

"Pardon? I think I'm gonna have to take some disciplinary action on you."

"Fuck you anyway." Schütz pushed his helmet into his face and formed a kissing mouth. Then he smiled broadly.

"But our dear Fourie, he got it easy," Calvert explained, sitting next to Moseneke and patting the giant on the shoulder. "All he has to do is pull out his eight-eight and the girls are lining up to lay the pipe."

"Hey!" Moseneke spread his arms defensively and allowed himself a long pause for thought. Everyone stared at him. "Fourie can't do it. I don't want to kill the women, okay?"

His comrades burst out laughing.

"Fourie's eight-eight only fits dark women."

The others snorted and cheered, while Moseneke was pleased about the laughter. His exotic accent only made his sentences more effective.

"The Frenchmen all have venereal diseases anyway," Schumann finally remarked, crossing his arms.

"You shouldn't take a Frenchman anyway!" Schneider shouted. The men were laughing tears.

"You know what I mean, assholes!"

This went on for a while until the truck finally reached the edge of the village of Bénouville. It passed a few farms on the side of the road, where dozens of Frenchmen were working early in the morning. Farmers fed the animals, while an old woman at the side of the road, with a girl holding her hand, suspiciously blinked in the direction of the German trucks.

"Look at the little girl, Schütz!" Calvert laughed and pointed to her. "After all they have girls your size here!"

"Man, she's only 13!" he returned insulted.

"So? You're 12, so what's your problem?"

"I'm about to kick your ass, Jack!"

"Oh, I want to see that. Do you think your little arms will reach that high?"

Schütz turned red in the face.

"Let it go for now," Schneider intervened and silenced everyone. The trucks chugged through the village until the density of the buildings subsided again. The road passed a few solitary farms, then a T-junction, surrounded by three large barns. Then the trucks turned right.

After 200 meters the bridge over the Caen canal could be seen. The first of the double bridges was the so-called canal bridge, a narrow, modern metal opening bridge that could be raised as a whole when ships passed the canal.

"All right, men, listen up!" Schneider started and pulled out a sketch. "As I said – but since you're too stupid to remember something like that, I'll repeat it again – the second bridge is ours – the one over there, the one over the Orne." Schneider stood up and pointed over the driver's cab of the truck to the second bridge, also made of metal, but without the typical slanted construction of the opening bridge, instead with a pivot point in the middle. This second bridge was located at the other end of a 500 meter wide strip of land between the canal and the river Orne.

"This one is called the Orne Bridge. We're taking it over from some gorgeous guys from the reserve together with 2nd squad. The others will take this one here in front, called the Canal Bridge."

The soldiers nodded eagerly. Rumbling, the truck crossed the first bridge, where a bored landser stood at the barrier. The truck jolted several times as it passed the bridge.

"This is just as stupid as that stupid mission near Orel,"

Schumann complained again.

"It's your own fault, if you let Russian bullets bite you," Schneider remarked, but Schumann continued unabatedly: "Why did we go through hell in training when we were made to be dogfaces after all? Why all the cross-country marches and exercises with the fucking constant drilling, why all the language and cultural training and all the filth when we're being made to be fucking bridge guards?"

"Now stop trying to make it look as miserable as sin, Mannerheim," Schneider whispered. "The final time in Russia may have been unlucky for us, but it's just the next logical step to be here now."

"Unlucky? Our last adequate mission was in Africa. Since then, all we've done is this front line shit. Seriously, I'm too good to be stuck in the trenches."

The others grinned, but Schneider continued with his lecture, which he had given several times before. He never tired of getting his men in the mood for what was coming: "Why do you think we haven't done anything proper since Africa? Look at us! We are not Ivans, so what are they going to do with us?"

"But even these companies were partly send to the slaughter," Schumann interjected. The Norwegian also never got tired of complaining about the situation.

"Yes, and our commander, and even more recently the OKW, have issued directives prohibiting such operations. It takes time until the wearer of fruit salads get to know, which our core strengths are."

"And our core strengths should be pushing up and down a turnpike"?

"You don't understand," Schneider moaned.

"He doesn't want to understand," Calvert interjected and smirked.

"Gee, Mannerheim, why don't you just keep your trap shut," Berger, a tall Rhinelander with sunken cheeks and a talent for foreign languages, exclaimed. The private first class pulled his stahlhelm over his face and indicated that he was covering his ears. Meanwhile the truck rolled over the road between the two bridges. The land to the right and left was nothing more than a narrow embankment enclosed by the Caen Canal and the Orne, which was at ground level and overgrown with grass, and in many places very marshy. But on each side of the road there was also a small part of forest. During the conversation on the loading area, Schneider noticed the terrain in the corner of his eye and had his first ideas of how he make use of it tactically – years of training and the experiences from the battle had skilled him to do such terrain analyses in passing.

"I do understand it," Schumann returned, then he first knocked Calvert and then Berger against the helmet. Moseneke smiled.

"But I don't want that crap."

"At least that's a ray of hope! Then I don't have to explain to you why the 804th has been assigned to Rommel. Once it starts and the Americans and the British arrive here with their bondsmen, we will be in great demand again very soon. And believe me, Rommel knows all about our core strengths!"

"Is that the reason why we should guard this bridge?"

Schneider rolled his eyes. "How many times have I explained this to you now? How many times, Jack?"

"Seven times, mon amour."

"Thank you. But I like to repeat it: These bridges that we are now taking over are incredibly important, and there is a danger that the enemy will try to get hold of them with paratroopers, once the invasion starts. That is why there will be no more Eastern battalion soldiers sent here as guards. If the enemy lands in Calais and these double bridges fall, the Normandy coast will be cut off and all forces that we wanted to move from the West to the invasion point would have to make huge detours."

"Gosh! I've never looked at it from this perspective before," Schütz joked.

"Shut the fuck up." Schneider leaned back and crossed his arms while Schumann shook his head.

"We'll rot on this fucking bridge. Why did I sign up for this unit?"

"You know how it is with us: It all ends sometime."

69

"It all ends sometime," Schneider's men repeated with one voice, only Schumann remained silent and twisted his mouth. In the early days of the Brandenburgers, some officer had come up with the saying, which has since even found its way into official letters and orders.

The Opel stopped just before the Orne Bridge, and the truck behind it also came to a halt. The other two trucks, with the 3rd and 4th squad on board, had already stopped at the first bridge, where the soldiers jumped off the loading platforms and were scurrying around.

"All right, ladies and gentlemen, get oooooouuuuut."

With these words Schneider drove his men out of the truck. The Brandenburgers grabbed their equipment and jumped off the loading area. The driver and co-driver also got out, pulling their equipment out of the driver's cab; then the whole squad formed a semicircle around Schneider. A few meters away, at the edge of the Orne Bridge, there was also a guard; a young guy who, when he saw Moseneke, made big eyes and looked around uncertainly.

"You already have an admirer," Calvert giggled, nudging Moseneke to make him aware of the post.

"I'm a handsome man," he grinned.

Schneider looked into the faces of his men, who had thrown their haversacks over their shoulders and carried their weapons casually on their long arms. Schneider did not think much of military formalities and would therefore never let his soldiers line up. With him, everything went off quite relaxed. Besides, they were tormented enough by the leadership with parade duty anyway, because the high officers assumed that this was the only way to discipline all the non-Germans.

"Good," Schneider began, studying the expressions of his men. Next to Moseneke, Calvert, the small Schütz, Berger and Schumann, stood in front of him the American-born Murray Foster with his puffy moustache; the Viennese Alfons Stückl, like Berger a linguistic genius who spoke seven languages fluently; Gerd Wildner, who studied law, with his over-proportionally large nose and his tendency towards Islam; private Pierre Valente from Alsace and the

70

Private Erich Mielke, who, according to his own statement, was wanted by the police for a murder in the early 1930s. The day after Hitler's death he is said to have turned himself in to the German authorities, months later he was acquitted of all charges for lack of evidence. In the middle of 1943 he joined the Wehrmacht and immediately volunteered for the Brandenburgers, because – as he always said – he wanted to change the world. Now he was 36 years old and still a private because of some faux pas he had allowed himself, although his abilities indicated that he had already gained military experience elsewhere. Moreover, Mielke always raved about wanting to become chief of the Abwehr one day.

"I'll look around and report to the platoon leader. Then we'll contact the unit responsible for this area. Wait here and try not to kill anyone until I get back." Schneider's men nodded and beamed before Schneider disappeared. The master sergeant marched over to the Canal Bridge, because the platoon leader, First Lieutenant Fritze, had been riding along with the 3rd squad. His men stayed behind waiting.

"I wonder what lil' Taylor is doing," Foster mused aloud, revealing his heavy American accent.

"He's probably sitting around somewhere fucking some girl right now. And he tells his boss that she is an important source," Calvert replied. Everyone laughed.

"The old womanizer," Foster grinned. Nice memories of days gone by came to mind.

Then suddenly the high and trembling voice of Mielke was heard through the laughter: "Don't you think you are using bad language when talking about women?" He looked around expectantly, but all he got was a shake of the head and a look of disapproval.

"What do you want?" Foster's voice sounded annoyed.

"If you talk about women as if they were mere instruments of the male sex drive, this society will never reach the next stage of evolution. Then even the little guy and the worker will still be oppressed in a hundred years, because there is a big connection between all of this. Finally, the historical dialectic of things teaches us that the change

71

to a classless society is an indispensable building block of the future. I recommend reading Max Horkheimer."

Everyone stared at Mielke. The private always managed to look like a foreign body in the circle of his comrades.

"Erich, seriously," Berger began in a fatherly voice and put his hand on Mielke's shoulder. "You are a nice guy, really. But leave us alone with this shit. Nobody cares. And you'll only get in trouble again."

Mielke looked to the ground disappointed.

South of Saint-Omer, France, April 3rd, 1944

In the course of the last months dozens of changes of position had been carried out within the regiment. Accordingly, the 9th Company had moved frequently in the canton of Saint-Omer-North and neighboring cantons. Currently Engelmann's platoon was South of Saint-Omer, a pretty little town with a cathedral. Engelmann and some others had taken the opportunity to attend some church services. Usually these were held in French, but sometimes the local priest, together with German field clergy, would hold a bilingual community mass, which was then attended mostly by German soldiers. Most French people preferred to stay at home on such days. Stendal and Nitz had often accompanied Engelmann; Jahnke, Ludwig and especially Münster, however, the lieutenant had not been able to convince to attend mass. Actually Engelmann himself was no friend of institutionalized religion. He did not need masses, churches or clergymen for his faith, but if a good pastor was at work with passion and a strong voice, a service could develop a very special atmosphere, which Engelmann again appreciated very much.

The first light of day poured over the land, transforming the darkness into colorless areas that only gave a hint of meadows and forests and slowly became saturated. It was a terrible storm. The wind tore at the trees with all its might, whistling over the roofs of the farms. Long strings of rain whirled around almost horizontally. The men of the 9th Company were lucky to be able to stay in the barns and farmhouses of the local farmers, who were royally rewarded for housing German military personnel. Engelmann, Nitz and Münster resided in a small country house, which a very old farmer lived in completely alone since the death of his wife. The man was reserved, but friendly, and provided the soldiers with good food. Engelmann even had a room for himself, while Nitz and Münster shared the neighboring room. The rooms were furnished with real beds with mattresses, with desks and wardrobes – all made of sturdy oak wood. Engelmann almost felt like being in a hotel.

After the lieutenant had washed and shaved, he stepped into the corridor. Engelmann looked at his Swiss watch. 6.58 German time. Breakfast time!

Nitz stumbled out of the next room and rubbed his eyes, then he stretched his back with a painful face.

"Golly," the master sergeant moaned, "all of this is nothing for an old man anymore." He grinned weakly, but there was pain and exhaustion in his expression.

"How's your back?"

"It has to, Herr Leutnant, it has to."

Engelmann nodded with narrowed eyes. Nitz worried him.

"Münster's already down?"

"Yes, he's washing himself."

"I hope he'll be at the table on time. Yesterday I was embarrassed that we had to keep the old man waiting, who after all prepares meals for us."

Nitz nodded silently, then looked out the window.

"They won't come today anyway," the master sergeant mused, tugging at his moustache. Engelmann also looked at the storm that was raging out there.

"Unlikely," he growled in a tired voice.

"I'm tired of waiting," Nitz hissed, turning away from the window. Engelmann agreed with a straight face, then both

73

went down the stairs leading to the ground floor.

"And when I have to think of all the things we have to do today...," Nitz's voice echoed.

In the kitchen everything was prepared on a wide wooden table: Bread, milk, eggs, butter, sausage and cheese made a sumptuous meal. It had been set for four people. The smell of fresh coffee filled the air. The farmer really spoiled the panzer men. Münster had therefore not only asked jokingly whether they would not be poisoned here bit by bit – but in the end, after years of sacrifices in Russia, they didn't care much and helped themselves every morning. Everything the old landlord offered tasted almost heavenly.

Münster was already sitting at the table, picking his ear as if searching for hidden treasures. When he saw the lieutenant, he jumped up and saluted briefly. A radio was playing BBC quietly, as it does every morning. Actually this was forbidden, but nobody cared about it, besides the Brits played groovy music.

"Good morning, Herr Leutnant. Morning, Papa."

"Morning son," Nitz returned.

"Where's Monsieur Grou?" Engelmann asked. Münster shrugged his shoulders.

"He wasn't here when I came down." Then the staff sergeant suddenly had a very broad grin on his face. "I bet he's got a bomb hidden in here. He's sitting with the Résistance now, drinking coffee."

"Keep such remarks to yourself," Engelmann hissed, wiping the smile off Münster's face. In the lieutenant's eyes, Grou was a man of honor. So he did not want them to speak ill of him.

All of a sudden the front door was opened. An old man with wrinkled, sunken cheeks and sagging skin stepped into the kitchen. His clothes were soaked and his cheeks reddened by the storm. The old farmer moved slowly and slightly bent.

"Bon jour, Monsieur Grou," Engelmann said friendly.

The Frenchman smiled kindly, then he presented what he was holding in his hands: a dead pigeon. The poultry had

74

not been shot down, at least it did not look like it had been. It seemed to have died in another way, and Grou had found it. The Wehrmacht had ordered the French, under threat of severe punishment, to hand over any pigeons they found to the Germans immediately, and the old farmer seemed to comply. He handed Engelmann the white bird, which was already quite stiff. The lieutenant didn't really want to touch the pigeon at first, but Grou kept holding it under his nose smiling all the time. So Engelmann grabbed it. He held the feathered animal up with pointed fingers while he pressed his lips together. Sometimes it wasn't easy with the old Frenchman: Grou couldn't speak German and in French he didn't want to talk for unknown reasons. So the mutual communication was limited to nodding the head, shaking the head and pointing fingers. Grou beamed, nodded, beamed once more apparently very satisfied and then sat down at the table.

With his bird fingers he touches the food now? Engelmann thought. He was shuddering in disgust. Grou had already grabbed the bread and butter and began to prepare a sandwich. Münster and Nitz also sat down, but they waited politely for the lieutenant.

"Get started," he told them, looking at the dead feathered animal in his hands. With his fingers he felt over the sticky plumage and finally found what he had been looking for: a narrow metal tube. He took it off the pigeon, walked to the door, opened it and put the dead animal outside next to the threshold. A strong wind blew into his face. Quickly he closed the door again and was greeted by expectant faces. Grou, however, calmly bit into a cheese sandwich.

"Well, was it loaded, Herr Leutnant?" Nitz asked.

"Apparently," he murmured and opened the tube. A small piece of rice paper fell into his hand.

"Well?" Nitz asked tiredly, but Engelmann shook his head. "The same gibberish as last time: Five, eight, B, K, four, nine, two, one, one, V, V." He shook his head once more. "And after that, another drawing. Looks like a fish."

Nitz thoughtfully frowned. "I really wonder what that could mean. Are we meant by it?"

75

"Maybe our position is right there on the slip of paper," Münster wondered.

Engelmann laughed: "I think a fish would not be the right symbol for us. Be that as it may, I'll pass the note on immediately and then let others worry about it."

*

At noon the storm raged terribly. The soldiers of the 9th Company drove long wooden stakes into the ground on the beach of Calais, on the tips of which the engineers would then place mines. On this day they fought mainly with the weather. The sea was rough and threw huge waves at them. The sky darkened, thick clouds drifted over the heads of the soldiers. Torrential rain pattered to the ground, soaking the men to the bone. Strong breezes whistled across the beach. The soldiers had thrown their tents over themselves as rain protection and peered only with their heads out of the cutouts provided for them. The tents fluttered in the wind, while hours of rain paid their tribute: The water finally found a way under the waterproof material, drowned the soldiers' uniforms and got through to their underwear. Engelmann froze and felt horrible. He could not have imagined a more unpleasant weather – at least for the moment, because he had experienced worse things in Russia. He looked into the faces of his landsers, who looked tormented, but at least they did not complain and kept pushing their spades into the sand.

Engelmann's palms were covered with blisters from the constant work. Like almost every day when the regiment's tank men were not busy with their panzers, they dug holes somewhere in the canton or on the beach. Together with Stendal and Jahnke, Engelmann dug earth out of a hole that grew deeper with every turn of the spade. At least the ground was not frozen anymore. On the contrary, the fine subsoil of the beach was easy to remove.

Engelmann felt his back in an unpleasant way. He stretched out groaning to relieve the pain. He barely could keep his eyes open. The storm blew horribly against his face bringing sand and burning salt water with it.

"Argh!" Jahnke groaned as he had hit a buried stone with his spade. He threw his tool aside, bent down into the hole, which was a good meter deep, and pulled out a large chunk, which he hoisted moaning beside the hole.

"Lousy weather!" Stendal complained in his typical Tyrolean way.

Ungrateful dirty work! The lieutenant thought. In the background soldiers of the 2nd Platoon sorted the delivered wooden stakes and dragged them to already prepared holes. They had to hurry to get them into the ground, otherwise the storm would close the holes again. Engelmann could only shake his head. It was Rosenkamp's idea that they had to work hard despite the circumstances. One day really didn't matter! Engelmann was not only concerned with the work, which was simply no fun in this weather. He was also concerned with the care for his soldiers and the fighting strength of the company, which was quickly endangered by such games.

If 25 soldiers with pneumonia go to the doctor tomorrow, we'll be in trouble! Engelmann was sure that if he were the company commander, he wouldn't have given such an imbecile order, especially since the commander had every opportunity to keep his soldiers away from work. After all, this morning the regimental commander had issued the order to carry out work only at the commanders' will due to the weather. But apparently Rosenkamp wanted to show once again that he was a great commander.

At the same time, the ox is just cruising around in his kubelwagen and has not yet been hit by a single drop of rain. Engelmann wrinkled his nose.

"Herr Leutnant?" a squeaky voice struggled through the storm. Engelmann turned and looked into the thin face of a private. The lieutenant sighed, for the soldier was the commander's driver. *Speak of the devil!*

"Hauptmann Rosenkamp would like to speak to you," the man who stood outside without rain protection was shivering. The rain splashed against the fabric of his uniform. Engelmann squinted past the man and saw the beige-colored kubelwagen with the spare wheel on the hood standing at the edge of the beach; where the ground was raised and the sand gave way to a narrow road. The folding roof of the car had been pulled up, the metal shining in the rain. Engelmann sighed once more, while the private turned around and ran back. He also wanted to get back into the dry car as quickly as possible.

Engelmann trudged after him. With every step he took, his feet got out the water that was ankle-deep in his boots, like a slimy membrane.

"I'll be right back," he told his two soldiers, and they replied with one voice, "Jawohl, Herr Leutnant".

Engelmann held one arm protectively over his eyes and pinched them together as he approached the commander's car. He recognized Rosenkamp, who, sitting on the passenger side, looked out of the window bored.

The captain was a short guy with a broad face and glasses with circular lenses on his nose. His hair had always been pomaded to form a wave that sloshed over his head.

The lieutenant stood by the window on the passenger side. With a disgusted look Rosenkamp looked outside into the rain, then he focused on Engelmann.

"Herr Leutnant Engelmann," he began, clearing his throat. "The officers are having a little get-together over by the 7th at Salperwick. Jump in, we'll drive over there. Oberstleutnant Sieckenius has brought some wine and French dance girls. There'll also be a hot supper."

Engelmann stared at Rosenkamp stunned. He couldn't believe what he had heard.

"What do you think?" he asked his superior. "We're supposed to bury 30 more obstacles today."

Rosenkamp made a disparaging gesture with his hand, then he smacked and replied: "Herr Leutnant, let your men work now, and jump in. The landsers can do it on their own. You sure you want to be out here in this shitty weather?"

"With all due respect, Herr Hauptmann, I will not sit and party in a warm room while my men have to work in all weathers."

The captain pulled a face.

"What kind of sourpuss are you? Digging in the dirt is for grunts. You're an officer, so act like one. You don't have to stand out here in the rain."

Engelmann was seething, but he remained calm. Instead, he dug his hands out and showed the captain his palms. These were covered with calluses and blisters.

"That's what the hands of every damn soldier in this company look like. I'd be ashamed, if my hands looked different!"

The captain lowered his eyes in annoyance and shook his head in incomprehension. He smacked his lips again.

"Whatever you say, Engelmann. Then you can go and freeze your ass off." Afterwards, addressing the driver, Rosenkamp said: "Come on, let's go. To Salperwick. And get going."

"Jawohl, Herr Hauptmann."

The kubelwagen rushed away and left Engelmann literally out in the cold.

Pointe du Hoc, France, April 6th, 1944

The 253rd Infantry Division had finally been withdrawn from Russia and moved to Northern France to reinforce the Atlantic Wall, where it was inserted between the 709th and 352nd Infantry Divisions, with the right border at Pointe du Hoc, a 30-meter high cliff on the Calvados coast. The division's left border was the small village of Saint-Marcouf on the Cotentin peninsula. Rommel had not yet been able to achieve his desired front width of ten kilometers per division, but with the troops supplied from Russia he had decisively strengthened the French coast as well as the coast of the Benelux countries. Around Calais, where the enemy was expected to land, the width of the divisions was even 14 kilometers. The sky cleared more and more with each passing day. Fine, white clouds floated over the firmament and were pierced by glaring sunshine. The sea in front of the cliff shone in a brilliant blue, while on the shore, where a 20-meter-wide sandy beach lay between the water and the cliffs, fine waves soared over the shores. On both sides the cliffs led to a long, rocky peak that pointed out to the sea. The elevated position of Pointe du Hoc made it a very important strategic point.

Both warring parties had recently recognized this: While the Germans had placed six 155-millimeter guns on the cliff in positions from which they could fire at any landing zone from St. Marcouf to Colleville, Allied bomber units had flown several raids against Pointe du Hoc in recent weeks. Truly, the Western Allies would hardly land in Normandy, which was evident from the fact that the air raids against the department of Pas-de-Calais were the fiercest, but they could provide enough planes to serve the entire Atlantic Wall.

Berning was very happy that he had only arrived after the last Allied air raid at Pointe du Hoc, where his squadron had been assigned the task of reinforcing the 120-man defensive crew of the 352nd as well as the 80 gunners. The terrain on the cliff was ploughed up by enemy bombs. Deep craters covered the entire space, but so far they had not hit anything of importance. Some concrete bunkers rose out of the crater landscape. A branched trench system, partly deep enough to be able to move upright in it, stretched over the cliff.

Berning stood not far from a rock shelter. 30 meters down the rock face was a narrow sandy beach. The sergeant adjusted his field cap and wiped the sweat from his forehead. At his feet the squad was busy extending the trench system with spades and shovels to create an additional machine gun position for Hege's weapon.

Berning looked out over the sea, which had a bright blue color all the way to the horizon. Sunbeams reflected on the water and made it shimmer. It was pleasantly warm, with a cool breeze blowing in from the sea. The sergeant was very happy to be here in Normandy, because it was said that the enemy would attack near Calais, which is far away from Pointe du Hoc – a linear distance of 270 kilometers towards the Northeast. So there was a good chance of having it pretty easy in the North of France.

And should the Allies still come, then – Berning thought – the Germans here on the cliff were extremely well-fortified. Not only did the rock ledge by its very nature offer a brilliant defensive position against attackers from the water; the sergeant couldn't imagine, with the best will in the world, that anyone would be stupid enough to climb a rock face under enemy fire. In addition more than 300 soldiers were now stationed on this small spot, equipped with two-centimeter anti-aircraft guns, machine guns, mines and tanks, waiting in the hinterland for the enemy. Well someone should try to land here!

In the distance the sergeant recognized some of the flaks, which protruded from position holes around the bunkers. The artillery guns, however, were hidden in an orchard near the farmstead in the hinterland and would only be brought forward when they were really needed. It was known that the Allied air raids in this sector were mainly aimed at these guns, so constructions made of telephone poles, which looked like them from the air, were placed in the cemented gun positions.

Berning's men groaned and complained as they dug the trenches. The sergeant felt that their displeasure was also directed at him, even if they didn't say so. After all, Berning didn't take part in the work, he just stood around, supervising the men like a slave driver in ancient Egypt. Even if he did not scramble to dig, this division of labor was not his idea. Pappendorf forbade his higher ranks to lend a hand. "An Unteroffizier isn't made to work, but to lead!" was his motto. So the Landser also had to dig out Berning's position, just as they had prepared Berning's sleeping place.

The sergeant scratched his head. He thought that Pappendorf didn't know what he was doing with his antiquated behavior. He didn't have the guts to tell his platoon leader. So he let Pappendorf calmly talk him into many things without offering any resistance. The master sergeant even forbade to take off the field blouses while working. As a result, the soldiers of the platoon sweated heavily in their uniforms, just because Pappendorf thought that the German soldier always wore his uniform according to the regulations. There was nothing more sacred to the master sergeant.

Hege dug very close to the cliffs, where he found more and more stones and the ground became rockier and hardly penetrable. The lance corporal jammed his spade on a large stone and howled up in pain. With the words "I'll get you, you bastard" he threw his tool aside, crouched down and dug further with his hands to expose the stone from all sides.

"Just do as much as you can," Berning said trying to help at least in some way.

"PARDON?"

"YOU SHOULD ONLY DO AS MUCH AS YOU CAN!"

"Great advice," Hege muttered, and pulled a large stone out of the hole. "If you hadn't told me, I would have dug right over the cliff." Hege spoke softly, and was drowned out by the pounding and hammering of the tools. Berning didn't hear him, at least he didn't want to hear him. He turned away from his men. He felt that feeling of dissatisfaction again. The weather was getting better every day and the sun was shining brightly. He wished he was at home now, lying on the shores of the Neusiedler See! But that was not possible. At some distance on the left hand Berning saw Pappendorf, who ran around between the positions of the 1st Squad and rebuked the soldiers loudly. The platoon had its emplacements directly on the rock ledge on that side of the cliff that roughly pointed towards Cherbourg. In case of an attack they should be at the edge with a jump to be able to operate down to the shore. The front line, in other words, a doubtful honor for Berning. But still he did not worry too much. As already mentioned, Pointe du Hoc was not exactly next to Calais.

Berning looked to the right where the top of the cliff rose. A large, multi-storey bunker had been built there, which was connected to other cliff positions by underground concrete tunnels. Berning looked back and let his gaze wander over the entire system of emplacements, and then suddenly he saw what he and the men had been waiting for all day: At some distance in front of him, between the craters and trenches, a crowd of soldiers had gathered at one of the "telephone pole guns". About ten men stood on the circular, concrete square, where there was an enclosure for the 155-millimeter gun. Berning clearly recognized the red collars that most of the men wore on their coats, as well as the distinctive peaked caps. Field Marshal Erwin Rommel stood in the center and looked at a map, while the division commander, Lieutenant General Becker, showed him a point in the terrain. Major General Speidel, Rommel's Chief of General Staff, a slim man with glasses, also accompanied his superior as usual on his inspections. Rommel's and Speidel's collar patches with the red and gold Larisch embroidery and the Knight's Cross in between made an awe-inspiring impression on Berning. Speidel had only been awarded his Knight's Cross this week. But above all it was the sight of Rommel – the serious face of the Field Marshal with the narrow mouth and the deep eye sockets hidden behind dark shadows – that encouraged the German soldiers and gave them a spiritual upswing. Among them, Rommel was a legend. What he had achieved in Africa with inferior forces and almost without supplies was still present in the minds of the soldiers, partly due to the targeted propaganda. So Rommel's almost daily visits to the emplacements of the Atlantic Wall not only served to control the construction progress, but were also an event for the landsers every time.

Other generals and officers surrounded the old Desert Fox. Berning recognized members of a propaganda company who brought their box-shaped cameras into position to take some pictures. Someone from the field gendarmerie was also part of the large group that followed Rommel. Berning also noticed that the commander of the 352nd Infantry Division, who remained in charge of defending the cliff despite the addition of the 253rd, was present.

"He is there," Berning whispered. His soldiers listened up, stopped working. Reuben nudged Hege, who had not noticed anything.

"The Jumper?" Weiss asked in a whisper. In the language of the German soldiers, Rommel's nickname had changed from the Desert Fox to the Jumper, after he had changed posts unusually often since von Witzleben came to power. The Chancellor also thought highly of his Rommel, and that's why he always used him where the fire was burning.

"Yes," Berning whispered in awe. His body stood to attention all by itself.

"UNTEROFFIZIER BERNING!" Pappendorf's voice roared over the cliff. Berning recoiled. Pappendorf stood between the soldiers of the 1st Squad with his mouth squeezed shut and an evil expression. He tapped his head with exaggerated gestures.

Berning flinched. He grabbed his field cap, fumbled around with it and finally had the feeling that it was perfectly on his head. Apparently this was really the case, because the master sergeant had already turned away from Berning, snarling at a soldier of the 1st Squad, whose uniform he didn't like.

The sharp voice of the master sergeant sounded all the way to Berning. Pappendorf was a very big admirer of Rommel and therefore even more than usual he was anxious to present his platoon in perfect shape. How often had the master sergeant raved about the Desert Fox during his instructions and training sessions?

At the front, Rommel left the crowd of officers and moved straight towards the top of the cliff – right towards Berning! The whole field-gray megillah with the red accents immediately followed.

The sergeant's heart made a jump, fresh beads of sweat formed at his temples. Actually, he and his men did everything right, but Berning was always nervous in the face of high-ranking superiors.

Then he was overcome by the fear that he had made some mistake that would be revealed in front of the high officers. Berning didn't manage to get his body out of the "Stand to attention", instead he hectically threw his head to the right and left and found out with relief that everything was really in order with his soldiers. Nevertheless sweat soaked his shirt. The cool wind took hold of the damp spots and made Berning shiver.

"He's heading straight towards us," he whispered to his men. Veneration gripped the men. They grabbed their tools tighter and looked up carefully.

"He's coming right towards us," Reuben repeated. He was also excited.

Weiss, on the other hand, tapped Berning against the boot. "I'm glad I'm not the man in charge here," he grinned, but somehow there was a trace of envy in his voice.

"Take it easy," Berning stuttered, not losing sight of the approaching officers. "Take it easy. Remember what the commander said: Just keep working and wait to be spoken to. There's no need for us to report."

"Yeah, right. We should just wait. We don't have to make a report."

Most of Berning's soldiers behaved very confidently and continued to work, although their eyes kept peeking over the edge of the trench, perhaps to catch a glimpse of Rommel. Berning turned around with a beating heart. He swallowed, suddenly his throat was dry. He could clearly hear the deep, rough voice of his division commander, who at that moment was explaining about the unit here and trying to depict in words what the cliff would look like when all work is done.

"Herr Unteroffizier?" Berning suddenly heard a Swabian voice behind him. He stopped breathing for a moment, then he turned around. Rommel looked directly at him. The old Field Marshal had pressed his lips together into a thin line.

"Yes, I mean YOU," Rommel snarled grimly. "Or do you see another Unteroffizier around?"

The sweat shot out of all his pores, but Berning tried hard to maintain his firm posture. "Jawohl... Herr Feldmarschall?" he stuttered. Berning's eyes darted across the faces of the other officers. They seemed to be expectant. Berning suddenly felt a weight on his shoulders that he was not able to carry. Uncertain what was asked of him, his right hand twitched. He lifted it up, but then let it sink again and only crossed his arms behind his back. He was content with himself that he had just prevented himself from greeting militarily in the field. After all, he did not want to make the Field Marshal a target for snipers.

"Good afternoon, Herr Feldmarschall," Berning said after a moment. Out of the corner of his eye he saw his division commander loosing composure.

"Do you think this is a battlefield, or is my person in your eyes simply not worth the respect of a military salute?" Rommel hissed.

Berning's hand immediately rushed up to his temple while opening his mouth, not knowing what to answer. More than half a syllable, which sounded like a cry for help, he did not produce.

"Come with me," Rommel ordered, turned around and walked away from the others. Berning hurried after the field marshal at the double. He felt the looks that followed him. He wished to get away from here – just far away.

Rommel and Berning were departed far enough from the others that nobody could overhear their conversation. But everyone who saw the angry expression on Rommel's face knew in which direction that very conversation would go.

"Explain to me what you are doing there, Herr Unteroffizier," the CiC France-Benelux demanded to know while looking the sergeant keenly in the eye. Berning could not escape the stern gaze, but at the same time could hardly bear it. "I... um... we..." Berning wiped through his fearfully distorted face, "We're digging the trenches as requested, Herr Generalfeldmarschall."

"Well, well. I was presented with another picture. I saw your men digging the trenches," Rommel leaned forward and was only a toothbrush length away from Berning. "But not YOU. You stood around twiddling your thumbs."

"I... I..." Berning twitched all over. "I watch over my men. I... am a sergeant after all, Herr Generalfeldmarschall."

"Now stop ending each sentence with 'Herr Generalfeldmarschall'! I know my frigging rank!"

86

"Jawohl, Herr Generalfeldmarschall."

Rommel rolled his eyes, which only made Berning more uncertain: "I mean... jawohl..."

"Get a hold of yourself!" Rommel suddenly yelled. That was definitely heard by Berning's comrades. The sergeant stood there shaking and blinking his eyes.

"Herr Unteroffizier," the field marshal continued, suddenly being quite calm, as if a lever had been pulled in his head, "the German army is facing the greatest invasion force of all time. This wall – the Atlantic Wall," Rommel spread his arms, "is all that will help us when the concentrated power of the enemy fleets, the enemy air forces and the enemy armies comes crashing down upon us. We do not have time to have manpower standing around with cheap excuses while our defenses are far from being able to resist. And for you to think that just because you are a sergeant, you don't need to work is an outrage. That only proves that you haven't understood what it means to be a sergeant! I expect every soldier under my command, no matter what rank, to get his fingers bloody every day the enemy does not show up, to dig even deeper, to put up even more obstacles, to fortify even more stretches of beach. That will be our only life insurance when the battle begins."

Rommel panted with rage. His infernal stare wouldn't let go of the poor sergeant.

Berning, however, didn't understand anything anymore. With wide eyes he looked at the field marshal. His lips trembled. First he wanted to say that the enemy would land in Calais anyway and not here, but that would hardly have given him any advantages. Instead, he replied quivering: "That... that was the order of Feldwebel Pappendorf that I was not allowed to work, but only to supervise. It's not my fault, Herr... um." Nervously Berning wiped his face with one hand.

"Aha! Even though you wanted to, you were not allowed to work? Well, we'll see soon!"

Berning's eyes grew wide and he suddenly understood what he had done, but it was too late. He wanted to say something more, but Rommel shouted over to his entourage at that moment: "Bring Feldwebel Pappendorf over! On the double!"

Pappendorf dashed in like lightning. Immediately he stood at attention, greeted according to regulations and spoke with shining eyes: "Herr Generalfeldmarschall, Feldwebel Pappendorf reporting!" Berning had never seen Pappendorf so... so... so... happy.

"Let me see your hands," Rommel demanded. With a questioning look Pappendorf presented his hands to the field marshal. He grasped them roughly, turned them over and looked at the palms of his hands. "They look like my adjutant's," Rommel growled. Pappendorf still didn't understand, however his eyes shone in the presence of his "favorite general," as he always said.

"Herr Feldwebel!" Rommel brought Pappendorf back to reality with a roaring tone of voice. "Were you possessed by the devil that you forbid this fine sergeant by order to take part in the entrenchment work? That man," Rommel pointed to Berning, "according to his statement, clearly pointed out to you that everyone has to take part in the work – that includes you, by the way! It is absurd that the German warrant officer is watching idly while his men are working. I resent that under my command! Do you understand?"

Pappendorf looked as if his world had just caved in. After a long pause he exclaimed, "Jawohl, Herr Generalfeldmarschall."

"You would do well to listen to this sergeant every now and then."

With these words Rommel turned away from Berning and Pappendorf and marched back to his entourage with a taut posture. The two soldiers remained behind. Berning was gripped by raging fear.

Pappendorf's eyes twitched, his whole face trembled with uncontrolled fury.

"You didn't do that for nothing, Unteroffizier," he whispered. "You didn't do that for nothing."

Berning was close to a nervous breakdown. With his mouth open he tried to form syllables of apology, but he couldn't make any sounds. At the same time a steady hum appeared in the distance, which quickly grew louder.

Things got restless on the cliff. The soldiers stopped working and stared at the sky. Rommel and his delegation also interrupted their conversations and looked up. At the next moment, everyone was running around, looking for shelter somewhere.

American bombers! The whole sky was covered! Like steel arrows they shot closer, then the bombs fell. Berning and Pappendorf threw themselves into the next bomb crater and held their arms protectively over their heads. Now they could only wait and pray. Around them the world broke in two. The earth vibrated. The bombs exploded with cracking sounds. Thick clods of earth poured over the soldiers. Each detonation caused an incredible air blow that swept over the crater where Berning and Pappendorf had sought shelter. Seconds later the German AA-guns started roaring and mingled with the concert of death. The enemy bombers turned around and took off. Flak shots, which buzzed through the air like glowing threads, chased after them in vain.

Huge clouds of smoke surrounded the cliff, roaring male voices provided the background noise. Berning and Pappendorf hurried back to their unit when someone shouted: "Rommel has been hit! They've killed the Generalfeldmarschall!" Soldiers were scurrying about. Meanwhile Berning was relieved to discover that there were no casualties in his squad. Gradually the dust that irritated his lungs began to clear. He coughed hard, then he looked up and saw Rommel, who was vividly jumping around among the men of his delegation. Blood clung to the field marshal's high forehead, ran down his face, sullied his coat.

It took quite some time before the soldiers realized that there had indeed been high-ranking casualties: Becker was taken to the military hospital with very serious injuries, as was the commander of the 352nd Infantry Division. And Speidel's skull had been split by a large splinter. For him any help came too late. It was a severe blow to the German forces in the West, so close to the expected invasion.

When all the fuss died away and the wounded as well as Rommel had left the cliff, Berning sat down in his cover hole that his soldiers had dug for him. He stuck his head between his arms and tried with all his might to get rid of that sinking feeling in his stomach. He would have liked to beat himself. Just a moment ago everything had been more or less okay and Berning had even managed to satisfy Pappendorf in the end. And now this! Now everything would start all over again! At that moment he heard Pappendorf's voice echoing over the cliff in a mixture of threat and complacency: "Unteroffizier Beeeeeeerniiiiiiiiing?! COME OVER HERE!"

Quelmes, France, May 20th, 1944

The platoon leaders as well as the company sergeant major had gathered in a farmhouse with the company commander, who had just informed them that they would be relocated once again: This time, however, there would not only be a change of position from one village to another. This time the whole division was moved – to another part of the Atlantic Wall! The decision was made by Rommel himself, who probably got a bad feeling about gathering all forces near Calais, while the other coastal sections were insufficiently secured. So no braving gaps, as Field Marshal von Manstein had demanded. It was planned to move the 16th Panzer Division into the hinterland from Caen to Bayeux, where currently only the 24th Panzer Division was located as a mobile force. The battered Großdeutschland Division was detached from the Eastern Front in order to close the gap of the 16th near Calais.

Engelmann nodded with a serious look as Rosenkamp shared the marching orders. So they were going to Normandy – Engelmann faced this decision with skepticism: He did not believe that the enemy would land anywhere else than Calais; it was the narrowest point of the English Channel after all. The Allies had to move a gigantic fleet that would definitely attract attention and, moreover, be an easy target for the German Luftwaffe. A landing in Normandy was therefore simply very unlikely. That's exactly why he was looking at the transfer with mixed feelings:

On the one hand he was happy that he would probably not take part in the battles, but on the other hand he was feverishly awaiting the upcoming fight, because only it had the potential to end this war. One way or another. Engelmann would have liked to take part, of course, to give his best and influence the fortunes of war in favor of the Reich.

"Any questions?" Rosenkamp finished as he looked at his men. They all sat around a large table with cake and coffee spread out on it. Everybody had helped themselves generously during the issue of orders.

"All right, if there's nothing else, one more thing from me. Leutnant Engelmann, in one hour you send me ten men from your platoon to dismantle my camp."

Engelmann crossed his arms. That Rosenkamp was really starting to have it in for him.

"Herr Hauptmann, I must object," he began dryly, without believing that he would succeed, "we are to get the platoon ready to march by tomorrow morning according to your words. If you take the men away from me now, we'll have to work a night shift to do it. And with all due respect, I think you and your staff could pack your bags yourself."

"I couldn't agree more, Herr Hauptmann." Unexpectedly, Engelmann was supported by Master Sergeant Kranz. Rosenkamp, on the other hand, grinned stupidly before he announced: "Herr Leutnant, if you tell me which part of my order you didn't understand, I'll gladly repeat it for you." Engelmann and Kranz looked at each other briefly and meaningfully. The lieutenant shook his head resignedly.

Minutes later, the gentlemen left the building to make their way back to their units. Münster waited outside next to a motorcycle with sidecar for his platoon leader. When

91

Engelmann came to him with a scowling expression and anger in his eyes, he saved himself any questions.

"We'll drive back immediately, then drum up all tank commanders. We'll assemble at my tank at eleven o'clock German time for the issue of orders," the lieutenant grumbled. Münster nodded. Engelmann got into the sidecar. Even before the staff sergeant could step on the gas, Engelmann had swallowed his anger and said: "We're moving to Normandy."

Münster's face dropped. "No, really?" he only said. Engelmann shrugged his shoulders.

"I thought the motto was to concentrate all forces where the enemy will land, and that is Calais."

"Apparently, Rommel is no longer so sure of that. The entire division is being moved to Normandy, as there are almost no mobile forces there."

"That's nonsense. Rommel never said that. Von Witzleben has meddled in his affairs again." Münster was furious.

"After all, Hauptmann Stollwerk believes the decision was the right one." Engelmann laughed ironically.

"I see." Münster was thinking. "Maybe the transfer isn't that bad after all. Who knows what the Yanks are up to?"

Bern, Switzerland, May 24th, 1944

The apartment door fell shut. Peace entered the Bernese apartment of the Abwehr. Even though Thomas experienced this almost every day, it was always a strange feeling when Luise went to work. Naked, Thomas let himself fall on the bed and blinked at the ceiling. The two of them had – as so often – already had a good time early in the morning before Luise washed and got ready. Allegedly Thomas would now also take care of his business, but the truth was different: Thomas had nothing to do at all. After all, his profession was Luise, even if he would like to undo that. So his days consisted of strolling through the city and spending the dough of the Abwehr, as well as a daily running training, which he used at the same time to check his many hiding places for emergencies, and to see if nobody had discovered his "iron rations". Or he squatted in his apartment, struggling with his feelings and thoughts. As long as Luise was with him, everything was perfect, but the time spent alone tormented and tortured him – and it got worse and worse.

Taylor lit a cigarette and took a strong puff. For a moment he glanced at the Swiss daily newspaper published the day before, which was lying on a rickety wooden stool next to the kitchen door. Luise sometimes read this democratic filth, but Taylor could not do that to himself. Reading a Swiss newspaper was often an unpleasant business for him. He longed for a Völkischer Beobachter that he could read as a German without feeling bad at once; even the VB had changed its tone a bit in the end, after its mother organization, the NSDAP, had lost power. Yes, even somehow critical articles about the war orientation of the new government had been printed. Von Witzleben's people also checked all the publications in the Reich, but no longer as strictly as Goebbels used to.

The complete silence around Thomas finally got on his nerves to such an extent that he stood up and opened the window. Cool air blew in. Outside, the busy hustle and bustle of the Swiss capital continued to rumble, for the streets were packed with people doing business or enjoying themselves. After years of economic crisis, during which public relief work and unemployment had dominated life in Switzerland, the country had managed to recover a little despite the war. According to this, on fine days many people were on the road to spend their money in restaurants, cafés or shops. The sounds coming through the window into Thomas' room were comforting for him, but he still didn't feel comfortable.

He was simply at odds with himself as to how things should continue. Every time he was alone, he thought about his situation. He then came to the painful realization that

Luise and he had no future together – yes, could not have a future together.

Taylor blew smoke through his teeth and looked out the window at the sandstone buildings across the street. Voices and the sounds of vehicles could be heard. Thomas sighed. What should he do? Actually there was nothing he could do. He could enjoy the time with her while it lasted. If he was unlucky, the Abwehr would soon come up with the idea of removing him from Switzerland; after all, he hadn't been able to provide any information worth mentioning for a long time. Perhaps in the end it would have been better if Thomas had met Luise's father. Luise, however, had decided against a meeting shortly before the arrival of the British officer. Her fear of his reaction was too big.

Thoughtfully, Thomas blew a long trail of smoke out of the window and squinted his eyes. The word "Abwehr" drifted through his mind, then the word "spy". Finally a completely different word burned itself into his brain: "traitor". At least he felt like a traitor. Although he was here in the service of his country, even though he no longer knew what use the Reich still had in him; yet he betrayed the person in his life who meant most to him: He betrayed Luise. He made her believe that he was someone he was not. Worse, he worked with those she hated deeply and who allegedly had done bad things to her people. Even him, she had put bugs in his ear about his employer. Him, who thought he was so steadfast! But Luise had made wild allusions about terrible things that the Gestapo and the Sicherheitsdienst, both of which were now operating under the umbrella of the Abwehr, should have done. Thomas sometimes wondered, when he was overcome by doubts, for what kind of people he was actually working.

Maybe it's best to leave Switzerland? he finally considered. *Or maybe I can at least make up for a little bit by not having to write a report for the German secret service about every word she says?* That was all he could do anyway.

Then there was only hope that the Abwehr would withdraw him soon. At some point, the master spies in Stuttgart had to realize that there was nothing more to get from Luise. Of course the separation would be painful, of course the time afterwards would be horror. But sooner or later he had to go through it anyway. "Better sooner," Thomas used to say. Finally, another consideration entered his mind as well. Taylor had once vowed to be of great service to his country. Here in Switzerland, he was no longer able to live up to that either.

"So it's decided," he sighed and flicked the cigarette butt out of the window. "I'll inform the fools that there's nothing more to be gained here and that I want to be withdrawn." Then something happened that he hadn't expected: He started crying. Thomas had to blink and rub his eyes to avoid it. Luise was the Jill to his Jack. She was the one he could be happy with. But he could not.

Maisy, France, June 5th, 1944

Once the defense systems at Pointe du Hoc had been completed, the men of the Reconnaissance Division 253 marched to Maisy every day. The beaches there were provided with sufficient obstacles, but the dunes lacked communication trenches between the shelters. Wood was brought in and cut to size, while the squadron was mainly busy with entrenchments. The men were suffering under the morning sun. Sweat ran down their bodies and drowned their uniforms. Despite the 30 degrees, despite the piercing sun and the hard work, Pappendorf still forbade his platoon to take off their uniforms or even to undo their buttons. With the support of Balduin, who lived according to the motto "everyone in his own way", the 2nd platoon had to endure the brutal heat with buttoned shirts and the thick, felted field blouses over it. The other platoons as well as the Grenadier Regiment 453, reinforced by an East Battalion, were working bare-chested or dressed only in the sweaty, light blue shirts of the Wehrmacht. Nobody made fun of the

2nd platoon, however, they all took pity on the poor soldiers. Also yesterday, when the heat was even more extreme over the Calvados coast and two men of the 1st Squad collapsed dehydrated, Pappendorf remained unimpressed. For him the regulations and only the regulations applied. These also stated that a superior had to take care of his subordinates, but the master sergeant felt that the uniform regulations were the more important instruction. "What will the Yanks think when they land here and see you without your uniforms?" he commented.

After all, the sea was rough and caused huge waves. In the morning a short rain shower had covered the land, and more rain was forecasted for the afternoon. This gave the sweating men some courage. In addition, the worsening weather meant that the enemy would not come for the time being – the German weather forecast for the next few days also said "no invasion weather".

Berning, Reuben, Hege and the others groaned and grunted under the blazing heat. Their uniforms were soaked. Pappendorf, however, had his eyes everywhere; and especially on the 2nd Squad. Berning and his landsers had no chance to open their blouses even for a moment. With Argus eyes Pappendorf ran up and down behind the trench that Berning's squad was working on. Of course, the sergeant now took part in the hard work, but Master Sergeant Pappendorf actually violated Rommel's order in this point.

He still considered himself too important to pick up a shovel. Instead, he kept his hands crossed behind his back and let his gaze wander like a robot over Berning and his soldiers. They were digging a communication trench that would connect some machine gun nests. Hege cursed softly. Reuben shoveled like a man possessed. The man demonstrated an incredible workload.

Berning felt how the terrible heat under his clothes became unbearable. He wiped his hand across his sweaty forehead and straightened his field cap. At last the bell rang – its metallic clang echoed loudly over the dune. Lunch break! Berning rammed his spade into the sand and looked up into the sky, which slowly darkened. The sun disappeared behind thick clouds. The other soldiers also laid down their tools, stretched themselves in their wet uniforms and looked up at the sky with twisted faces. It looked like storm and rain, and then they would certainly freeze in their sweaty blouses.

The men sat down on the sand of the dunes and breathed loudly. In a moment the company sergeant major would arrive and bring the rations. Pappendorf was actually not to be seen for a moment, but Berning did not dare to open his field blouse or allow his men to do so. Instead he lay down on the sand and closed his eyes briefly. Thus he only heard the chattering and cursing of his men and the roaring of the waves that thundered against the beach. Soon more noises were added: Shouts were heard – some in foreign languages, while men laughed and puffed hard. Even the sound of a leather ball being kicked, joined the soundscape; down on the beach some of the soldiers used their lunch break for a football match.

"Look at the Slavs," Hege noticed and dragged on a cigarette audibly, "they must still have excess energy." According to the sound, Hege seemed to get something from the bottom of his lungs and spit it out.

Berning opened his eyes and looked towards the cloudy sky. The breezes that came from the sea became stronger. He sat up and saw Reuben, Weiss and Hege crouching beside him in the sand. Down on the beach, two dozen men in undershirts or blue tops ran after a ball and shot it at improvised goals made of wooden stakes.

"What did General von Schlieben write in his report?" Berning pondered with narrowed eyes. "It's too much to ask that the Russians fight the Americans in France for Germany. These poor devils should not wear German uniforms."

Hege took a last drag from his cigarette butt and flicked it away. They scored. The men fell into each other's arms, cheering.

"You see the one who scored?" Reuben asked. "That gook there. They say he's Korean. He had to fight for the

97

Japanese against the Russians, but then he got captured and had to fight for the Russians against us. Then he was captured again and now he has to fight here for us," Reuben explained. Weiss put him off with closed eyes.

"Don't believe every crap they tell you," he muttered.

"As far as I know it's true."

"Oh, what do you know?" Weiss smirked. Berning had to grin too. "What you know fits neatly on the back of a stamp!" They all laughed. Meanwhile, the clouds above their heads got darker shades.

"At least they're not coming today," Berning shouted against the wind. Reuben nodded, then the sergeant continued: "And probably not for the rest of the week either. The weather's too bad, says the weather service."

"Yeah, yeah, the weather's too bad." Reuben nodded.

Then they did come – no boats and infantrymen, but bombers... dozens of planes, roaring with noisy engines from the sea. The alarm sounded and suddenly the men at Maisy ran around like ants. Field-gray crowds squeezed into the bunkers, but the American planes – giant Liberators covering the sky like an olive colored icing – seemed to have other targets. Peacefully they flew over the beach fortifications and disappeared into the hinterland.

Somewhere far away, a German AA-gun started to bark. The repeated banging of the mighty eight-eight echoed as a muffled beating over to the beach. Allied bombers had been flying into France all day, attacking German emplacements and infrastructures. The enemy planes were able to move almost undisturbed and freely over Western Europe; accordingly, air raids had become a gruesome routine. Nevertheless, the quantity of attacks on this day reached a new level.

Bénouville, France, June 6th, 1944

The clock had just struck midnight. All afternoon and evening Allied bombers had been flying over the area of the double bridges. Reports of attacks against the surrounding towns, against runways and barracks as well as against the beach fortifications along the entire coast had been coming in since noon.

"I don't fucking like this," Schumann murmured, while the low hum of Allied bombers was already droning over the double bridges again.

The platoon leader, First Lieutenant Fritze, counteracted the routine, which was extremely dangerous during the war, by constantly rotating his four squads. Two were deployed at each bridge. One squad on each side of the river, secured with machine gun positions and barbed wire. Narrow entrenchments stretched along the embankments. On the West bank of the Canal Bridge as well as on the East bank of the Orne Bridge two additional guns were ready to defend against tanks.

To the North of the Canal Bridge there was also a bunker, to the South a tower with machine guns for air defense, both of which were operated by a squad of a Grenadier Company – the 2nd of Infantry Regiment 744. This company was located as a reserve in Bénouville and was reinforced by four tanks of Czech design, while another Grenadier Company was stationed in Ranville.

Schneider's squad secured the Eastern bank of the Canal Bridge. Calvert and Foster lay in the alarm position, a turret at the side of the road piled up out of sandbags and equipped with a machine gun. The rest of the squad spent the night in the adjacent bridge house, where the control panel for the bridge's opening mechanism was also installed.

The Brandenburgers tried to sleep, which was not easy that night. Enemy bomber formations flying in continuously brought a constant threatening roar over the country. Sleep was hardly to be thought of.

"Shut up and go to sleep," Schneider complained with clenched eyes. Over at Troarn, the flak spit fire. An air combat was raging in the distance. Sometimes even the German Luftwaffe could be seen in the sky. Schneider squeezed himself into his sleeping bag and covered his ears. The allied planes were annoying! Moseneke slept and snored next to him like a bear. The others were also lying in their sleeping bags and stared – lost in their own thoughts – at the ceiling.

"Why do they fly endless attacks today?" Schumann murmured and stuffed a piece of bread in his mouth. He leaned against the wall and stared into the darkness.

"Maybe they've smashed up everything in Germany and are going after France now." Stückl's dry humor combined with his Viennese accent always had an effect on his comrades. This time, however, the others did not say anything, but Stückl's words filled their thoughts, where pictures of destroyed German cities appeared.

The droning was getting louder. More and more enemy planes filled the sky.

"Did it start after all?" Schumann whispered.

"Stop driving yourself crazy all the time. And us on top!" Schneider snorted. "The weather is way too shitty. They won't come before the middle of the month! And now shut up!" The master sergeant pressed his hands against his ears with all his might and gritted his teeth. But it didn't help, the roaring got through and engulfed his hearing. Schneider could have gone through the roof.

"But why else would they suddenly start bombing everything so much?"

"Because they have the planes and the fuel and the people to do it. Shut up now, Schumann! Lie down and sleep! In three hours you must be at your post!" In Schneider's mind, enemy planes were dancing.

"Gosh!" he suddenly yelled. Schneider jumped, grabbed his helmet and threw it against the ceiling at full speed. It rattled and banged, which made his men look up. But nobody said anything. The soldiers of the 1st Squad had learned to live with Schneider's choleric streak.

100

"Don't the bastards know that it is night time," the master sergeant complained aloud, then he rummaged between his clothes that were tucked away at the head of his sleeping bag, felt his field blouse and pulled out a cigarette and matches. He lit his cigarette and puffed out the smoke annoyingly. Finally, he sat back down in his place and nervously dragged on his cigarette.

"If they don't move soon, I'm going over to Troarn, put myself behind an anti-aircraft gun and shoot all the boys down," he murmured.

Minutes passed, the bomber hum went away. Slowly Schneider's eyes closed. The last thing he noticed was that one of his comrades left the room in the darkness.

*

Erich Mielke, who was still just a private, grabbed his Gewehr 43 and left the narrow bridge house. He looked a bit topsy-turvy: He was not wearing a field blouse, but a civilian cap; from his trousers one suspender had come off, hanging down. But what should happen? After all, Mielke only wanted to have a leak and not go to a parade. Moreover, Schneider did not mind such a thing.

Private Mielke, who always put on a serious face and whose hair formed a quiff all by itself, stepped onto the road that connected the two bridges. The moon in the sky covered the area in a dim light.

To Mielke's right was the Canal Bridge, which on this side of the bank had the steel structure that made it possible to open.

He could just about make out the barrier guard, who had been positioned by the grenadiers and apparently slept standing up. In front of Mielke, on the opposite side of the road, lay the machine gun nest of his squad, which appeared as a dark gray area in front of the black background. Nevertheless, Mielke recognized the two very distinctive steel helmets, which stuck out above. Slowly he waddled across the street and stopped in front of the machine gun nest.

101

"Schütz?" Calvert's tired voice fought its way through the darkness.

"Mielke," the private replied sparsely.

"I see. Hope you brought some hot food."

"And two French women," Foster added.

"It's fucking cold for early June," Calvert concluded, rubbing his arms as he made a sound of discomfort.

"I'm just taking a piss."

"Well..." In the middle of the sentence, Calvert stopped and listened. Foster and Mielke also remained motionless. Slowly Calvert pushed his helmet back into his neck, while the hum of large propeller machines could be heard from the North again. Allied planes were approaching.

"Not again," Calvert moaned and grabbed his machine carbine tighter. "They don't leave us any peace today."

Mielke shrugged his shoulders, then he turned away. *Stupid capitalists with their bombers!* He thought and trotted away. *Stupid fascists! Stupid war! And I'm just guarding a bridge. How am I supposed to give important information to my comrades?*

Up in the sky, whole clusters of enemy planes passed exactly over the double bridges. At such a moment the roar was particularly loud and made the earth shake, but the soldiers were used to it. Quickly the planes disappeared again, and with them the rumbling.

"Don't get bombed," he heard Calvert shouting behind him when the machine gun position was long since covered in darkness again. Mielke stepped onto the meadow.

To his right, the Caen Canal flowed through the countryside. At the bottom of the bank there were two narrow trenches, which were supposed to serve as alternative emplacements in case of an attack against their main positions. In front of him was a large open space with a long row of trees covering the canal bank, to the left there was a pond. Anyway the ground here was all swampy.

Mielke noticed how his boots got stuck in the mud and came loose again with a smacking sound. But he had to go this way – had to move well away from the others.

He just couldn't empty his bladder when someone was

102

around. While the bomber formations moved further away and the constant mechanical buzzing decreased with them, suddenly a huge dark object hissed through the air directly in front of Mielke. The next moment it banged loudly, then it rattled. Mielke froze and clasped his rifle.

*

Calvert and Foster clearly saw the large object floating in the moonlight before it hit the ground somewhere in the darkness. Both stared in the direction of the crash, but there was nothing to hear or see.

"Did a bomber really just go down there?" Calvert asked, tapping against his helmet. Foster, who was lying by the MG 34, waved his gun over and looked through the iron sights into the night.

"Seems to be," he returned.

"Nice to see that our flak can hit something."

"Why don't you go over and report to the Greek – just in case. Don't want a stray pilot stumbling into our sleeping quarters at night."

Calvert nodded and tugged at his helmet, then he snuffled his nose loudly.

"And what about our *best boy*?"

"Let Mielke polish his dick in peace."

Both grinned, then Calvert climbed over the sandbag wall, swung his machine carbine on his back and trotted back to the bridge house. Foster remained at his post and stared into the night. Nothing! Not a move or a sound in the area. The pilots were probably dead anyway.

*

The moment Mielke realized that something of the Allies must have gone down there in front of him, the moon of course did not play along. Thick clouds moved in front of the Earth satellite and stole the light away of Europe.

Mielke heard noises in front of him. He did not dare to move. On the one hand, there was barbed wire everywhere

where the thing had landed, on the other, pure fear overcame him. Mielke stood there and clasped his rifle with all his might. He stared into the darkness, pricked up his ears. There was movement in front of him, something... someone was roaming around! No! Several figures! Mielke turned to stone. Not a fiber of his body moved. In his shocked rigidity his own breathing, which suddenly raced like a train, drowned out all other sounds. He sucked the air into his lungs, expelled it again with a rattling sound. He could clearly hear his pulse, which climbed up his throat and thumped murderously.

"Able... able," someone whispered in front of him. Mielke did not move. Moments became eternities. Then the clouds that covered the moon disappeared, and once more a slight glimmer settled over the landscape. Mielke was terrified.

Two meters in front of him stood a figure in a half bent position. He was holding a blade in his hands! A violent twitch went through Mielke, then everything went off in a flash: The figure attacked and wanted to ram the blade into Mielke's side, but the private pulled up his weapon and struck the attacker on the chin with his shaft. The man staggered and groaned, then he fell on his behind. Mielke pressed the buttstock of his weapon against his shoulder, aimed the muzzle of the barrel at the fallen attacker, who seemed to have recognized his fate and looked motionlessly into the German rifle. Putting his finger on the trigger, he aimed precisely at the solar plexus. He had the attacker in his sights, his finger resting on the trigger. Mielke hesitated. Suddenly he dropped his rifle, put his hands up in the air.

"No, please, don't, don't!" he begged and threw himself on his knees. For a moment, the attacker seemed stunned, then he stood up.

"Please don't hurt me, I'll do whatever you want!" Mielke cried. "I'll show you where the German positions are! I'll do anything!"

Other figures approached from all directions. Mielke held trembling hands above his head and closed his eyes in fear. "Please!" he begged. "Please, please."

"Get Howard!" One of the figures commanded, with a

104

heavy British accent. A second one went away.

Strong hands grabbed Mielke at the back and pulled him up. Immediately he felt the cold barrel of a machine pistol, which pressed itself roughly into his side.

"Move, Jerry!" the man behind him whispered. Mielke obeyed. While the guy with the submachine gun led Mielke away from the bridges, the private recognized other figures in the moonlight, who were arranging their equipment, preparing their weapons and whispering instructions to each other. There was no doubt about it: lanky uniforms, circular jump helmets covered with camouflage material, revolvers at the belt and Bren machine guns as well as Sten automatic pistols.

These figures belonged to the British armed forces! Mielke's eyes widened.

What are they doing here in Normandy? He asked himself. He had just passed a soldier who was preparing his machine gun. The curved magazine, which sat prominently on top of the weapon, gave the Bren a unique look. But before Mielke could really wonder about the strange British weapons, something much bigger and more incredible came into his field of vision: In front of him, a small airplane appeared out of the darkness, which had apparently crashed into the middle of the barbed wire entanglement and tore it apart. More British soldiers climbed out of it, then another one of these planes flew silently over Mielke's head and landed rattling in the darkness a few meters further back.

What are these devices? Mielke's thoughts raced, while the man with the submachine gun signaled him to stop and remain standing there. Mielke nodded and obeyed, the barrel of the weapon still in his side. It became hectic around him. The figures were gathering, there must be about 20 of them! Suddenly a British Major positioned himself in front of Mielke. Dark, full hair peeked out from under his helmet.

"You speak English, Jerry?" he whispered. A threatening shine shone out of the major's eye, glaring in the moonlight. Mielke shook his head. The Major ordered a man named

Tappert to approach, who appeared in Mielke's field of vision one blink of an eye later.

"So you declare you give us any information we need on the German sentries at these bridges," Major Howard asked in English, raising one eyebrow. Apparently he wondered how little resistance Mielke put up. Out of the corner of his eye, the German could hear other heavily armed men coming out of the darkness, dividing into two rows. They also carried grenade launchers with them. Suddenly the moonlight revealed a small AT-gun, which was pushed across the meadow by two men. Mielke realized that many more British had come down here than he had initially suspected. Further south, there was another rumble as another one of those strange planes touched down on the ground and glided over the grass before it came to a halt.

"You are willing to testify about the German forces in the area of the two bridges?" Tappert translated with a slight accent.

Mielke nodded quickly and answered, "Jawohl, jawohl!"

*

Schneider and his men slipped into their uniforms and loaded their weapons, when Calvert stood in the entrance again. Schneider had radioed Fritze immediately after Calvert's report about the wrecked plane, and he ordered him to investigate. So they would now set off to look at one of those damned bombers in the middle of the night. Great night!

"Two more have come down!" Calvert gasped in a strained voice. Schneider's eyes widened. So there would be something to do that night after all.

Outside there was a long whistle. A split second later a grenade hit in front of the bridge. The detonation blasted across the area and echoed right into the bridge house. Schneider looked at Calvert, who turned on his heel and raced back to the machine gun nest; meanwhile, Foster's gun began to speak. Long bursts of fire roared through the area. Rifle shots and submachine guns mingled with the noise. Schneider was about to give his orders when a small, egg-shaped object rolled into the room. The eyes of the master sergeant focused on the British grenade, which came to rest in the middle of the room and would wipe out all life in here. Unable to act, the sight paralyzed him. But sometimes the God of War was merciful to some, punishing others with unspeakable misfortune. Only after a good five seconds Schneider understood that the grenade must be a dud. He pulled up his machine carbine, set the button switch to full-automatic and fired his entire magazine into the wall to the left of the entrance. Usually the stone would be capable of withstanding a bullet, but not a whole magazine. His gun rattled for only a few seconds, then all 30 bullets had gone into the wall. The muzzle blasts blustered incredibly in the small room and made Schneider's ears ring. Among the noise of the battle was the screaming of a man right in front of the entrance. At the same time a real shower of shells hit the Canal Bridge.

"Come on, get out of here!" the master sergeant urged his men on and put a new magazine in his gun. He grabbed his helmet and put it on his head, then he stormed forward through the room to the outside. He almost tripped over the enemy he had hit. Schneider stumbled and threw himself to the ground, where he immediately turned on his right shoulder.

He saw how the MG 34 spat death and destruction into the darkness on the road by the sandbag turret. Every burst of fire made the weapon and Foster behind it briefly visible. Glowing tracer bullets chased through the night. In between a merciless hail of mortar rounds fell, but Schneider could not see the impacts. All he could hear was the whistling of the approaching rounds and the detonations that lifted the earth and the grass. Behind Schneider, the remains of his squad rushed out of the bridge house and took up positions all around.

"Flare gun! Alarm!" Schneider shouted. Moseneke loaded the weapon accordingly and fired into the air.

Now everyone should have noticed that, Schneider said to himself. He stared into the darkness. The enemy mortars were about to dig everything up. Schneider slid back to the bridge house and leaned against the wall.

"Well?" he gasped and meant Schumann, who was crouching over a screaming opponent, while another figure lay beside him – dead.

"That's a bloody Englishman! With gun, uniform, all that shit!" he said. Schneider listened up. He thought they'd be attacked by the Resistance. That it was the British added a whole new quality to the story – and a whole new dimension.

"Everything's covered in blood, damn it!" Schumann complained.

"Shut up, Mannerheim. For all: Prepare to jump, first half of the squad. Target is our machine gun position. Wildner leads the second half and provides covering fire! My intention: from the MG nest, we engage the enemy on his left flank."

His men confirmed. Schneider had no idea where the enemy was, so he held on to Foster's machine gun fire, which sprayed bullets into the open area.

"What about the Englishman?" Schumann groaned.

"Leave the son of a bitch alone. There's no time."

"Jawohl."

"It all ends sometime. And now fire!" Schneider yelled. His soldiers had quickly taken up positions. They bent their triggers, chasing bullets in the presumed enemy direction. The projectiles disappeared in the darkness. Schneider charged off, Moseneke and Schütz followed right behind him. They ran across the road, reached the turret of sandbags and dropped to the ground.

"Norway!" Schneider yelled upwards. Norway was the squad's watchword, confirmed by Foster only a fraction of a second later.

At the same time the mortar fire died away. Foster once again released a firing burst into the unknown. Schneider picked himself up, climbed over the sandbags and dropped into the machine gun nest, where Calvert immediately helped him to his feet.

"Report!" Schneider demanded, and at the same moment

Foster started babbling without taking his hands off his gun: "We had figures in the forefield - four or five – then we fired and they disappeared. Then came the mortar fire. I've been shooting blind ever since, trying to make the guys understand that there's nothing to get here but sadness! The post of the dogfaces ran right over to give the alarm."

"That's good. Prepare for covering fire for the second half of the squad. I'll move them over here, and then we'll get the bastards on the counterattack!"

But this plan was suddenly thwarted when the mortar fire resumed and their rounds came whistling over. This time they hit the bridge house. Some other weapon joined in the concert. A moment later there was a terrible blow over at the second half of the squad. Schneider couldn't see that the bridge house flew apart, but he could hear it very clearly. The noise was finally drowned out by the cries of pain from his men.

"Scheisse!" the master sergeant said, "Fourie, turn on the light!"

"Okay, jawohl!" The black Wehrmacht soldier sat up halfway, then he shot a flare into the sky, which burst into a small sun and illuminated the battlefield for a few seconds.

Moseneke had shot the bullet far to the North to light up the possible enemy positions, but their own forces remained in darkness. Schneider could not believe what he saw. His heart was pumping wildly. In the light of the flare, a At-gun and more than 40 enemy soldiers, divided into two groups, appeared. Foster immediately shot into one crowd. Men went down, while the others were pressing their bodies against the ground and returned the fire. Bullet impacts were dancing over the sandbags and tore open the fabric. Sand trickled out.

Before the light was gone, the AT-gun fired again and tore a big hole in the road right next to the bridge house that was just a pile of rubble. Several men lay in front of it and writhed in pain. Schneider was worrying. They couldn't win this fight anymore, at least not without help from the other side of the bridge.

"Calvert, come with me! We've got to get to the second

half of the squad and get the wounded across the bridge. Foster, cover our asses. I'll pull you over as soon as the wounded are safe!"

Foster nodded with a serious expression, then Schneider and Calvert climbed over the sandbags and out of the turret. Moseneke and Schütz were still lying there on the ground, firing aimlessly into the open – only single fire, because they didn't want to waste too much ammunition. Who knew what else would happen that night?

"Follow me, we'll get the wounded! And then over to the other side of the bridge!"

Behind Schneider, Foster's machine gun started talking again. Tracer bullets shattered the gloom. The English fire also came at random. It tore up the asphalt and scorched the grass. It drilled into the sandbags of the machine gun nest and banged clinking against the metal structure of the bridge. Schneider instructed Moseneke and Schütz, then they ran off and crossed the road again. Around them mortar rounds hit the ground releasing deadly fragments, but the Brandenburgers were lucky. Meanwhile at the Orne Bridge shooting started too.

*

Foster fed his gun a new belt and pulled the trigger. Enemy bullets bounced off his cover. Again, the AT-gun thundered in the blackness and tore another hole in the ground somewhere near the bridge house. Foster was glad that the enemy hadn't had the idea yet to use it against him! Anyway, he had to give Schneider a little more time, otherwise his comrades would bleed to death. With no regard for his own life, he fired more hammering bursts of fire.

Foster's hearing, tormented and hardened by countless hours at the machine gun, suddenly noticed a noise right in front of the sandbag wall. He stopped. Uncontrollable heat rose into his skull.

There's someone! Foster thought startled. Immediately he let go of his machine gun and pulled out his Colt, a

110

souvenir from home. He raised his gun and leaned forward slowly to look over the sandbags, when suddenly a thin, strongly accented voice called out the word "Norway". Relieved, Foster slumped down a bit and put his gun back into the belt.

Gosh, Mielke! His thoughts jumped for joy, while he completely ignored the fact that the voice did not sound like the private at all. But Foster had no time left to identify the moment of relief as the fatal mistake of his life. Two grenades rolled into his machine gun position and detonated immediately. The explosives tore Foster's body apart and transformed it into a bloody and fleshy mess, while the force of the detonations blew up the sandbag emplacement like an over-inflated balloon.

*

Schneider heard the double detonation behind him, which stood out clearly from the mortar impacts and also from the fire of the AT-gun due to its short but violent blows. Those had been hand grenades! The master sergeant had just reached the second half of the squad and was about to see what was left of it. As projectiles of all calibers whistled over him and mortar rounds ploughed the ground in front of the bridge, he realized that he no longer had a machine gun nest. After seconds without fire from Foster's gun – seconds could be a very long time in combat – the matter was clear to Schneider. Slowly the situation became critical!

Moseneke, Schütz and Calvert jumped past him and dragged the bodies of their comrades. Stückl had been hit hard, with several thick splinters in his chest and both shoulders. He spat blood and was about to pass out into the world of unconsciousness. Valente was dead. So was Wildner. Berger had been badly hit in the leg by a mortar fragment. Maybe he'd lose it. But he was still breathing, he was still awake and he even had his gun in his hands.

Suddenly the enemy fire died down. From the Orne Bridge the noise of the firefight continued undiminished.

111

Schneider listened into the darkness. The British man he had hit earlier whimpered and gasped, having survived all the attacks against the bridge house. Once again clouds covered the moon and took the last bit of light from Northern France. It was pitch black so that Schneider could not see his own hands. He groped his way until he found one of his comrades.

"Who is here?" he wanted to know.

"Fourie."

"Man, you're hardly visible." Then Schneider whispered his idea into the soldier's ear: "We have to get out of here. We'll try it without covering fire. With luck, they don't know over there whether there's still resistance or not. But in any case, they'll soon attack the bridge. So we gotta get out of here!"

Moseneke hit his helmet against the helmet of Schneider as a sign of confirmation, then both felt for their comrades and passed on the squad leader's plan.

"Fourie and Calvert grab the wounded and go ahead! We'll stay behind you and provide covering fire in case of an emergency. Take the fastest way to the bridge!" Schneider hissed.

"Where's the Finn?" Schütz' question made Schneider wonder. Yes, where was Schumann?

Schneider looked around. *No idea, no time!*

"We have to go," he hissed. Moseneke and Calvert loaded the wounded onto their shoulders and trudged away quickly. It was quite a feat to be almost running in total darkness with 80 kilos on their backs, but the approaching enemy moved them.

Schneider and Schütz followed the carriers attentively. It was suspiciously quiet behind them. In the distance, the battle that was currently taking place around the Orne Bridge was roaring, but the enemy had certainly not given up at the Canal Bridge either.

Schneider finally got to the head of his remaining squad to show the carriers of the wounded the way. He stormed past Moseneke and Calvert and stepped onto the road. Determined he marched towards the bridge. Slowly the moon fought its way out from behind the clouds and once again unfolded a minimum of light. Schneider recognized the metal structure of the bridge, then suddenly a person with a gun and steel helmet appeared out of the darkness. Schneider stopped and pulled up his weapon.

Are the island monkeys already at the bridge? Thoughts and fears chased through his mind.

"Norway... Norway," the figure stammered in a thin voice. Relieved, Schneider lowered his gun, for he could not have known that the enemy had already found out the password. He approached the person who was standing there in silence. It turned out to be Schumann. Schneider got to his soldier and hit him roughly against the helmet.

"Mannerheim, boy! Where have you been?"

"Wildner had sent me out to get reinforcements from over there. When I left, everything at the house was smashed to pieces."

"Yes, it's quite a mess! Get on behind – with Schütz - we've got wounded and some dead and have to get to the other bank as fast as possible."

Schumann nodded in horror; the realization that he had lost comrades that night was clearly affecting him.

They had just reached the bridge when the Tommies fire started again. Bullets from handguns cut through the air, hailing the bridge structure. Schneider and his men threw themselves to the ground.

"Bring over the wounded," the master sergeant barked, took up his machine carbine and shot aimlessly into the darkness. Moseneke nudged Calvert and demanded that he would hand over his wounded. At first Calvert stared wide-eyed, but then he obeyed.

Gently Moseneke took Berger, the second wounded man, put him on the ground and grabbed him by the back of his field blouse. With Stückl on his shoulders, he dragged Berger behind him, who, awake and with his weapon raised, could have prevented even the worst from happening.

Calvert joined Schneider and Schütz so that at least three German weapons shot into the night. But there were to be no more losses. The three of them swerved over the bridge, which Moseneke had already crossed. If they had been really unlucky, they would have been hit by their own people on the other side of the river, who didn't really know what was going on. But Schneider remained true to his luck. A three-man squad of 4th Squad, who was supposed to explore the situation, met them halfway across the bridge. Schneider reported in brief and heard that the grenadiers and tanks had already been alerted.

Shortly after Schneider met the company commander of the grenadiers, a captain, older than 50, with a pipe between his teeth. The officer pulled Schneider to him and signaled the master sergeant to follow. He led him to the left side of the bridge and into one of the two multi-storey buildings that lay just behind the embankment. In the moonlight, Schneider recognized the barrels of machine guns protruding from windows on the first floor.

"Your dark friend already told me about the situation, but I wanted to hear it again from a German," the captain began, as he stopped in the corridor of the building.

"I'm Greek," Schneider admitted with an evil eye.

"Oh, my God. You're a bunch."

Schneider ignored this remark and described the situation without taking a breath. The captain listened attentively.

"All right, Feldwebel. Your colorful circus troupe can take a break. We're in charge now!" He laughed out loud. "The Tommies are in for a treat!"

"Treat? How?"

"Well, with our treat-tools!" As if on cue, the engines of the Czech tanks started up by the roadside at the back of the buildings. They rolled off, moved into the street, turned around and rumbled towards the bridge. The small tanks 38(t) with their 3.7-centimeters cannons were certainly no colossuses of steel, but they were better than nothing. Some of the tanks that had been taken out of service were used as infantry support for grenadier units off the Eastern Front, but otherwise they were no longer used.

"Herr Hauptmann. I must once again point out to you that the enemy has at least one AT-gun," Schneider

114

instructed the officer in a forceful voice. But the man just grinned, then he cackled: "Oh, AT-gun, AT-gun, AT-Gun, balderdash, AT-Gun! My tin cans are over there so quickly that the Tommies won't even know what's happening to them. Watch this, Feldwebel!"

The captain pulled on Schneider's field blouse and thus dragged him into the next room, from whose window the Canal Bridge could be seen. The first 38(t) just passed the crossing, rattling. Schneider recognized the tank as a large, dark surface which pushed itself over the barely visible steel bridge. The armored fighting vehicle was almost over it, when the driver let the engine roar and accelerated. Suddenly a thunder shook the air. A ball of fire formed, engulfed the tank and ignited an inferno. At its climax, the ammunition depot blew up and sent the turret into the sky. A burning tank man had been disembarked shortly before and had fallen over the railing of the bridge into the canal. The other tanks stopped and went into reverse.

While the pipe fell out of the mouth of the captain at the sight of his burning tank, two things were clear to Schneider: First, the invasion had begun, second, the invasion would not take place in Calais, where the majority of the German forces was concentrated.

And Rommel's on convalescent leave. Splendid! the master sergeant thought.

HMS Empire Anvil, English Channel, June 6th, 1944

Corporal Tom Roebuck spent the last hour before his unit would board the landing craft in the ship's mess, where he sat with some of his comrades and poured cheap coffee into himself. The food on board had been disgusting from the start, and the coffee was only edible because Roebuck almost poured a pound of sugar into each cup. He had just washed the last of the brown broth down his throat when a tinny voice sounded from the ship's speakers: "Hour H minus 60 minutes."

Saviano, a.k.a. Pizza, looked at his watch and said, "It's time, boys."

The others who sat at the table with Saviano and Roebuck nodded; these were Timothy Juergens, John D'Amico and the slender wearer of glasses with the protruding Adam's apple: Joe Constantin.

"Let's see what you've got," Roebuck demanded, pulled an unopened letter out of his uniform jacket and laid it on the gray mess table. His comrades also rummaged around in their uniforms, revealing letters they had received in the last few days. Meanwhile the kitchen boy trotted over with a new pot of coffee and filled the cups. With a bored expression on his face, he was constantly creeping back and forth between the kitchen and the dining room. He apparently couldn't share the tension that lay on the marines of the 4th Marine Raider Battalion. After all, he didn't have to jump out of a landing craft into chest deep, ice-cold water in just a few hours to run 400 yards over uncovered terrain against German positions that were perfectly entrenched in the dunes. Although the Navy and Air Force promised to level the German bunkers and MG nests prior to the landing, and the Airborne boys promised to wipe out all remnants of the bombing, Roebuck by now knew what to make of such promises.

The Marine Raiders were lucky to exist at all, because at the end of 1943, it was considered to dissolve this branch of the Corps in order to free up more personnel for the regular Marines. Almost at the last moment, Roosevelt had ordered that the Corps' overall staffing level be increased due to the difficult war situation in both theaters. The breakup of the Raiders would have been a severe blow to the sworn fighting community, which that night was to participate in the largest military operation in the history of mankind.

Roebuck took a big sip of coffee. Then he lit up a Chesterfield and inhaled the smoke with closed eyes. The tiredness pressed noticeably against his eyes, but he

116

couldn't sleep now anyway – as it was about to start. So coffee and cigarettes were his remedy for the fatigue – and of course the adrenaline of the battle, which would flood his body as soon as he got caught in enemy fire.

"Hey, what's wrong with you, you selfish fuck?" Juergens complained and pointed to Roebuck. "Gimme one too, man." Juergens bent over and signaling Roebuck to put a cigarette in his mouth. Roebuck sighed, pulled out the white cigarette pack again and snapped his finger against the bottom of the pack so that a cigarette slipped halfway out of the opening at the top. He handed the Chesterfield box to Juergens, who picked up the cigarette with his lips. Grinning, Juergens leaned back. Suddenly, his features distorted into a grimace, and he whined again: "What's wrong with you? Where is my fire?"

Now Roebuck leaned back, showing his comrade his middle finger, while he made an obscene gesture with his tongue.

"Do I look like your nigger, Batman?"

"Fuck you, asshole."

Shaking his head, Juergens brought out his own storm lighter and lit his cigarette. He took a deep puff and blew a wisp of smoke around Roebuck's ears.

"Can't you please just get a room and cut the crap?" D'Amico grunted. The Marines laughed lustily. When the men had regained their composure, they turned their eyes on Constantin.

"Go ahead, Joe," Roebuck demanded, nodding to Constantin. He looked a little embarrassed for a moment, but then tore open the envelope and took out the letter. Most of the time Constantin received mail from his mother – and her letters were usually very funny. This time it was unfortunately only a message from Constantin's cousin. The private first class read aloud, his bright voice getting tangled up in the letters again and again and twisting words. The content of the letter was not important: Constantin's cousin reported with a few lines about his life in Italy with the Air Force. As a ground crew member he worked in the officers' mess in Polistena and therefore had a quiet life. Although he had been involved since Sicily, he had not seen anything of the war so far.

"Lucky bastard!" Saviano commented, whose turn it was. He too tore open the envelope and pulled out a letter. He read: "Ciao Bambino..." Saviano looked around. "Should I really read this? It's in Italian." He hadn't finished his sentence when Juergens reached across the table and grabbed the letter from Pizza. He looked at the letters, jumped up and threw it at his Italian comrade's feet.

"You fucking liar! It's in English!"

"It's all right." Saviano looked ruefully and picked the letter up off the floor.

"You can't speak the spaghetti language anyway," D'Amico remarked, grinning.

"You wouldn't believe what I can do!" Saviano returned.

"Well, from what I heard, you'll show me everything you can for 10 bucks."

The Marines were jeering. Saviano said, "Fuck off," then crossed his arms and played the "prima donna". When the laughter subsided, Roebuck said, "Go ahead, read it."

"I don't really want to."

"Don't be like that," D'Amico teased.

"Yeah, Pizza, go ahead," Roebuck urged.

"You're a fine one to talk, Tom. You only get letters of the idyllic world from your wife," Saviano replied. Bitterness determined his voice. "But in my case, any letter can tell me that my brothers are KIA."

The Marines understood that, of course; still, ritual was ritual. Juergens finally reached over the table and put the burning cigarette in Saviano's mouth. He took a puff, handed the cigarette to Constantin and began to read: "Ciao Bambino, here's Mama. I have received news from all your brothers in the last few days. They are well..." Roebuck could feel Saviano exhaling as he read. Like many American families with Italian roots, the Savianos seemed to have a particularly strong bond between family members. "Marco is not allowed to say where he is, but his ship still sails the Pacific. And he will be coming home soon, for a few weeks. Adolfo is in Catania... in our old home country! And far away from the front, thank God! Franco is now in Melbourne on a stopover. I hope old Maripone keeps his hands off the Australian women! Oh, Tony, my Tony..."

Roebuck and the others grinned, but Saviano didn't notice. He read, absorbed in the words of his mother: "what I would give to have our Franco be more like you..."

"She means 'virgin'," Juergens whispered.

"Franco is always so bold and impatient. But you have become a righteous man! Papa and I are very proud of you. By the way, you surely remember Vera? We sometimes meet her family at Sunday mass."

"Ohhh... Vera?" D'Amico smirked.

"Vera... Vera," Juergens mused, "dirty little convent girl, eh?" Again the GIs grinned, but Saviano was not provoked. He continued unconcerned, "Vera has been asking about you a lot lately. You should write to her, bambino! I have enclosed her address. Love, Mom." Saviano looked up. Roebuck thought he saw a short twitch in his eyes – a moment of emotion. But Pizza quickly recovered and put the letter down. Emotions were not exactly what the Marines Corps expected from a man.

"Who is Vera, Pizza?" Juergens demanded to know.

"Yeah... and why didn't you tell us about this girl?" D'Amico said.

"There's nothing to tell, you fools!" Saviano replied.

"So she's still available?" D'Amico kept asking. The others grinned.

"Just fuck you," Saviano hissed.

Juergens jumped up and made obvious movements with his abdomen and hands: "Oh... Vera... yes, Vera! Give it to me hard! Give it to me hard!" D'Amico also joined in the concert of mockery. He made an appropriate gesture with his right hand and mouth. Roebuck was silent and enjoyed the scene.

"You're such bastards," Saviano finally protested, throwing the cigarette, burnt to the bitter end, into his coffee cup. The Marines continued to fool around, while Constantin asked in between – addressed more to himself

119

than to the others – if there was any Coke in this mess. At some point, when the murmuring had subsided and the kitchen boy had poured the next round of coffee, Juergens asked Roebuck to read his letter. He didn't want to be told twice, as he was already anxious to see what his wife had written to him. Often she had sent him indecent photos of herself with texts that made him want to go home to her immediately. But as long as he was trapped in this war, his hand would remain his only girlfriend. That was often the problem of married people: In the Pacific, apart from a few untouchable nurses, there was in fact hardly anyone of the opposite sex – at least not where Roebuck's unit had been operating. Only Japanese and bullets had been waiting for him in the field. But since they were roaming in England from the beginning of the year – the president had ordered to increase the invasion troops with battle-hardened Marines from the Pacific after it had become known that the Germans had significantly strengthened their troops at the Atlantic Wall – the Marines had found their true land of milk and honey: Besides training and preparation for the invasion, the soldiers had always had enough time to visit the local pubs and have a good time. In England, if you wanted a girl, you didn't even have to go to a brothel. Roebuck's comrades quickly noticed that the English girls quickly got involved with the Yanks; after only a week, most of Roebuck's unit had a liaison. For some of them, a real relationship even began to develop, and there were discussions about bringing the girls to the States after the war and marrying them. Juergens was one of those cases. Roebuck, however, had always had to watch the colorful hustle and bustle of his comrades. For him, the only distractions in England were alcohol and sports.

Now he tore open the envelope with nimble fingers and pulled out the paper.

"And... pictures?" Juergens wanted to know right away. Roebuck shook his head. *And I wouldn't show them to you either*, he added in his mind.

The stationery he held in his hands felt rough. It was folded in the middle, but Roebuck saw Marie's writing shimmer through. He even thought at that moment that he could smell her. Roebuck's heart made a leap and heat rose to his head. He had already killed tens of Japs in this war and he would soon run into the Krauts' machine gun fire. He could handle that. A letter from her, however, brought him down every time. Roebuck unfolded it and was surprised at the few words of the message. Immediately he read it out: "Dear Tom, I am very sorry, but I am leaving you. Marie." Tom's mind had not yet understood what he had just read. He went over the short message again in his mind: "Dear Tom, I am very sorry, but I am leaving you. Marie."

His comrades were silent, every grin had disappeared from their faces. Tom himself sat there like a rock. He stared at the letter, stared at the characters, but he couldn't grasp a single thought. Then something struck him: She was so far away, on the other side of the world. She was absolutely not within his grasp. If there was no war and she would leave him, then at least he would still be around and could try to win her back. But what could he do here in Europe? She was beyond his reach. Every letter took weeks to get home. Up to that point, there were absolutely no emotions in Tom. He only felt a great emptiness.

"Shit, Tom..." Juergens finally cleared his throat and put his hand on Roebuck's shoulder. The others nodded silently.

"Imagine, tomorrow night we'll be sitting together in Sainte-Marie-du-Mont, drinking French wine. The world will look different again."

Still Tom just sat there motionless. Juergens kept on chattering: "Believe me, there are plenty of girls in France just waiting for a guy like you. We can expect some great months."

"Great months?" Constantin interfered. "Ask the Krauts!"

"Shut the fuck up, will ya?" D'Amico yelled at his skinny fellow soldier. Roebuck had turned to stone. At some point, he put the letter on the table and lit a new cigarette with empty eyes.

"Ask the Gunny," Juergens hissed, addressing Constantin.

"He was already here in the last war. He also says the Krauts are a gift. They're supposed to be tough, but at least they're not as crazy as the slit-eyed yellow apes. The Germans know when they're beaten and surrender. You don't have to pull them out of every goddamn hole in the ground and be afraid they'll come at you with swords or blow themselves up!"

Roebuck's mind completely blanked out the discussion. Slowly, very slowly, an irrepressible rage flared up inside him.

Pointe du Hoc, France, June 6th, 1944

The dull rumbling of the eight-eight flak woke Berning. Slowly he opened his eyes and looked into the darkness of the night, which transformed the room furniture into gloomy racks. Berning's palms made an unpleasant impression. Large calluses had spread there. He had spent too much time planting Rommel asparaguses and digging trenches in the coastal embankments.

His unit had set up camp for the night in a large farmhouse in the hinterland of Pointe du Hoc, not far from where the artillery guns were hidden. Since the previous day, the cliff had also been fortified by a battery of eight-eights, which were distributed over the entire place. During the day, these guns had already caused a hell of a noise when American bomber formations had repeatedly passed over the cliff. In the evening hours it had become quieter, and although severe bombing raids were reported from all over Northern France, the coastal units had not been put on alert. Berning liked that. He did not understand the whole excitement, after all there were enemy air raids in France every day. So even in the night of June 6th, only the alarm posts were in place, while the rest were sleeping at night. After all, the Wehrmacht weather service predicted that the weather that night and in the next few days would prevent the enemy from landing.

Half asleep, Berning rubbed his eyes. He heard that his comrades around him – he was with the other warrant officers of the squadron in a room that had probably served as a dining room for the landowners – had also been woken by the flak noise out there.

"Oh, scheisse! Can't they at least leave us alone at night?" someone complained.

Berning sat up. The moonlight entered the room through the windows and gave the soldiers lying on camp beds and partly on the ground a dusky appearance. Berning wished that the eight-eights had never been moved to Pointe du Hoc.

Suddenly the door was ripped open. Pappendorf stood in the room.

"Alarm!" he shouted.

Berning was blinking his eyes.

My God, they're just planes, he said to his platoon leader in his mind. Pappendorf howled at a horrible volume: "Enemy airmen approaching! Alarm! Rise and shine."

Immediately the soldiers were sitting up straight on their beds. Within seconds they threw themselves into their pants and jackets. The squadron had never been on its feet so fast. In clusters, the soldiers stormed out of the building onto the road that led both inland and down to the cliff. They had to run 500 meters from here to their emplacements. The moonlight prevented it from being pitch black. Berning saw his comrades as dark shadowy creatures running around, preparing their weapons for battle and gathering. The lights of an anti-aircraft searchlight battalion cut everywhere through the darkness.

Berning looked into the air and froze. American planes were passing overhead. The 2-centimeter AA-guns, which were hidden away from the cliff positions, sputtered red-hot projectiles in between. Berning counted eight large bombers. The eight-eights also fired continuously. The flak soldiers sent up one round after the other into the sky.

Berning clearly saw one of the Allied planes catch fire and

123

quickly lost altitude. Only then he became aware of the real danger, which was approaching at enormous speed. Against the moon he noticed tiny airplanes, which came from the sea at low altitude straight towards the cliff. It was difficult to spot the fast objects in the darkness. Berning saw that there were several, without being able to count them exactly. For a moment, he lost his breath. What was flying towards them were not planes! They were gliders that had been pulled by the big bombers behind them and which had cut the ropes just before Pointe du Hoc.

Oh, no, Berning thought. *Enemy paratroopers! Elite soldiers!* He grabbed his rifle as tight as he could. His heart was pounding like a machine gun.

At the cliff and everywhere fire from German handguns flashed up. The soldiers of his squad gathered around Berning, ready to strike. Only their sergeant was not ready. Now the first glider rushed almost silently over their heads, turned away and went down behind a row of trees. It rumbled and rattled a lot after the pseudo airplane had touched the ground. First Lieutenant Balduin loudly took the 1st Platoon and stormed after the enemy airmen in order to engage them as soon as they landed.

Terrified and full of horror Berning stared at the remaining gliders that were floating right towards him and would probably also descend into the hinterland of the cliff.

"Fire!" Pappendorf ordered and ran around wildly gesticulating between his platoon and the 3rd Platoon. "Get those gliders down!"

With rifles and submachine guns, the German soldiers opened fire on the gliders blurring in the night sky: pudgy objects with long, straight wings. Silently, the next gliders passed over the heads of the Germans. Suddenly Pappendorf stood next to Berning, in his hands a MG 42.

"Berning, go, meat mount!" he shrieked. Berning looked at his platoon leader questioningly.

"Yes, do I have to say please, you carnival prince!? GO, MEAT MOUNT!"

I hate the meat mount, the sergeant complained in his mind. At the same time he grasped the bipod of the machine gun and hoisted the muzzle onto his shoulder. With a jerky movement he closed his right ear with his left hand, then Pappendorf started firing the MG. The weapon rattled terribly on Berning's shoulder, striking him repeatedly against the bone as it rang in his ears. But Pappendorf's firing worked. He had taken aim at one of the enemy gliders, which was moving right towards them. One third of the machine gun belt was loaded with tracer bullets that sparkled as they hurtled towards the glider. Berning recognized clearly that Pappendorf landed massive hits. Glowing rounds pierced the enemy flying object, which consisted of wood and light metal. Some bullets ricocheted off and flew through the night like drunken fireflies.

The glider crunched and bucked under the fire, then it jerked, tipped over at the front and rushed towards the ground, front first. It crashed and broke into a thousand pieces. The 3rd Platoon stormed off to secure the crash site. Further back with the 1st Platoon, firefights flared up, their noise echoing over the cliff.

Pappendorf opened the top of the machine gun with lightning-fast movements, inserted a new belt. Then he repeated his trick again. He unleashed a real rain of fire on the next approaching glider, which started spinning, went off course and crashed hard into one of the farmhouses. The platoon leader of 3rd Platoon realized the situation and immediately sent a squad, which rushed forward and threw hand grenades into the crashed glider. The occupants – probably Americans – stood no chance.

Further gliders, three or four, hovered over the heads of the 2nd Platoon just at this moment. They floated towards an open space behind the farmhouses, where they went down one by one.

They are heading straight for the Rommel asparaguses, Berning thought in a mixture of joy and fear. Pappendorf barked to attack. Meanwhile, the 3rd Platoon stayed on the spot to secure the farmhouses. Pappendorf rushed towards the gliders' landing sites, his unit chased after him. Carrying the heavy machine gun, the master sergeant ran past the buildings and fought his way through a row of bushes leading to the field with the Rommel asparaguses. Berning hurried after him, panting. Quietly he cursed that of all people the fastest master sergeant in the Wehrmacht had to be his platoon leader.

Berning pressed his rifle to his body and turned his head away as he fought his way through the bushes. Meanwhile, Pappendorf fired a flare into the night sky, illuminating the field, which looked like a nail board because of the closely placed Rommel asparaguses. When Berning had crossed the row of bushes, he immediately threw himself on the ground to avoid possible enemy fire. But what he saw relieved him: Three gliders lay on the ground, smashed by the Rommel asparaguses like flies under a rolled up newspaper. The flanks of the gliders were torn open, their fronts completely destroyed. Pieces of wood and equipment parts were scattered. Between the wooden stakes there were bodies everywhere, motionless or trembling in pain. Wounded people were screaming terribly. There was no fight to be fought here, there were only prisoners to be taken. Pappendorf was already organizing the platoon and giving new orders. From over there, where the 1st Platoon was operating, machine gun fire and grenade blasts echoed. After a short speech by their platoon leader, parts of Pappendorf's platoon set out to secure the field and recover the wounded.

"Berning!" Pappendorf finally yelled. Immediately the sergeant stood at attention.

"Here, Herr Feldwebel!"

"Do you hear that?"

Berning listened into the night. Shots and shouts from over there filled the scenery, but mostly German weapons and German words were heard.

"They're still fighting over there! I'm sure the 1st Platoon will need support." Pappendorf grinned maliciously, then he sneered: "Here is nothing more for you to do, Unteroffizier. Take your men and report to platoon leader of the 1st."

Berning sighed. He ran off.

126

Bénouville, France, June 6th, 1944

The veil of the night was still covering the double bridges of Bénouville and Ranville. The moonlight, which had finally overcome every cloud, continued to give Normandy a minimum of light. A few raindrops fell on the earth.

The British had just failed in their attempt to storm the West bank of the Canal Bridge. Their wounded and killed men were within the range of the German machine guns – and the Germans did not let the enemy get close. The tank, which was slowly burning out, threw an eerie light on the scenery.

Over the telephone the Germans on the West bank of the Caen Canal learned that their comrades at the Orne Bridge had been pushed to the East bank where they were surrounded by paratroopers and had to fend off attacks all around. Parts of the 744th Infantry Regiment, which were deployed to replace the bridge defenders, would advance in mass first towards the Ranville area, as this was suspected to be the center of the enemy air landing.

Still the humming of enemy planes filled the sky, which flew in wide-ranging formations again and again and again to Northern France.

"Bombers again," Fourie groaned, who had just returned with Calvert and the others from the casualty assembly for the wounded. The land on this side of the canal had not yet been invaded by enemy forces. Schneider pondered. He stopped and shook his head.

"They're not bombers," he whispered. Fourie looked at him questioningly. But Schneider had no time to explain. Suddenly he stormed off. Seconds later he had reached the building where the Captain of the grenadiers had set up his command post.

"There will be more," Schneider sighed when he saw the old man. "We must think of something and throw the Tommies out now before they gather and bite!"

"Ha!" The captain tapped the tip of his nose with a wink. "No fear, Feldwebel! The English will soon be finished. My grenadiers are preparing to attack the bridge!" The officer tapped Schneider on the shoulder, smiling.

"Assault?"

"Of course! Let's go in head-on and then we'll knock the noodle off the Englishman. It'll be a good blow!"

"Herr Hauptmann, there are forty Tommies over there. At least."

"And I have 132 men. One to three, so it fits! Don't worry, Feldwebel, I did this a thousand times during the Great War!"

With these words he left Schneider standing in the hallway of the building and stepped out into the street. The master sergeant followed the officer with an apathetic look.

Outside, in the moonlight, he saw the grenadiers line up in two long rows in the street, equipped with French rifles from the last war. They didn't even have hand grenades; moreover almost any of the men could easily have been Schneider's father.

Poor bastards, the master sergeant thought. He flinched; a new zest for action seized him. He rushed past the old men, chased across the street, felt his way down the embankment and finally found the trench on the canal bank, which was occupied by the 4th Squad of the Brandenburgers.

"Is Wolle here?" he asked the soldiers in the position.

"Here!" Sergeant Wolfgang Huber replied, the squad leader.

Schneider squeezed past the soldiers. Breathless, he made it to Huber, a goldsmith from Erlangen, who was sitting on the ground at the end of the trench. Huber rose and hit Schneider against the shoulder.

"It sucks about your people. Especially Foster. Oh, boy, oh, boy, oh, boy," he whispered in a choked-up voice.

"Yeah, but it's not over yet. This Hauptmann is about to send his men to their doom."

"Who, the madman with the pipe? I'm surprised he hasn't driven the Tommies away with his own sword on horseback. He should just let the English come! I'm sure they know the bridge is ready to be blown up, so they won't wait long to attack."

128

Schneider nodded before he replied, "I need some of your boys, Wolle. Then I'll try to prevent the worst from happening."

Apparently Huber pondered for a moment, because he hesitated. After seconds that seemed like hours to Schneider, the sergeant agreed: "Go up to the front building and take the Dschibril brothers. I can't spare anyone else if I want to stay effective."

"Thank you." Schneider and Huber banged their helmets against each other, then the master sergeant turned around and made his way back to the road, where he could see the long faces of the poor grenadiers in the flickering light of the burning tank. Their captain had placed himself at their head, where he gave a speech: "Men, a long blast of my whistle is the signal to attack!" He held up his whistle. "We'll storm over, spread out and give the English a good thrashing! A motorized battalion is to arrive here in an hour to reinforce us. Then I want to be able to tell the gentlemen on their steel steeds that the situation is in perfect order! To get you in the mood for what is to come, I will tell you the story of the battle of Augustów, where a young platoon leader, who liked to smoke a pipe, took twelve prisoners of war all by himself..." All Schneider could do was shake his head as he ran into the building Huber had mentioned, collected the Libyan-born Dschibril brothers and finally gathered his men to explain the procedure. He had to hurry, because the captain could sound the attack at any moment. Schneider fervently hoped the guy would tell a long story.

*

Schneider had ordered his men to take weapons, magazines and grenades. Anything that rattled, however, had to go. In a hurry, they had also cut strips out of their tents and wrapped the ammunition in them. Schneider hoped that that was enough to keep them dry, otherwise it would become... interesting on the other side of the river.

As the squad searched their way down to the canal bank north of the bridge, the captain was still in the middle of his history lesson. Meanwhile, he was babbling about Operation Michael.

Schneider climbed ahead and slipped several times on the steep slope. The country was still covered in darkness, but this would soon change. So they had to hurry for several reasons.

Schneider reached the water of the Caen Canal. He put his right boot into it and immediately recoiled. It was icy! Moseneke, who had been unusually tense during Schneider's quick issue of orders, but who had assured that everything was alright when asked, was pushing behind him. Perhaps the events of the night, including the death of a few good comrades, were affecting him – after all, that is how everyone felt. But the Brits had not done this for nothing, Schneider had sworn to himself. So he forced himself into the water and waded ahead with his gun held high.

The master sergeant did not know how deep the water was. Since the canal could be passed by ships, he prepared himself to definitely have to swim. It only took a few steps until he could no longer feel the ground under his boots. While he held his machine carbine up with one hand, he tried to swim as best he could. The icy cold water poured into his uniform and sloshed against his body. He was exhaling loudly and quickly as the cold pressed the air out of his lungs. Schneider gasped, but it worked.

"God, how I hate France," he heard Schumann groaning.

Moseneke was panting and snorting behind Schneider. Suddenly he began to kick and flap his arms around him. He uttered a loud curse, then he spat water. His limbs wriggled like fish on land.

Schneider was swimming as best he could. The weapon left only one arm free for swimming movements, because his right hand gripped the metal shaft of the Stg 44. His hand began to tingle under the weight of the weapon. Schneider swallowed water, spat, forced himself to close his mouth. They had to be as quiet as possible. Moseneke, however, was paddling his arms like a man possessed. The water splashed. Schneider turned around swimming. In the moonlight, which broke on the surface of the water, he recognized Moseneke, who made great waves, disappearing again and again and wriggling completely uncontrolled in the cool water.

Was he hit? Schneider thought, accompanied by a shudder. He immediately swam back, reached the kicking private first class and pulled him up. He struggled for air, coughed water and sucked in air loudly. Calvert approached from behind.

"What's wrong with you?" Schneider asked with a slight panic in his voice.

"I... I..." Again and again the dark-skinned soldier disappeared and had to be pulled up again by Schneider and kept afloat.

"I can't swim," Moseneke finally said. Schneider's eyes widened, then rage overcame him. But he couldn't lose his temper now, not here! Not in the middle of the Caen Canal and not now, when they didn't have time!

"What's wrong with him?" Calvert asked at the same time, but then understood and swam up to Moseneke to lift him up over the surface of the water.

"Why don't you tell me, you fool?" Schneider lectured him.

"I was embarrassed."

"Jack, help me!"

Together they pulled the wheezing and water-spitting Moseneke through the canal, while the latter held the weapons above water. Firefights flared up in the distance. In Ranville, the fighting resumed.

Snorting, the Brandenburgers reached the other bank of the river. Schneider fought his way out of the water and lay flat on the embankment. He felt the soaked uniform pull at him, restricting his freedom of movement, but it had to work. All of a sudden the air was filled with the roar of aircraft engines again. The enemy planes approached quickly, while Schneider's men waded out of the water and took up positions to his left and right. Above them it became loud as an apparently gigantic swarm of enemy machines thundered over them.

Are they dropping a whole army group? Schneider thought. The hammering of the countless propellers, the rumbling of the clumsy planes drowned out everything else which Schneider was very pleased with at that moment. It was necessary to regain the East bank of the canal in a hurry before the parachuted Brits could form up and before the crazy captain would sound the attack.

Too late! Schneider heard the shrill sound of a whistle, which echoed over from the other bank. He pulled himself up. Not far from him the British machine guns started barking. There was a flash of lightning up ahead at the bridge. Guns roared, then men were screaming. Schneider signaled Calvert to go through the communication trench in front of them together with the Dschibril brothers. The three glided silently into the darkness. Schneider took the rest of his squad, jumped up the embankment and ran towards the bridge. Behind him, he heard the sound of Calvert detonating hand grenades, then it became silent. The two Libyans were masters of the blade. They wouldn't waste ammunition.

There was a bang in front of the bridge. Bullets blew around and tore apart soil, stones and bodies. The rounds of the English glanced off at the still slightly smoldering tank wreck and sparkled in all directions. Schneider clearly saw figures that collapsed in the enemy fire. Suddenly there were several violent blows when tank cannons sounded from the German bank. The Czech vehicles with their 3.7-centimeter barrels were completely outdated for the year 1944, but in this case it was enough. Apparently in an uncontrolled manner the tanks attacked the enemy bank and tore up the road and meadow. Schneider heard hectic British voices. He and his squad had worked their way up to the back of the enemy, which was within throwing range of hand grenades. Glowing tracer bullets of the Brits chased through the night, smashing into the bridge where some banged against the metal and blasted up into the sky. Suddenly the battlefield was illuminated. Apparently one of the German grenadiers had fired a flare, which now, dangling from a parachute in the air, bathed the battlefield in a glaring white light. Schneider recognized dozens of German bodies lying motionless on the bridge. He saw old men cowering fearfully behind the wrecked tank, while the British fire hammered mercilessly at them. In any case, the gunner with the flare pistol had fired poorly. Instead of just illuminating the enemy, at that moment everything was in the light; the British, the Germans, the bridge. An English machine gunner had taken up position in the ruins of the sandbag turret, and next to him stood another Englishman at Foster's very weapon. More British soldiers had taken up position near the destroyed bridge house, while the enemy AT-gun stood 30 meters behind the bridge beside the road. The enemy gave the grenadiers a hell of a beating, shooting right in the middle of them. Already there were cut up and dismembered bodies scattered in front of and on the bridge. A half torn up German tried, sluggish as a worm, to crawl away.

The English, however, made the classic mistake at that moment: All eyes were on the place from which the attack was launched. So none of the Tommies could see the doom approaching.

Schneider pulled two hand grenades out of his belt, turned the caps off and tore off the string while still running, before he hurled the two explosive devices into the British near the destroyed house. It was only when the sound of two detonations was heard, the resulting blasts of air tore at the soldiers and splinters were piercing through earth and flesh, that the British realized that the writing was on the wall. Schneider, Moseneke and the others fired their weapons and let a true hellfire break out over the enemy.

The battle did not last long. Moseneke jumped over to the bridge house, where he shot the remaining Englishmen with one magazine – almost all of them, because two of them dropped with the rest, but were not hit. Immediately they pulled out pistols, while Mosenekes weapon was empty. But the British soldiers had chosen the wrong opponent for a close-quarters dance. A far-reaching blow with his machine carbine knocked the pistols out of the hands of both Englishmen. With one leap Moseneke was in

133

front of the first of his opponents, who knelt before him as if in prayer. The dark-skinned giant reached out with his right leg and slammed it against the face of the man, who then flinched for a moment, while a cervical vertebra splintered inside him, then he collapsed like a wet sack. At the same moment the second Englishman had thrown himself at Moseneke. Both wrestled with each other like monitor lizards in a mating clinch, but the brave Englishman, who reached up to the chin of the Brandenburger, was hopelessly inferior. With a tremendous effort Moseneke grabbed the man at the front and back of his upper body and lifted him up. The Englishman roared with surprise, kicked his legs and tried to hit for his opponent's head, but Moseneke quickly set off for the final. He tore at the Brit with all his might. He hurled him towards his knee, with which he simultaneously took a dangerous blow. The knee and the upper end of the British man's coccyx crashed into each other, then the Englishman went down screaming – unable to get up again. He was still flailing and ailing, but the man was no longer able to fight.

The rest of the English were severely hit by the nasty surprise of the attack from the canal. As if in shock, they looked around terrified and tried to understand what was happening. Schneider and his men mercilessly used this moment of weakness. They fired from all barrels, threw more grenades. Within seconds a dozen Englishmen were on the ground – they twisted and writhed or remained motionless. The grenadiers on the bridge had also understood what was happening. In the shimmering twilight of the moon they pulled the triggers of their weapons. The gruesome struggle for the bridge at Bénouville began. Faceless creatures fought each other to the death. But this battle would be won by the Germans, which the leader of the enemy unit seemed to have understood. In a flash, he organized a withdrawal. Schneider threw himself to the ground and pressed a new magazine into his machine carbine. Enemy fire swept over him so close that he could feel the whiff of the bullets.

The grenadiers at the bridge launched one flare after the

other. The battlefield was lit up as bright as day.

Schneider shifted his fire, now holding on to the enemy AT-gun, which had no shield. The operators of the cannon were at Schneider's mercy without protection. He immediately hit one of them, who simply collapsed. The other two looked for cover and kissed the grass.

The English now threw smoke grenades, which covered the street and the sandbag turret in white smoke. As soon as a thick wall of fog had built up, the Brits were gone – vanished into the night. But they had left the AT-gun behind.

Schneider gathered his men, while the German grenadiers swarmed onto the West bank of the canal, taking care of the wounded on both sides and preparing to defend themselves again. Who knew how many enemy forces had landed in the area? In any case, the British would not be content to have lost the bridge.

Slowly dusk set in, the noise of some fights still echoed over from Ranville. Schneider urgently needed to contact his platoon leader. In the worst case, the Tommies were occupying the West bank of the Orne Bridge, which meant they were less than 600 meters away. That would become exciting once the sun had risen and you could look over to the other side. With these antiquated grenadiers, you couldn't go anywhere against these English elite soldiers. But then Schneider had another idea: Maybe he should go after the British before they could gather and reach full fighting strength again. A daring undertaking for sure, because Schneider could only guess how many enemy soldiers were in the area. But it was better than waiting here at the bridge for the next assault.

Always keep the initiative! the voice of his old teacher echoed in his head, then Calvert and the Dschibrils appeared out of the darkness. The three of them held British mortars in their hands, while Schneider noticed that Yusuf Dschibril's trouser leg was torn open and soaked in blood.

"Are you all right?" he asked, pointing to the injury. Yusuf nodded.

"Got caught in barbed wire, you know?" he returned,

135

while Calvert unloaded the mortars at Schneider's feet.

"We got six dead Soutpiels over there and about 60 rounds for these babies here." Satisfied, the South African pointed to the mortars.

"Let's see if Tommy rounds can kill Tommies." Schneider grinned. Calvert and the two Libyans seemed to understand and also looked happy. After all, they had to pay back the death of some good comrades.

Out of the corner of his eye, the master sergeant could see that the crazy captain, cocky as a rooster, was stalking across the bridge. Although he was only visible as a shadow in the fading darkness, the slightly bent posture with his arms constantly whirling around like pudding was unmistakable.

Seemingly confused, the captain first strolled around among his grenadiers, then he seemed to have discovered Schneider and trudged straight towards him.

Seconds later the captain stood between the Brandenburgers. The officer had his pipe stuck between his teeth, causing the smell of tobacco to get into Schneider's nose. He patted the Brandenburgers one after the other, beaming with joy.

"Gosh, Feldwebel. You're here, too? I didn't realize you were with us during the attack. That was a good hit, what do you think? The Tommies ran like the French. Ha! How could they withstand a German assault?"

Schneider's wet uniform stuck to his body like clay. This only increased his thirst for action, because if he didn't move soon, he would start to freeze violently. So he nodded and replied: "Herr Hauptmann, we have to leave again. Orders from above." Schneider didn't want to have to explain everything to this second greatest commander of all time.

"Oh, boy," the captain returned. "Everything's fine. My men and I will hold position until the cavalry arrives."

"We'll be back in four hours."

"And I'm going to interrogate the English POW. The bastards!" The captain dragged on his pipe, raised his clenched fist to make his words more forceful, and left.

Schneider turned to his men, explained his intention in short sentences. Finally he turned his attention to Moseneke: "Fourie, you can walk better than swim, can't you?" Moseneke lowered his head in humility.

"Up and over to Huber. He shall report to Fritze as soon as possible and tell him my intention. You'll be back here in two minutes. We've lost too much time already!"

Moseneke sprinted off.

Saint-Côme-du-Mont, France, June 6th, 1944

Colonel Richard Schmidt had already experienced too much that the events of the night could have let him sleep. No, things were different this night. This time, something was up.

Schmidt, commander of Grenadier Regiment 473, had gone to the Great War as a volunteer in 1917, spent a year in captivity and then joined the police. So he had undergone all the political unrest and chaos of the 20's and early 30's at first hand.

He had experienced how the monarchy had been torn away from the country he loved so much and replaced by the American system of democracy. He had seen how this democracy had plunged Germany into disaster, how it produced opposing governments; incapable of making decisions. Incapable of ruling! He had experienced how the National Socialists rose up and "cleaned up" the Reich. They were the ones who brought back the old strength to his country; they liberated Germany from political confusion. The price for this was high, but Schmidt – like many Germans – had been willing to pay that price. In 1935 he had joined the resurgent army as a captain. His heart had been warmed by the first sight of German Luftwaffe planes in the sky and the first time he saw German tanks rumbling through the streets in a military parade.

Hitler had shown a finger to the Allies and simply done what Germany was forbidden to do: Within a few years he had turned the meager Reichswehr into the most powerful military force in the world – and overrun all of Europe. Schmidt had been there from the beginning. And despite all the hardships of the war, despite the privations and despite the bad things that this fight brought with it, he had enjoyed it.

It was his generation that had to live in the trenches in the rain and cold during the World War. It was his generation – he and his comrades – who had been betrayed in 1918 by the office sitters at home. Schmidt's blood was boiling when he thought back to the horrors of the Great War; and to the fact that it had all been in vain because the socialists he hated so much had stabbed the German army in the back. He was firmly convinced of this.

Betrayed by our own people! Thoughts of anger raged through his mind. And now that Hitler was gone, fear came over him that history might repeat itself, as history had repeated itself many times before. Schmidt spat as he closed the door of his kubelwagen. It was just dawning, and the steeple of Saint-Côme-du-Mont gleamed slightly in the twilight.

Schmidt turned to his driver and told him to wait. The young private first class nodded.

Pah! Young man, in his early twenties, Schmidt pondered as he moved towards the large wooden gate of the church. *These young people have no idea what this is really about!*

He entered the church, marched straight up the spiral staircase that led up to the church tower. He knew that the war would be difficult should the Allies make a successful landing in France.

His excellent instinct also led him to not dismiss the unusual things of this night simply as an enemy diversion, as many did. The omens were too much of an invasion for that. First there were the unusually violent bombing raids, which concentrated mainly on Normandy and only secondarily on the most likely landing site Pas-de-Calais. In this night the enemy steel birds also dropped their bomb

138

load near the coast.

Everywhere along the Calvados coast the glowing threads of the Pathfinder airplanes stuck in the air. In addition, the enemy bombers had destroyed some bridges over the Loire and Seine during the night, apparently trying to close off Brittany and Normandy. Also, many telephone lines had been cut during the night, probably by the French, perhaps even by Allied commandos. All connections from his command post to the staff of his namesake Lieutenant General Arthur Schmidt had been dead since five o'clock in the morning.

Then there were reports of enemy paratroopers coming in from all over Normandy. There was great confusion within the Wehrmacht about this. In the hinterland of Cherbourg and at Coutances on the West coast of Normandy, puppets on parachutes are said to have descended, scaring the German soldiers with firecrackers. Were these only diversionary tactics? Did the other units reporting the landings of enemy soldiers perhaps also report only dummies? Did the Germans in Normandy witness a spectacular diversionary operation to cover up the landing at Pas-de-Calais? Many believed in a diversionary operation – unfortunately also many who had something to say. Schmidt's instinct, however, suspected something else: The invasion would take place in Normandy. What gave him that idea? Well, quite simply: He would do it that way himself – landing where the enemy least expected it.

It all stinks to high heaven!

His steel reinforced boots clacked loudly on the stone steps as he climbed to the top of the tower.

The Americans and the British are smart guys, he continued to ponder. *But they don't fool me.* After all, the Navy had spotted a huge fleet heading for Pas-de-Calais. But Schmidt was sure that the relatively young technology of radar could be deceived in some way. History finally showed that the Western powers were true masters of deception.

After all, Arthur Schmidt had already put his 6th army on alert, while Geyr von Scheppenburg did not consider this necessary for his 7th army.

139

Idiot! Schmidt internally accused the Commander of the 7th. *There's something going on! I'd bet my wife on it!*

Lydia's image briefly crossed his mind. He hadn't seen her for ages – at least it seemed like an eternity to him. The time he had been born into had never allowed him to lead an excessive private life. His existence so far was marked by the fight for Germany, not by love and holidays. He had dedicated his life to his country; but he did it also in order that the children of Germany might one day live in peace in a great nation; peace which had been denied to his generation.

Schmidt reached the top of the church tower, from where, in good weather, one could look down to the beach of Saint-Marcouf.

In good weather... the words echoed in his mind. He looked out through the big windows into the twilight. Misty fog lay over Cotentin, but the hedges and orchards for which the region was so famous slowly emerged from the night. In the distance the sea could be seen.

The German Weather Service believes there can be no invasion today? Then I would come exactly today! Schmidt was furious in his mind about his superiors; meanwhile he took his binoculars in his hands and positioned himself behind one of the windows.

"Let's see..." he growled, holding the binoculars to his eyes. He adjusted the focus, then he scanned the coast. At first, his gaze fixed itself on one of the emplacements, code name W5. As prominent points of W5 he spotted the tank wall, which ran parallel to the coast along the beach, and the dome with the machine gun nest inside. The defensive positions were the responsibility of the 7th Army, which remained deployed at the coast, while his 6th Army had taken over the rear, except for a few emplacements at the coast, which had been staffed by some companies of the 6th Army. The 7th Army, however, was behind schedule with the construction work everywhere. At least Colonel General Geyr von Scheppenburg made up for some of the omissions of his predecessor.

Suddenly all of W5 disappeared behind a veil of thick

smoke. A bang in the distance was heard only seconds later. Schmidt was startled. That bang in the distance had not remained a single sound, but quickly built up to a crescendo of gunfire. Thundering in the distance the shells went down and attacked W5. Schmidt was concentrating on his binoculars and searched the coast. Finally he let his gaze glide out to the sea. He stopped.

What he saw there on the sea – barely visible in the twilight – took his breath away for a moment. What he saw exceeded his worst fears: A vast fleet had made itself comfortable off the coast of Cotentin. Cruisers, destroyers, transporters, surfaced submarines – millions of tons of tonnage resting off the coast, in front of W5.

Battleships! Huge battleships sailed around the horizon. Schmidt saw the flashing of their guns as further impacts leveled the coast near W5. Protected by tethered balloons and partly fogged in, thus obstructing Schmidt's view, the most gigantic armada the world had ever seen lay off the coast of Northern France. The German Navy had nothing to compete with this.

Nevertheless, Schmidt also recognized that one of the enemy cruisers was slowly sinking into the water. Tiny boats swarmed around the large ship like water fleas, whose front part of the bow had already been completely swallowed up by the sea. Von Witzleben had ordered the majority of the German submarines back from their missions in the Atlantic. While some of these units were also on missions far away from Germany – which many people could not understand – many submarines had been assembled off the coast of Northern France. In addition, the Kriegsmarine had ordered all the torpedo boats and other small barges into the English Channel in order to be able to deliver quick, surprising blows to enemy ships in the event of an invasion. The German naval units were by far not up to the invasion fleet. Schmidt's eyes narrowed at the sight of the sinking enemy cruiser. The guys from the navy had shown some guts. Many sailors of the Reich would die in the coming battle in the English Channel, but at least they showed the Tommy and the Yank that the Channel was not entirely theirs.

Schmidt turned on his heel and ran down the stairs of the church tower. He had to get back to his command post as quickly as possible. Who knew how long it would take the navy to report the beginning of the invasion to the army. Unfortunately, the inter-branch cooperation in the German military was sometimes a catastrophe.

With bounding strides Schmidt dashed through the aisle of the church and pushed open the large wooden gate. In front of him stood the kubelwagen, but its driver had disappeared.

"Damn kid," Schmidt exclaimed.

"Hands up, Jerry!" he was suddenly screamed at from the side. Schmidt turned around in horror and looked at the faces of several American soldiers, smeared with black paint, who were pointing their weapons at him.

Paratroopers, Schmidt immediately recognized.

Northeast of Bénouville, France, June 6th, 1944

Wherever the other British paratroopers had descended, thank God they had not landed on the narrow strip of land between the Caen Channel and the Orne. Schneider guessed that the enemy had deployed the bulk of his forces North and East of Ranville – on the other side of the river. He further believed he had understood the idea behind the enemy battle plan: A small unit, deployed by gliders, was to take the double bridges in a surprise attack and hold them for several hours until reinforcements had parachuted in and reached the bridges. But while the British plan had not yet worked out, the situation remained extremely dangerous. Firefights flared up again and again in the East – sometimes farther away, sometimes close to Ranville. From the North, from the coast, a monstrous drumming and thundering could be heard since it slowly dawned.

142

That was artillery! The Normandy coast sank under an infernal bell of fire from guns of the Allied invasion fleet. Not only bombers, but also fighter bombers, reconnaissance planes, naval aircrafts and enemy fighters were populating the sky. Schneider was aware that something big was about to happen. He had not seen a German aircraft in the air since the first British attack against the bridges.

However, if he and his squad are discovered by an enemy fighter bomber, thing could quickly go south. A German pilot usually would not attack infantrymen, since it was not a target valuable enough, but the Allies had planes in such expansive numbers that they would probably pounce on any detected German forces. So Schneider and his men moved through a narrow strip of forest along the banks of the canal. Thick treetops protected them from views from the air. During their advance they had spotted three enemy Horsa gliders that had cut furrows in the meadow north of the Canal Bridge. Of another glider, only the tail rudder could be seen, which protruded from the Caen canal. And over in front of the Orne Bridge, other gliders had surely gone down.

Schneider knew how dangerous his action was: If the British were to hold the Orne Bridge and decide to come to the aid of their defeated comrades whom Schneider was currently chasing, they would stab his 1st Squad right in the back. This could end badly, because one could not miss each other on the narrow strip of land. However, Schneider accepted the risk with approval. His motto was: no risk, no reward. Under no circumstances should the British commandos be allowed to gain a foothold here.

In a rush, the Brandenburgers stamped down the undergrowth, staying close on the heels of the Tommies. Twice during the waning night they had fought small skirmishes with the enemy without this leading to anything. Each time the British managed to break away again. Schneider did not know how many enemy soldiers he was facing. He was also not sure how many soldiers could fit into such a Horsa. Maybe there were really only a few left, which is why they let themselves be chased like

143

that by the few Brandenburgers, or the English thought they would be pursued by far more Germans instead of just seven men.

Schneider would soon find out.

The Brandenburgers crept through the thicket, with swamps dominating the land between the canal and the river Orne on the right. A few hundred meters in front of them, however, the swamp ebbed and the forest occupied the entire strip of land, which became narrower and narrower towards the North, pushed in by the canal. That was almost in Ouistreham just off the coast, so that was the end of the line, unless the British dared to go into the water.

Schneider slowed down his pace. His men followed him, fanned out in skirmish line. Calvert had tied the three mortars together and carried them on his back like a duffel bag. He had one hand free, clutching a Walther P08. Schneider looked at his wristwatch. Already past seven o'clock! Everywhere around them, all hell was let loose in the distance. Battles were in full swing and sounded all the way to Bénouville. Lightning flashed across the sky, enemy planes swarmed around.

It was hazy. Some rain drops fell like long strings from the clouds. Schneider whistled through his teeth while his eyes meticulously scanned the forest area in front of him. He still couldn't imagine that a water landing was possible in this weather, especially at low tide, which was the present situation! The wind was not as fierce that day as it had been the day before, but it blew hard enough that no German barge would try to land in England. But well, that was out of the question at the moment anyway.

Suddenly Schneider's squad was fired upon. Muzzle flashes flickered in the forest in front of them and bullets buzzed through the air. Schneider threw himself down, firing a single random shot. Immediately afterwards a bloodcurdling scream broke out over there. Lucky shot!

Schneider and his men fired back. Every British resistance died away after only one minute. It seemed that the man who had been hit and was still screaming like a banshee had spoiled their morale. Under sporadic fire the English

144

set off again. The screaming of the injured man was also disappearing. But the British had reached the end of the road, and Schneider knew that. He gave the firing command to Calvert, who together with the Dschibrils had prepared the mortars. The Libyans opened their rucksacks in which they had stored the mortar rounds and loaded the barrel. It was lucky that every Brandenburger was trained on all kinds of weapon systems and also on enemy weapons. Of course, they were not as accurate as a mortar squad, but it would be enough to roughly rake the area between them and the sea. The first rounds were already shooting into the sky and went down whistling over there.

Schneider instructed the others to advance under cover of mortar fire to eliminate the British once and for all. They had to use the momentum of their hunt for the British NOW! The master sergeant shouted over to Calvert, that he should look for flares, with which Schneider wanted to direct the mortar fire. The South African confirmed before sending more explosive rounds into the sky. Schneider and the rest of the squad sprinted off under cover of the undergrowth. The master sergeant saw figures in front of him, veiled in the morning mist, scurrying to the right, accompanied by the earth fountains of the mortar shells. Schneider rushed after them.

Further to the North there was a tiny private harbor, where the English could have provided themselves with boats. But now they jumped over to the Orne. The Brandenburgers sent bullets after them and apparently inflicted further losses on them. British soldiers broke down. Occasionally the enemy fired back. The Germans threw themselves to the ground, took cover and held the British down with continuous fire from their machine carbines. Considering the ammunition reserves, Schneider could not continue this wasteful game for much longer, he was aware of that. But he had the enemy at a critical point, so he had to continue for the time being. Once again the fire of the enemy stopped. Headless, the British ran to the banks of the Orne, where there were no trees and no cover.

"Flare!" Schneider shouted in the cackling of the weapons.

145

"Okay, jawohl!" Moseneke pulled out his signal pistol and fired; the flare went off right over the British's new position; and Calvert's mortar fire followed at its heels.

Meanwhile Schneider had an idea. He signaled his men to move into position here and keep the enemy under fire. Then he waved Schütz over to him, who immediately jumped on his feet.

"Follow me!" Schneider yelled. "They want to cross the river!"

Schütz nodded, then Schneider ordered to hand him over the flare gun and ammunition. At that point the master sergeant and Schütz dashed off. From their position they ran sharply eastwards, where they soon broke out of the forest and came to an area littered with young trees. Ducked, they sneaked forward in the protection of the bushes until they reached the embankment. Schneider lay down flat on the ground, crawled out of the young trees and looked to the North. A cool breeze brushed over the land and also over his wet uniform, but in battle such things faded into the background. Therefore Schneider did not feel how much he was actually freezing. At that moment, the senses that were of immense importance for killing and survival dominated his mind.

Looking up the Orne, he actually found what he had suspected: In front, where the mortar rounds were lashing the embankment, some British had gone into the water to get to the bank on the other side. Schneider suspected that after the failed raid on the bridge, they wanted to join the other paratroopers to try again later with joint forces. He didn't know that in the meantime Fritze had also taken complete control of the Orne Bridge again and thus the first attempt of the British had been defeated altogether. However, enemy airborne forces had landed east of the Orne in divisional strength; and they would certainly not accept that the double bridges still belonged to the German forces.

Schneider counted 16 Englishmen, and the majority of them were in the water. On the opposite side two British soldiers were positioned for securing the river bank.

146

Schneider touched Schütz, the sniper, and showed him the boys on the other side of the river. He nodded and got behind his rifle. As the Gewehr 43 was semi-automatic, Schütz shot down both opponents within an instant. After that, Schneider opened fire, targeting the soldiers in the water. Schütz also directed his firing at the British in the river, who did not understand what was happening to them. They panicked, ploughing through the water with hectic swimming movements. Schütz and Schneider mercilessly shot down the helpless men; floating bodies became playthings of the current.

Again, the two Brandenburgers were met with sporadic enemy fire. Lead filled the air, projectiles buzzed around and went into the trees, slashed leaves and branches from the bushes and penetrated the ground, where they threw up small fountains of earth. Schneider pushed a new magazine into his gun, which clicked into place. It was his second to last.

"Let's put the pressure on once more," he hissed and sent a long burst of fire to the plain in front of him, where the rest of the British, who seemed to have given up fleeing through the Orne, entrenched themselves in the mortar craters. More explosive rounds went down on them and tore up the landscape. Schneider guessed that in the meantime Calvert had also fired two thirds of the mortar ammunition.

The Tommies hardly put up any more resistance. From time to time one of them stuck his upper body out of a crater and fired a shot in the direction of the Brandenburgers. Schütz remained completely calm. He pressed his weapon stock to his shoulder according to regulations, chose his next target over notch and bead sights and let his index finger fly over the trigger. The projectile tore into a Briton's shoulder, where it burst and threw bloody pieces in all directions. Groaning, the hit man sank into the crater, after which the enemy fire died down completely.

Schneider and Schütz could no longer make out any targets. Seconds passed. The master sergeant sat up halfway and tried to overlook the surroundings. Again a volley of mortar rounds went down in the forefield and dug new craters into the ground. Walls of dust and dirt built up, but immediately collapsed again. The moans and screams of the wounded mingled with the soundscape.

Only now Schneider felt the speed of his breathing. His gaze was frozen on the British position. Still nobody showed up there, meanwhile the next salvo of mortar rounds hit the ground. When the dust had settled, suddenly something happened. Two hands – unarmed and held high – became visible in one of the craters. Very slowly the owner of the raised hands, a British lieutenant, recognizable by his epaulettes, scrambled out of the crater. Bent, with the look of a good fighter who had suffered a defeat, he stood on the open field. Again, rounds from Calvert's mortars rushed in.

The enemy officer flinched, threw himself to the ground, and was lucky. Unharmed, he was able to stand up and again pulled his hands up; this time with emphasis, probably in the hope that the mortar fire would finally stop.

Schneider immediately grabbed his flare pistol, loaded the purple ammunition and fired into the air. With a loud popping sound the projectile took off into the sky, where it wandered across the firmament as a purple stripe. The mortars fell silent. Schneider picked himself up; the wet uniform stuck disgustingly to his body.

"Stay here and keep your eyes open," he told Schütz before he dared to go out into the open field. He held his weapon at the ready to signal the enemy that the capitulation has been accepted.

Slowly he walked towards the lieutenant, whose expression radiated pride and professionalism, but also bitterness over the defeat. Schneider nodded at the man appreciatively; and indeed, he had to admit that the English had fought well.

The Tommies are very tough bastards anyway and bold guys, he mused as he approached the British officer. *Very different from the Russians.*

When only ten meters away from the British lieutenant,

he looked over to the place where Moseneke and Schumann were in position. He waved at them, and moments later both of them emerged from the undergrowth as gray figures. The Englishman made a surprised face when he spotted the dark-skinned man in a Wehrmacht uniform before Schneider stood opposite him and attracted his attention. Both stared at each other and then nodded at the same time. Silence had returned to the scene, only the moans of the English wounded filled the air – and the roar of the battle in the distance.

"Who are you?" Schneider demanded.

"Lieutenant Den Brotheridge, 1st Platoon, D Company, 2nd Ox and Bucks Light Infantry," the officer replied. He was young and a slim fellow. Schneider estimated him to be in his late twenties.

"How many of you are left?"

"It is just me and three wounded."

Schneider nodded again. A single glance across the plain, into the shell craters and into the forest in the West, and he recognized several fallen Britons; some of them horribly disfigured by the blast, the heat and the thousand splinters set free with each explosion; torn open, lying there in a strange posture. Then he had to think of his people; of Valente, Foster and the others. That morning, both sides had had to pay their death toll.

"My men help you with the wounded, carrying them back to the bridge. I see that I get hands on a medic. Agree?"

Brotheridge nodded with clenched lips.

"What's your mission?" the master sergeant then demanded to know. Schumann and Moseneke appeared behind him.

"I have nothing else to say," Brotheridge confidently returned. Schneider pressed his lips together. He had expected that. He turned to Schumann and said, "Get Calvert and the others in here. Schütz will hold his position until we leave."

"Yep." With that brief word of agreement, Schumann disappeared. Afterwards, addressed to Moseneke, Schneider added: "And you take a look around here."

149

"Okay." Moseneke also left.

With Schneider's permission, Brotheridge climbed down into one of the craters and began to care for the wounded. Schneider himself squatted into an empty crater – he did not have to parade around as an invitation for snipers – and lit a cigarette.

After one minute Schumann returned together with Calvert and the Dschibrils. Calvert grinned.

"Damn Soutpiels, must have thought there were only old men and greenhorns in France," he exclaimed. But suddenly Moseneke rushed over, shouting: "Please Pantelis, come. You must see this!"

Moseneke had led Schneider back into the forest where the British had barricaded themselves before jumping over the road. The rest of the squad had stayed with the prisoners. Moseneke trudged through the undergrowth where mortar rounds had destroyed bushes, trees and soil. Several dead enemy soldiers who had fallen victim to the fragments were also lying here. Chests, limbs and heads were broken open, sometimes torn to shreds, sometimes torn apart by razor-sharp metal splinters the width of a hand. Shiny fragments, some as big as the blade of a circular saw, were stuck in the thick trunks of the old trees. But between all the khaki-colored uniforms there was also a field-gray one. A German soldier, apparently a prisoner of war of the British – had also fallen victim to Calvert's shelling. Schneider came closer and recognized the face. There was a dark hole in the man's neck from which blood and tissue emerged like millipedes. The dead man was Erich Mielke.

"Don't tell Jack," Schneider ordered. "They shot him, okay?"

Pointe du Hoc, France, June 6th, 1944

They are coming!

From his position Berning could see the tiny landing crafts approaching the cliff.

Oh no, Berning thought in view of the 22 landing crafts that were slowly but steadily moving towards the cliff. The alarm, a protracted warning sound that kept howling and then flattened out, was activated and covered the future battlefield with the distorted monotony of its call.

Why can't they land at Calais? Berning pleaded. On the right flank of his squad, Hege pressed the MG 42 against his shoulder, put his index finger over the trigger. At any moment, the boats would be in range.

"God, they want to climb up the cliffs under our fire?" Weiss shouted, so that Hege could understand him too. "It will be a massacre!"

"The question is, for whom?" Hege showed his rotten teeth. Then he explained, "Those are certainly not last month's recruits in the boats."

Everyone looked spellbound into the forefield -- observing the approaching attack forces. Berning was sure: A catastrophe was on the horizon in France. As in Sicily, the Allied superiority would simply sweep over the coast and into the heartland; and worst of all, he was already right in the middle of it again!

Everywhere on the cliff the order to fire was given. The machine guns rattled off; those of the platoon, the squadron, the artillery gunners and the company of the 352nd Infantry Division. The time frame, in which the enemy boats were within range of the German machine guns, but had not yet disappeared into the blind spot of the rock faces, turned out to be very small. Once the enemy had disappeared below the cliff walls, the Germans would have to jump out of their positions, overcome the barbed wire and bend over the rocky edges with their weapons to pepper the narrow sandy beach at the foot of Pointe du Hoc.

German artillery from the hinterland joined the concert of weapons. Pillars of water rose up where their shells disappeared into the sea. The resulting waves tore at the landing crafts, throwing them around, shaking them. One boat developed a list before it capsized. Desperate men were waving their arms. They tried to escape from the sinking boat, but the undertow pulled some of them down into the deep.

Hege whirled his gun around, shooting on the shipwrecked men. The waving arms became motionless bodies that slowly sank into the sea. But the enemy's attack was enormous, and they could cope with a lost barge. The German bullets roared sparkling over the metal skins of the landing crafts. Tiny helmets protruding from the cargo holds ducked away - or stumbled before they disappeared from the Germans' view. But despite all the defensive fire, the enemy was inexorably moving closer. The machine gunners of the boats also fired. Dozens of projectiles went into the cliff, into the positions, into the piled up sandbags; also into German bodies. Men who were hit screamed like babies. They were pulled out of the line of fire by their comrades.

The first boats had already disappeared under the rock face.

"They're at the beach!" someone yelled. Weiss just pulled the red-hot barrel from Hege's machine gun and pressed it into the sand. He cursed obscenely as he burned his hands.

"BERNING!" Pappendorf's voice cut through the battle noise. Berning looked along the long trench in which almost the entire platoon was positioned. The master sergeant squeezed his way through firing soldiers and approached Berning. Judging by Pappendorf's expression on his face, the master sergeant had some special orders up his sleeve again.

"BERNING!" Grasping for breath, Pappendorf reached the position of Berning's squad. Detonations sounded. The alarm howled in between.

"Berning! Grab hand grenades and head for the ledge. Prevent the enemy from coming up! 1st Squad, take cover

152

on the left flank. Your machine gun stays here."

"Jawohl, Herr Feldwebel. I have been ordered to..." Pappendorf interrupted him violently: "No time for that shit! Come on, up!" The last word hadn't left his lips yet, when the platoon leader turned around and made his way back to the other platoon members. Berning gathered himself; immense fear paralyzed him for a moment.

Explosions were cracking down by the water, guns were barking. And now he was supposed to go to the edge and throw down hand grenades? Berning snorted.

Fucking Amis! Hateful thoughts flooded his mind. *Can't they just leave us alone?!*

Berning pushed himself out of the trench. His rough hands felt furrowed, the skin had cracked in many places. He turned to his men and gave his orders in short sentences. Moments later, the landsers were struggling to get out of the trench with the exception of Hege and Weiss.

"Grenades ready for action," Berning grunted, who himself took a stick hand grenade from his belt. His men followed suit. They twisted off the caps, wrapped the fuse cords around their fingers and followed the sergeant to the front.

Suddenly one of the soldiers slipped on a stone and slammed sideways on the stony ground. With eyes wide open, the man stared at his hands: In one of them he held the grenade, in the other the torn fuse. Reflexively he turned on his stomach and buried the "potato masher" underneath him. Lightning flashed as the grenade detonated and the soldier's body became a plaything of the blast. He flew up a good meter before he fell back onto the rock with his abdomen ripped open. Berning froze in his movement, turning to the dead man. Motionless, wrapped in a bloody uniform, he lay there as if he had fallen asleep from exhaustion.

"I would have thrown it away," Reuben remarked apathetically. Pappendorf sent two comrades from the 3rd Squad to drag the dead man back into the trench.

Only a strange, metallic clink brought Berning back to reality. In disbelief he turned to the left where a three-

153

pronged hook had wedged itself into the ground. From the hook a thick rope ran to the edge of the cliff, where it disappeared down the rock face. More such hooks, pulling ropes behind them, suddenly rose everywhere over the rocky ledge, forming an arc in the air and landing in the barbed wire enclosure and in the crevices. Immediately the ropes got under tension. Sometimes the hooks slipped a few more meters over the ground before they got wedged in a crevice. One of the hooks could not find a hold, was pulled back to the edge of the rock and fell down into the depths.

The bastards really want to climb up that wall! Berning moaned in his mind. He still couldn't imagine it – but it happened, at that very moment. Berning tore the fuse from his hand grenade and threw it over the edge. His soldiers did the same. Detonations roared up the rock face, but they couldn't see if they had caused any damage. The men of his squad worked on the hooks. They cut through the ropes with their knives or loosened the hooks from the rock. The ropes disappeared immediately behind the edge of the cliff, as if heavy weights were hanging on them. But more hooks whizzed through the air, clinging to the rock. More and more climbing ropes were brought into position in this way.

Pappendorf propelled the 3rd Squad forward. All over the cliff the soldiers of the Wehrmacht rushed out of their positions to repel the American attack. Huge ladders were braced against the cliffs. Some Germans climbed between the barbed wire and down the rock walls to knock over the ladders. They went down with screaming Americans clawing at the rungs. But more and more ropes and hooks and ladders were brought into position by the enemy to overcome the rock face. One man of 3rd Squad was caught by an approaching hook on his shoulder. Before the soldier knew what was happening to him, a strong jerk went through the rope and pulled the man forward. He disappeared behind the edge of the cliff, shrieking.

The first pairs of hands of the Americans reached over the edge of the rock and grabbed for something to hold on to. Immediately the Germans were on the spot. They shot the hands to shreds at the shortest distance, which threw their owners back into the deep. But the enemy was numerous – and he seemed to have taken casualties into account; otherwise it could not be explained that the GIs hanging on the rope and ladders were climbing the rock face without a care in the world; no matter how many of their fellows fell past them to the ground, where they smashed into the sand as if into concrete and all bones burst under the pressure of the impact. Man by man they climbed the cliff; and from now on the fight claimed more and more German victims. With small machine pistols or revolvers, which the Americans, hanging on the rope, could fire, they suddenly shot into the Germans as soon as they raised their heads over the edge of the cliff. Berning and his comrades in turn threw themselves to the ground. Further back, several Germans had torn an entire segment of the barbed wire running along the cliff edge from its anchoring and threw it blindly into two Americans scrambling over a ledge. The one in front was hit by the razor-sharp wire. The fine metal cut open the man's hands and face before he staggered and fell against the GI behind him. He dragged him with him down the rock face.

Hege repeatedly used his machine gun to shoot along the edges of the cliff; or he aimed at one of the hooks until it was smashed to pieces.

But they were coming. They were coming and they were coming.

In panic, Berning threw his head to the left and to the right. His vision had become a narrow tunnel of undersaturated colors. His heart was pounding in his throat. His hands flooded his rifle with sweat. Right in front of him an American suddenly looked over the edge of the cliff, wearing the typical US Army circular steel helmet. Berning raised his gun and fired. The bullet penetrated the rock centimeters in front of the American, but it hurled up splinters that sprayed into the GI's face. The man cried out, grabbed his eyes with both hands and fell out of Berning's field of vision. The sergeant put a new clip into his rifle and cocked it. Then he realized that the Americans were about to run over the cliff.

155

The edge of the rock was uneven and jagged by many breakthroughs. Berning noticed that those Americans, who had climbed into the German fire so defenselessly, had not sacrificed their lives in vain. With ladders and ropes the enemy had climbed everywhere into the breakthroughs in the rock, and had waited there until small shock troops had gathered. Together they now threw grenades in the direction of the Germans, who fell back onto the trench of the 2nd Platoon. Berning, too, just ran when one of the explosives eggs fell in front of his feet. Behind him the explosions roared. The sergeant threw himself recklessly into the trench, hitting his helmet hard against a wooden supporting beam. By the time he staggered back to his feet, the Americans were already everywhere. Covered by the hand grenade detonations they had managed to climb the last few meters up the cliff, taking cover between barbed wire and protruding rock formations. A merciless firefight at the shortest distance began. The Americans were still outnumbered, but every second more soldiers pushed themselves over the rocky ledge. Every second, the power of the Americans on the battlefield increased. They also had the better weapons at their disposal. The Germans were mostly equipped with the Karabiner 98k – a bolt-action rifle – which did not bear the "98" in its name for nothing. The Americans, however, had brought the most modern firearms in the world to this battle: machine pistols en masse, handy, portable machine guns; and even their carbines were semi-automatic – a huge advantage in battle. A single American could easily hold down five German riflemen; and the Americans now attacked with concentrated firepower.

Bullets whipped around the ears of Berning and his men and trapped them in the trench. They hardly dared to lift their heads any more. Another soldier from his squad was already killed; another had a bullet through the shoulder. Men were screaming, men were killing all over the cliff. One by one, the Americans pulled the pins out of their hand grenades and threw them into the trenches. Immediately they jumped after them under bursts of fire, perfectly

156

coordinated with the detonations. The Germans died like flies, having no chance. Private Lenz was lying in the grass directly in front of Berning with his skull split open. On the side of the USA absolute specialist were at work.

Berning pressed himself against the wall of the trench. Chunks of earth rolled into his collar where they mixed with sticky sweat. Bullets buzzed over him, further back at the emplacements of 3rd Platoon the Americans were already standing in the trench. Bloodiest close combats took its course. Usually soldiers didn't hate each other, but in combat the sheer survival instinct drove hatred into the men's eyes, making them beat their opponents with spades and fists. Everywhere the bullets of the Americans struck. Once again they shattered the terrain, which had already been ploughed up by hundreds of bombs. Thin fountains of earth spread along the edges of the trenches like stakes shooting out of the ground. Suddenly a tubular projectile raced over Berning, drawing a tail of fire behind it.

Further back it covered one of the gun emplacements in fire and smoke. The fake cannon, made of telephone poles, burst into million fragments that flew away on all sides and penetrated the limbs and bodies of soldiers. The GI's seemed to be making a targeted attack on the guns.

The position could no longer be held, 3rd Platoon was down. Dozens of men in gray uniforms were lying in the trench with chalky pale faces or writhing on the ground in pain like earthworms in the blazing sun.

The Americans climbed over them, reached the back of the trench and jumped into the bomb craters behind them. There they spread out in all directions, seeming to attack certain points of the German defense in shock troops. The Americans knew exactly where to find what.

The commander of the squadron ordered the withdrawal, and Pappendorf grudgingly passed the order on to the men. But they wouldn't have lasted another blink of an eye anyway. Accordingly, they rushed out of the trench in panic and ran unordered into the hinterland. Berning also hurried out of his cover and onto the open field. Quickly he dashed from crater to crater, always keeping the large bunker in

157

view, which was the squadron's point of retreat. There was hardly any covering fire left. Pappendorf got Hege and let him shoot some more bursts of fire. But then they were also on the run, because otherwise they would have lost touch and would have been overtaken by the enemy. The Americans pursued the Germans without a break. They shot them in the back, killing many of the absconding.

Berning didn't look back. He just ran, ran, ran, on and on. The bunker was getting bigger in front of him. He had a stabbing pain in his side, his pulse pounding in his skull. But he ran and ran. Around him were his comrades, just as hopelessly on the run. One was hit. Blood and tissue ripped from his chest. His hands rose up, his legs gave way. At full speed, his face hit the ground. His body flipped over, somersaulted over his head and lay on his back. Berning raced further. He finally dashed into a hollow leading to the entrance of the bunker. Perhaps half the squadron had made it while the Americans were flooding all over the cliff.

Northeast of Pouppeville, France, June 6th, 1944

A hazy, smoky blue fog covered the coast, which crept closer with every screw movement of the small landing craft. The men of 1st Platoon of Company L stood tensed up on the loading area, staring at the bare steel of the raised ramp. The vibrations of the engine constantly pulsated through the boat; gripping the soldiers and making them tremble. The spray splashed over the side walls and showered like rain against the steel helmets every time the landing craft broke a wave. With eyes narrowing to slits, the helmsman stared over his steering wheel at the Normandy coast, which was peeling out of the fog in front of him, and which his comrades would be storming in a few minutes. The soldiers clasped their rifles. One of them

158

whispered a Shacharit – the Jewish Morning Prayer. It smelled of salty seawater, of fish, of vomit – not every stomach could stand the ride to the shore. Tom Roebuck needed no prayer at that moment. The anger in his chest had gone to his head, dominated his thoughts. At least the anger repressed all other emotions for the moment.

They made progress – slowly but steadily. Almost unstoppably, the landing crafts, which dominated the English Channel from here to the horizon, struggled through the waves of the sea. Battleships of all sizes were lying in the water behind them. During the night they had already supported the paratroopers with their fire, who had jumped off in this section directly behind the German dune fortifications in order to create confusion among the enemy and, if possible, to eliminate some resistance nests and guns. The Jerries had massively reinforced the Atlantic Wall with troops in the last months, so that the planners of the invasion finally came to the conclusion that the landing troops alone would not be able to overcome the beach – not even with massive support from the Navy and Air Force. Therefore, the plans to deploy the Airborne forces far inland to conquer important bridges were rejected. No, one was not allowed to think that far ahead. First, the beach had to be secured to clear the way for landing more troops. Only then it was possible to start fighting to free Normandy. Therefore, the paratroopers had jumped off immediately behind the dune fortifications that night to do their part for the success of the operation. Meanwhile, a British airborne division had descended North of Caen at a double bridge, crossing the Caen Canal and the Orne, to block off the operations area to the East. Under no circumstances should the Fritz be able to move additional troops from Eastern France to Normandy. Even now the German defense units in the area were actually already too large and were deployed in a massive manner. Rommel had positioned the mass of his forces directly on the beach. Despite the Navy's bombardment of hell, the landing troops on all sections of the beach – on the British and Canadian ones in the East between Caen and Bayeux, called "Sword", "Juno" and

"Gold"; and on the American one, called "Omaha" West of Bayeux and "Utah" North of Carentan - would run into an equivalent hellfire of the Germans. And then there was a cliff called Pointe du Hoc, which had to be taken by all means, and on which both the Rangers and the Airborne boys were set. That's where the Jerries had placed strong artillery guns capable of firing at both Omaha and Utah. A total of 180,000 men were to enter French soil by nightfall – a huge force – but any impressive number would be wasted, if the Jerries did not leave the beaches. The beaches were the key, they would determine the success or failure of the greatest invasion operation of all time.

"Utah," Roebuck whispered. This would be his beach, his unit's beach. He had to think of the massive decoy maneuvers that had been carried out in the run-up to the invasion to convince Jerry of a landing on the Pas-de-Calais. He tried to distract himself with such thoughts from the things that were currently on his mind. Things that really didn't belong in this war or in this operation. But he did not succeed. Again and again the image of his wife, his beautiful Marie, captured his mind's eye. It tore his heart apart.

Unstoppable the landing crafts worked their way through the floods. The natural dunes of the Normandy coast appeared in front of them. In a moment a strong blow would hit the boat when it touched the sandy ground. Then the whistle would sound and the ramp would lower. After that they would rush into the German machine gun fire. If there was one good thing about Marie's letter, it was that it took Roebuck's fear away.

"Two things!" the gunny yelled at the front against the noise of the ship's engine and the beating of the waves. He was still the same man who had fought with them on the Solomon Islands. He held his steel helmet with his hands tightly encircled in front of his chest, then he stroked the gray stubble on his shaved skull with his right hand. A huge wave broke on the ship, throwing it foaming into the hold. The men were dripping with water, and the water level on the loading area had risen a little.

"First: You never travel to France without a condom!" Grinning, the gunnery sergeant pointed to the condom he had slipped over the barrel of his gun; as had all the members of the company. The Marines smirked, though a little pinched.

"Second: Today we're not going against the fucking yellow monkeys. Today it's the Germans. With this opponent, you can almost speak of real people. I experienced the bastards in 1918, right here in France. They will fight bravely, but of course they have nothing against us. In a month, we'll be sliding over French hookers in Paris! And we'll be celebrating Christmas in Berlin! On that note: Semper Fi, men. Take care out there!"

"Amen," Saviano whispered. Some shouted, "Aye, gunny!"

"And now, heads down! The Jerries will greet us with their artillery before they hand out 7.92 millimeter welcome gifts on the beach!"

Juergens patted Roebuck on the shoulder from behind. He returned the silent huntsman's salute with a nod. But his mind was still somewhere else.

"Fucking bitch," he murmured. "I bet she's got someone else!"

"Yo, Roebuck!" the gunny, who knew about the problems of the Private First Class, shouted. Despite the swell, engine and weather, the gunnery sergeant proved to have ears like a lynx. "There's no room for your private shit!"

Roebuck gave the gunny a reproachful look. Immediately, the aging man set in motion, pushing the Marines aside and standing up in front of Roebuck. He looked him straight in the eye.

"Listen, boy, you're our gunner! The men need you! So don't wimp out and concentrate! I'm divorced too, so it's not the end of the world."

The gunny hit Roebuck rudely against the helmet, then he went back to his position. Roebuck looked after him and wrinkled his nose. But for him, it was the end of the world! He felt as if she had torn all his organs out of his body with her short, emotionally cold message, leaving nothing but

161

emptiness behind. But it was no use, in a few minutes they would reach the beach.

Six fighter bombers suddenly roared low over the landing crafts. They displayed the white star on blue background of the United States Army Air Force on their fuselages. The Marines raised their fists in cheers as the planes turned and flew towards the coast.

Then they waited for the first impacts of the artillery, but it didn't happen. Finally, the bow of the landing craft pushed into the sandy sea bed. A jerk went through the men before the ramp fell down and landed splashing in the water. Immediately the whistle sounded, although the men did not need to be ordered to leave the steel coffin at last. They jumped out of the boat, raced down the ramp and stood waist-deep in the water. Wading, they scurried towards the beach. Wooden constructions, which rose up into the sky everywhere like the skeletons of giant primeval lizards, were the only cover there was. The Marines kept on charging.

Roebuck felt the cold wet seeping into his uniform. He groaned in strain, for with all the equipment on his back and the machine gun in his hand, it was no chicken feed to wade through the water. On the right and on the left the ramps of other boats lowered. The Marines dashed out into the water. Hundreds of men threw themselves towards the beach.

Roebuck squinted his eyes. At any moment the German bullets would strike beside him, whipping up the water, killing comrades. The Marines kept on charging. A gigantic, olive-colored mass struggled out of the water to reach the beach, which was extended by the low tide. Sherman tanks, surrounded by large rubber protectors, rose from the water like turtles and rolled rattling towards the beach.

Roebuck gasped and puffed. The machine gun, which he carried with both hands on his shoulders, weighed heavily and pressed his wet boots into the soft ground. Every step robbed him of precious strength. The water of the Channel seemed to behave like pulp; it stuck to Roebuck, tugged at him.

162

Rude curses and calls from superiors were heard. The water gradually became shallower. Behind a fine curtain of fog, Roebuck spotted large bunkers embedded in the dunes. The embrasures were clearly visible in the form of black lines. Sandbag positions also appeared on the top of the dunes. But there were no German bullets, no German artillery. Well, were the Krauts sleeping?

The Marines fought and struggled and dug themselves out of the water and ran across the bare sandy beach. Not a single shot was fired. Only when Roebuck had charged towards the dunes at 150 yards he recognized the American flag hanging from one of the German bunkers. It fluttered in the wind.

The Chief of Company L was received by an officer of the US paratroopers at the access to the dunes. The airborne boys had taken the Germans completely by surprise during the night and in a coup de main they had brought all the emplacements from Pouppeville to Saint-Marcouf under their control. The Utah section was almost in the hands of the Allies.

The gunny rounded up the men. Back at the bunkers, Roebuck spotted about 20 German prisoners who were guarded by some paratroopers. Most of the Jerries were old men, their faces encrusted with dirt and their expressions were hopeless.

"What did I tell you?" the gunny laughed, showing his teeth. "The fuckin' Krauts won't give us any trouble. They're greenhorns. Let's go. We're marching into the hinterland. We got a continent to conquer!"

Roebuck stared at the sand dune. In times of peace one could certainly have a good holiday here, if there were beach chairs instead of bunkers in the dunes. But now he did not want to think about holidays. Instead in a rush of action he pulled up his sleeves.

So, we are done here for Christmas? he had to remember the words of the gunny.

Pizza, carrying the matching mount to Roebuck's gun on his shoulders, tapped Tom against his helmet, signaling him to follow the rest of the mob that had already started

163

moving. Roebuck trotted along, but his mind was not on the matter at all.

France we have as good as in our pockets, he recalled the situation in his mind. *And doesn't France border directly on the land of the Krauts? Then it really could be over by Christmas. Or sooner! Maybe I'll be home by Christmas! And then I'll handle Marie …*

West of Cairon, France, June 6th, 1944

It was dawning. The darkness of the night turned into a shimmering twilight that bathed the world in gray shades.

With very small eyes, Engelmann stared at the still gloomy vacant space that opened up in front of Quasimodo's staging area. Chewing the last piece of chocolate, he made sure of the time, which his Swiss clockwork told him.

What's taking so long?

On this day, the company was to set off early in the morning to do some target practice with live ammunition. Accordingly, ammunition and fuel were to be at 100 percent.

Allied bombers were humming in the distance. Unusually many seemed to be flying into France that night, perhaps they were flying massive attacks against individual cities again. Quietly the engines of the panzers rattled to the hum of the distant propeller machines. Engelmann looked around to all sides, recognizing the tanks of his platoon as leaden shadows emerging between the trees.

All of a sudden Nitz stepped out of the darkness. He climbed up the hull of Quasimodo and leaned against the turret that seemed out of place with a grin.

"It's about to start, Herr Leutnant," he announced in his Leipzig dialect.

"Well, finally." Engelmann was pissed. He and his men

had been on their feet for three hours, because actually the company wanted to practice shooting in the dark. They could forget about that now.

"3rd Platoon has overslept completely," Nitz also gave the reason for the delay.

"Damn philistines!" Engelmann whispered, before he spoke into his throat microphone: "Anna 1 to all: It seems to be about to start."

"Anna 2," the voice of Nitz's driver was heard.

"Anna 3."

"Anna 4, understood."

"Anna 5."

"Stay combat ready. March along ordered route on my command. I'm taking the lead."

Nitz suddenly held a letter right in front of Engelmann.

"For me?"

The master sergeant nodded with big eyes. "It's from your wife."

Immediately Engelmann grabbed the letter, but at the moment he had no time to read. After the exercise he would concentrate on the letter, alone in a quiet place. Engelmann folded the letter carefully and put it under his field jacket.

"Thanks, Oberfeld."

Nitz nodded softly, indicated a military salute with his hand, then jumped off the hull and hurried over to his tank.

"How's the back?" Engelmann shouted after him.

"About to break through," Nitz groaned as he walked away.

Engelmann nodded seriously before announcing the first command over his throat microphone: "Unteroffizier, please give me the company frequency."

"Jawohl, company frequency," Stendal replied.

There was a crack in Engelmann's loudspeakers.

Minutes went by. Slowly the Normandy countryside, with its low hedges and vineyards, brightened up. But nothing happened. The ether remained silent. Engelmann exhaled air from his lungs in annoyance and looked at the clock once more.

Suddenly Rosenkamp's voice crackled from the

loudspeakers: "Rita to everyone. Report according to order! Come."

"Anna here," Engelmann began, then the voices of the other platoon leaders sounded one after the other, and finally those of the commander of the so-called Leader Group:

"Berta."

"Claudia here."

"Rita 1 hearing."

"March off in..." Suddenly Rosenkamp's voice stopped, which sounded quite contrite. "Wait...," the company commander announced, then there was silence in the radio circuit for a few moments. When Rosenkamp's voice returned, it had taken on a completely different tone, a serious and worried one: "The exercise is cancelled," he revealed to his men and repeated the message once more before continuing: "Enemy landings North of Caen. Probably a commando operation to divert attention from their main push against Calais. Nevertheless, we have received our orders for action. Platoon leaders will assemble at once at my panzer!"

Pointe du Hoc, France, June 6th, 1944

The sun was just peeking over the horizon, casting its light on the cliff. As if breathing softly, the sea sloshed up and down in front of Pointe du Hoc. Gentle waves pressed against the cliffs, where they melted into millions and millions of drops. The American landing crafts rested on the edge of the water, their lowered ramps having dug deep into the sandy ground. Some amphibious trucks, which looked like small rowing boats with wheels, had been driven up to the sandy beach and placed under the protection of the rocks. Few Americans had stayed on the beach; they cared for the screaming and wheezing

166

wounded. A priest went from doomed man to doomed man, giving each one his final blessing. And the bodies! Corpses everywhere! Burst open by the impact, because a drop from over 30 meters turned every sandy beach into granite. Other bodies were ripped open by fragments of shells. 40 dead lined the narrow beach, brooding in the developing heat. Some had been swallowed up by the sea. A small rearguard collected ammunition and heavy weapons off the bodies, then they also set out on the ropes and ladders to climb Pointe du Hoc.

Meanwhile the majority of the Rangers – those who had not died while climbing up – had long since reached the German front line, through which they now dug their way like a hot knife through butter.

Of the initial 300 men, just over 200 were left, but the Germans also had suffered heavy losses. On the top of the cliff the fight roared in all facets. Anti-tank missiles and explosives sawed through the firing positions of the assumed artillery guns. Small arms fire produced vast racket.

Men shouted orders, other men cried in agony. Men were dying. Men rolled over the earth, intertwined like lovers – but there was no room for love. They drove bullets, blades, even teeth into each other's flesh; tore open the bodies of their enemies by all means. They did everything they could to wound their enemy. They beat each other bluntly, broke limbs, fired at each other. Everything was right to inflict injuries on the enemy. A bloodlust had broken out across the cliff, and it took both sides equally.

The close combats finally subsided, the trenches and craters filled with bodies. The Americans were on the advance, chasing the defenders into the bunkers which were to be fought over next. The entire cliff was already controlled by the Americans, only the bunkers on the edge, which blocked the way into the hinterland, were still under German control. If these bunkers fell, the path was clear, the path to the artillery guns.

Berning, Pappendorf and Hege looked out through the narrow embrasure of the bunker. A turbulent, barren land opened up in front of them. Somewhere out there was the enemy, hidden in the bomb craters and trenches. He was probably gathering at this very minute to attack the last German bastions. If these were to fall, the way would be clear to the hinterland, where twenty German tanks were ready and waiting – but in a country with low hedgerows and small forests, it would be easy for the enemy infantry to fight the combat vehicles. No, if the Americans ever broke out of the cliff, they would find the guns and destroy them. There were also some Frenchmen loyal to the Reich – yes, they existed – with old hunting rifles in position at the farmstead behind Pointe du Hoc, but they were certainly no obstacle for the GIs either. Therefore the attack had to be stopped on the cliff.

Suddenly two US steel helmets appeared in the forefield. Dark green figures scurried from one crater to the next. Hege pulled the trigger, sending half a belt after the Americans. But where the earth fountains now rose, the figures were long gone, they had disappeared again into a crater. The game was repeated once more, then again. Finally Berning noticed that one of the Americans was carrying a big box on his back.

"I think one of them is a radio operator," he revealed his discovery. Pappendorf narrowed his eyes to slits and bent over. Again the figures rushed from a crater across to a trench. Machine gun fire pursued them, but once again Hege didn't hit anything.

"Fact," Pappendorf murmured, who seemed to have recognized the radio as well. Hege uttered an obscene curse.

"Do the bastards spy on us?" Berning asked. He turned to his platoon leader. Pappendorf's face frightened the sergeant. Totally compressed, with trembling features, the master sergeant looked at him. Slowly he got down on his knees, then lay flat on the ground, pressed his hands against his helmet and closed his eyes.

Berning startled.

What's this guy up to now? he thought with grave concern in the back of his mind.

"Believe me, men. Get your heads down!" Pappendorf whispered in a surly voice. At the same moment, the bunker door to Hege's machine gun nest was pushed open and Balduin stood in the room panting: "No connection to our panzers, all lines dead! Damn French resistance..." he snorted, before he stopped and stared at Pappendorf lying on the floor in bewilderment.

"Herr Feldwebel, what the hell...?" That's all the officer could say. An insane bang, under which the whole bunker trembled, the walls shook and cracks in the heavy concrete ceiling formed, initiated the enemy ship fire. Shells, big as suitcases, rushed onto the roof of the bunker, where they became huge balls of flames. Shivering and begging every higher power, the Germans clawed into the ground. The noise was deafening. Every bullet was banging and cracking, shaking the bunker as if it was made of jelly. Too short bursts went into the ground in front of the shelter and piled up brown walls of humus. Pieces of earth flew inside through the embrasure, more shells hit the bunker. They blew up large pieces from the roof, hurling rocks and metal away. The stench of burnt gunpowder drifted into the bunker rooms, lay on the soldiers' lungs, made them cough and croak. Mercilessly, the grenades drilled down on the shelter, half burying it, digging up the earth. The embrasure of Hege's position was half buried. Dirt and boulders blocked the view. With every salvo that whistled over from the ships, another layer of the German bunker was removed, widening the cracks in the reinforced concrete. With every salvo the gigantic explosive projectiles went deeper into the bunker. They hammered on the roof like gigantic sledgehammers, crushing layer after layer of the thick concrete armor. They were drilling deeper into the bunker, deeper and deeper – following the promise that there was soft flesh to be shredded inside the hard shell.

Berning was doomed to passivity. He lay flat on the floor, pressing his hands against his ears and breathing fast and loud. The air burst from his lungs every time another salvo came down on them. The bunker vibrated and shook like a wet dog. Fine concrete dust drizzled down Berning's neck.

Thick chunks of plaster were thrown around, further parts of the bunker were blasted off.

"Pappendorf!" the shaky voice of the First Lieutenant struggled through the roar of the impacts. Berning raised his head only a few inches and saw his commander lying on the ground.

"Jawohl, Herr Oberleutnant?" Pappendorf's voice was once again above the noise, clearly audible. But the master sergeant was also curled up on the ground, holding his head. At that moment his face also showed the naked fear of being buried alive in this shelter. His face was also furrowed, distorted, as could only be the case with a person whose fate was entirely in the hands of others.

In this case in the hands of the American naval artillery crews, and their ability to hit the bunker; and of course in the hands of the radio operator, who was hiding somewhere in the forefield, watching his target and ordering salvo after salvo, until the last fragment of the bunker was nailed into the ground of the cliff.

"Send someone down to the panzers immediately! They have to come here or we're history!" Balduin ordered. Pappendorf nodded his lips pressed together.

Our tanks will teach the scumbags a lesson! Berning thought, while pressing his palms so hard against his ears that all that remained of the artillery's drumbeats was a muffled cracking sound.

"Jawohl, Herr Oberleutnant!" Pappendorf's voice, in spite of everything, reached Berning's ears. "Berning!"

The sergeant looked up.

"Grab two men, down to the tanks. On the double!"

"You want me to go out there?"

Pappendorf's look gave him the answer.

Oh, no, Berning cried in his mind, then he pulled himself up. The next salvo went crashing into the bunker. Everything was shaking and quivering. The pressure turned Berning's knees into a soft mass, then he buckled to the side and hit the bunker wall with his shoulder.

"Wait for the pauses between each impact," Pappendorf's piercing and menacingly sharp voice instructed him.

170

Yeah, thanks for the advice, great commander! Berning wiped over his mouth and ducked down. The next salvo brought another burst of fire over the bunker. The loud crescendo of the large ship's guns, whose artillery shells once again tried to smash the bunker, materialized into dust-laden shock waves that pushed through the embrasures. Dirt and fine particles lay in the air, obscuring the soldiers' view; they obscured everything. Dust fell on the sweaty skin of the people and crusted into a black lunar landscape. It was inhaled again and lay biting on the lungs of the soldiers. Berning's men coughed and wheezed, wailed and groaned. They were at the mercy of this foreign power, which rained down on their bunker in the form of heavy shelling.

When the next salvo of fire had detonated, new cracks had formed in the walls and the dust was pouring through the bunker from all sides, Berning lifted himself up, grabbed Reuben and Weiss by the shoulder and signaled them both to follow him.

They rushed through the heavy door out into the corridor, went along it and suddenly threw themselves on the rough stone floor as the next salvo of artillery shells hit the bunker. But then they pulled themselves up, ran towards the exit and pressed themselves against the wall. The next salvo thundered onto their stone protective cocoon; and tore at it terribly. In the following moments of peace, the three rushed out the door and ran as fast as they could – away from the bunker! When the next shells approached, they dashed blindly into a bomb crater.

"What are we supposed to do, anyway?" Weiss asked through the roar of the impacts.

"They want us to go down to the panzers and get them over here."

Weiss' eyes became wide. "What? That's over three kilometers!"

"Yeah, yeah, three kilometers." Reuben nodded.

"Anyway. We gotta..." Berning broke off in mid-sentence and listened into the noise. The last burst of fire from the ship artillery had just faded away, when a completely different noise started to roar in the hinterland of the cliff:

171

Several overlapping drumbeats roared over Pointe du Hoc.

"These... these are our cannons," Berning noted with astonishment.

"What...?" But Weiss didn't even have to ask the question. He and the sergeant looked at each other silently... and understood: They had not fallen victim to an enemy commando raid here on the cliff – no - the Allied landing had begun. Here, in Normandy!

Berning felt a strange feeling in his stomach. He ignored the rising fears in him as best as he could and grabbed his rifle again.

"We gotta get those tanks!" he ordered, more to himself. But that was no longer necessary, because just at that moment Panzer IV each with a thick Balkenkreuz on their flanks came from the hinterland onto the cliff area. With explosive rounds they attacked the positions of the Americans.

"Then we can go back," Weiss remarked.

Berning waved off.

"No, we'll hold position here," he commanded.

"What?" Weiss was terrified.

"We'll let the panzers do their job, we don't have to put ourselves in unnecessary danger."

"There's no way they can handle themselves in that terrain."

"Of course. It's coordinated with Pappe. We are to remain under cover until the situation is cleared up," Berning lied to keep Weiss quiet. The latter swallowed it. "I see," he exclaimed. Then he and Reuben let themselves slide to the bottom of the crater, while a tremendous noise and an angry drumming hissed over them. Berning, however, slowly pushed himself up the earthy slope until his eyes could see over the edge. Thus he followed the firefight, in which direct sphere of influence he was, as an uninvolved observer: The German tanks rolled forward, but in the rugged country they made only slow progress. With machine gun and HE rounds they chased the American attackers to hell. Under their fire, the enemy withdrew bit by bit to the edges of the cliff, but by no means they gave up

172

the area without a fight. A rocket rammed a Panzer IV into the tread and smashed it. The naval artillery also shifted its fire from the bunkers to the tanks, which then quickly scattered. The first salvos of fire nevertheless hit two panzers directly, crushing them like a thumb did a fly. Then Berning saw German soldiers squeezing out of the battered bunkers and joining the attack. He clearly recognized his comrades from the squadron, who also charged forward with Pappendorf and the platoon in the lead. Finally, they entered a trench and took up the firefight with the retreating Americans.

"So? Do you see anything?" Weiss wanted to know.

Berning slid down to the bottom of the crater, then he shook his head. "No, just the panzers chasing away the Americans."

South of Banville, France, June 6th, 1944

While the PzRgt 2 had marched towards the beach, the incoming reports increasingly darkened the faces of the German taner. It was reported that the German defense nests from Caen to Longues-sur-Mer had been destroyed in a combination of artillery fire, air attacks and landing ground troops. The British-Canadian landing head, from which the enemy troops swept into the hinterland, had opened up in the assembly area of the 16th Panzer Division. From Caen to Longues-sur-Mer on a width of 30 kilometers they were on the advance. There were also repeated reports of landings elsewhere, even the Cotentin peninsula seemed to be under attack. There were reports of enemy tanks – tanks that rose from the sea like Phoenix from the ashes and rattled towards the hinterland. Engelmann didn't really want to believe this, but enemy tanks were only right for him. He could deal with them better than with the infantry.

And we are at the mercy of the enemy ship artillery here on the coast! His thoughts were rattling to the beat of the engine. He wished to return 30 kilometers to the hinterland, where he would let the enemy come and crush him out of reach of the allied battleships.

The panzers of the III Abteilung moved over a wide meadow, broke through narrow hedges and rolled down a small stone wall, which connected two farms. Then they reached the road to Banville. From their present position it was less than five kilometers to the coast. The roaring and murmuring of guns in the distance formed the background noise like a steady, deep melody.

After a short drive, the outermost houses of the little village of Banville appeared on the horizon. White timber-framed buildings with black gabled roofs lay there peacefully. They did not look as if they had ever witnessed a fight.

Stollwerk's 12th Company had taken the lead as vanguard and approached the village from the left to cover the left flank of the battalion. Engelmann saw the Panzer IV of the captain, which pushed through a terrain covered with low hedges a few hundred meters from Banville. Meanwhile Rosenkamp's 9th Company was to cross the main road, pass through the village and take position behind it. On the right the 10th advanced, should bypass the village on the right and keep this flank free for the battalion. Unstoppably the German steel flood poured over the tiny village.

Suddenly there was a tremendous bang at the front between the timber-framed houses. Smoke was coming up. Almost at the same moment the turret of a Panzer IV from Stollwerk's company took off. The hull came to a halt and spat fire, the turret crashed into the grass at some distance.

Two M4 Shermans appeared out of Banville and rolled onto the scene. Their hulls were surrounded by strange, shapeless rings. Stollwerk's tanks stopped and fired – the Shermans were destroyed in an instant. Tank men disembarked and were caught in German machine gun fire. Burning, the wrecks came to a standstill. The fire swallowed the red signs on the flanks of the Shermans, which identified the combat vehicles as Canadian units.

174

This quick clash was the prelude to a tank battle. Everywhere in Banville the muzzle flashes of fired tank main guns flashed. Earth was torn out of the meadows surrounding the village; hedges were torn up and leaped into the air. Stollwerk's tanks surrounded the village on the left side as planned, slipping between some buildings and an adjoining forest. The 10th set out to take the path on the right, which led away from Banville, and thus circumnavigated the village from this side. Again and again the cannons of the German panzers sounded. At Banville, buildings burst apart under the fire; roads were torn up. Glass was blown out of the windows. Shermans got enkindled under AP round hits, others moved, returning fire.

"Step on the gas, Hans!" Engelmann demanded, clutching the flaps of his hatch with both hands.

"Jepp, Sepp."

"We have to keep up." Engelmann turned to Stendal: "Pass on to the platoon: Step on the gas, I want to get to Banville as fast as possible. We're taking the main road."

Stendal passed the orders to the platoon, waited for the confirmation of the commanders, then switched his headphones to company frequency; apparently at just the right moment, because Rosenkamp's voice was heard through the airwaves.

Stendal listened and frowned. Meanwhile, Engelmann's panzers accelerated, took the lead of the company and raced straight for Banville. A scattered armor piercing shell strayed in the direction of the platoon, hit just before Anna 3 and tore a deep hole in the earth. Engelmann dived down into his copula.

We gotta get closer, if we want to get at the Shermans, he thought. That's another reason why he ordered speed. A Sherman could only be pierced at a distance of a few hundred meters by the short 5-centimeter cannons of his tanks.

Stendal returned to the intercom and passed on the new orders of Captain Rosenkamp: "The Hauptmann has ordered to stop," he said soberly.

175

"Pardon?"

"We are to stop at once, return to the village at 1000 and take position there."

"Give me the company frequency."

There was a short crack in Engelmann's headphones.

"Rita, this is Anna," the lieutenant began.

"Rita is listening."

"Please repeat last line."

"Immediate stop, go back to the village at 1000. Observation stop!"

"Observation stop? The 10th and 12th are already on the flanks when we..." Engelmann shouldn't have let go of the press to talk button, then Rosenkamp wouldn't have been able to interrupt him: "We have enemy sightings in the village... there... so we can't just go in there. We have to investigate the situation calmly... observe, then I can make a decision."

"Investigating the situation calmly?" Engelmann raved. "Wels and Brunsbüttel are counting on us to take the village. Back at the village we are also a splendid target for enemy planes and their ship's artillery. They'll tear us apart!"

"Well... now... um... but first we have to... no discussions, Anna! If the others surge ahead, that's their business. Understood?" Rosenkamp floundered several times.

"We have to..." Engelmann sighed, then he released the press to talk button.

"UNDERSTOOD?" Rosenkamp urged.

"Copy that."

For a moment Engelmann hesitated, thought hard. It was so damned important not to stop now! But finally the lieutenant submitted to the order, transmitted the corresponding instructions to Münster and had them passed on to the platoon via Stendal. The tanks stopped; then they started moving backwards towards the village. About 1000 meters away from Banville the company's panzers gathered and formed a long wedge. In the distance the guns of various tanks were thundering, but on the outskirts of Banville there was no sign of fighting. Clouds of

176

smoke stood over the houses, the two Shermans were burning, as well as the turretless German tank hull.

"We'll... uh... observe the forefield... for... 20 minutes." Rosenkamp's nervous voice cracked. "Enemy sightings to me... I'll use my... binoculars and map... to get an overview of the area..."

Engelmann saw the command tank of Rosenkamp standing by the vehicles of Leader Group in some distance. Rosenkamp looked out of the hatch, rowing with his arms while he tried to spread out a huge map. While doing so he yelled at a tank man standing next to the panzer. Engelmann heard Rosenkamp's high voice, but the wind did not carry more than incomprehensible sounds to his ear. The lieutenant turned to Banville. The place lay quietly, no movement could be detected. In the distance, the tank battle roared – and the tankers of the 9th Company enjoyed the view!

Pointe du Hoc, France, June 6th, 1944

The American attackers were pinned to the edges of the cliff, with the abyss behind them. The Germans were only a trench away from the enemy, less than 100 meters. Both sides had been waiting for hours for the enemy to make a mistake.

The air was filled with the incessant cracking of German guns firing from the Pointe du Hoc hinterland at the American landing at Colleville-sur-Mer.

The attackers of the cliff had failed to stop the German cannons, but as long as they held on to the edges of the cliff, the guns could not be let into their actual firing positions – they could not use the full range they would have on Pointe du Hoc, which juts out into the sea. That is why the Germans had to overthrow the Americans, why they had to reconquer the cliff.

Berning's squadron had 55 percent losses; for the other company stationed at Pointe du Hoc, the one belonging to the 352nd Infantry Division, the numbers were similar.

Of the 80 artillery gunners, 62 were still left to operate the guns. In addition, four tanks were destroyed, the rest of them had moved out of sight into the hinterland.

If the Americans should show up somewhere or try an attack, the panzers once again would storm onto the cliff and cover everything with high explosive rounds. But otherwise it was too dangerous for the tanks to show themselves, because the Americans still used the ship artillery with unbelievable precision to eliminate targets. Thus an iron stalemate prevailed at Pointe du Hoc, which neither side was able to overcome at present. The German infantry had moved too close to the Americans for the enemy to use its naval guns against them; but neither warring party was able to defeat the enemy – at least neither warring party dared.

From the German side, Pointe du Hoc was denied any priority by the leadership. Most of the units in the area moved against the landing at Colleville-sur-Mer, or against the Cotentin peninsula, where the Anglo-Americans had settled over a wide area.

Moreover, no one had noticed that Berning had not been involved in the counterattack, which had pushed the Americans back to the rocky ledge. Weiss and Reuben did not ask any further questions either, because the sergeant had been able to make them believe that he really hadn't noticed anything about the attack of the platoon. So the three had spent the time of the further fights carefree in the bomb crater, and they could move in unnoticed in the aftermath of the fights.

Berning leaned against the earthy wall of the trench, Hege and Weiss were with him. The weather was uncomfortable – constant drizzle, cool temperatures, strong breezes sweeping over the cliff from the sea. Berning had crossed his arms and pressed them against his body to warm himself.

He looked over to Weiss and Hege, who were leaning

against the wall and dozing under the MG 42, which was propped up on a mount. Two men with scissors telescopes from 1st Squad, who thus monitored the positions of the Americans, acted as alarm posts. In the meantime nobody dared to stick his head out of the trench. The Americans were damn good snipers.

Berning was hungry, but he did not touch his iron ration. It was only allowed to be eaten on order; and Pappendorf applied severe punishments to anyone who violated it.

"When will the food supply arrive?" Hege asked, licking his bad teeth.

The sergeant shrugged his shoulders. "About 6 or 7 p.m., I guess."

"WHAT?"

"6 OR 7 P.M.!"

"I see."

Hege nodded contently.

"That's the thing I'm not worried about," Weiss said.

Berning looked at the private first class questioningly.

"Well, that makes sense. We sit here in the trenches and fill our bellies every day. And the Yanks?" Weiss grinned.

"I wonder how long they'll keep this up," Hege mused.

"Maybe this will all end without a fight." Berning's face lit up. Yes, the Americans were trapped on that goddamn rock. They were out of supplies, they had a lot of wounded and probably not much ammunition left. How long could this stalemate last? A few days? How about a week? Not much longer. So all the Germans had to do was wait. A big smile appeared on Berning's face.

Apparently the alleged superiority of the Allies didn't help them after all, he thought in silence. *And I just have to sit here until this stupid invasion is over.*

Banville, France, June 6th, 1944

At last things kept going again. After von Burgsdorff himself had rushed over in his command tank and conducted a loud, one-sided conversation with Rosenkamp from hatch to hatch, the company's panzers were allowed to start moving again. With a delay of almost 45 minutes they rolled through Banville, but they could not move too fast in the urban terrain, the danger of enemy anti-tank troops hiding in the buildings was too great. So the tanks moved through the streets at half speed, passing collapsed houses and exploded cars. Fallen German soldiers were scattered along the roadsides. A machine gun nest in a bakery, fortified with sandbags, was filled with thousands of bullet casings, their brass shining in the sunlight.

Quasimodo was in the lead; Engelmann peered out of the copula with a serious look. He scanned the rows of buildings that crept past him again and again with his eyes. Nothing moved. But when he looked to the right, the wrecks of shot tanks shimmered through between the old timber-framed houses, clouds of smoke rising to the sky. These were German tanks, which burned out slowly. Charred bodies lay in the grass. The 10th Company had lost a dozen panzers in the area East of Banville when the Canadian tanks driving out of the village had fallen into their flank. Now the enemy tanks had retreated behind the dunes, which formed the last piece of ground North of Banville in front of the English Channel. According to Stollwerk they prepared for a counterattack over there. Stollwerk's panzers were also already in the dunes, where they had to fight off infantry and tanks on all sides. More landing crafts approached. Every minute the enemy invasion force became stronger. When Engelmann put together the chaotically arriving pieces of information via radio, he had to assume that an entire armored brigade of Canadians was coming ashore in this section of the front.

Engelmann let Münster slowly gain momentum. Anti-tank troops or not, they had to catch up with the other companies, otherwise they would get into serious trouble. German grenadiers, who followed the progressing tanks, could not keep in step with them and thus fell back.

The further way through Banville was quickly done. Once again there was a short delay at the exit of the village, when a French man with a beret and wet eyes stood in front of a badly battered building. A hole so large that a truck could fit through was prominently visible in the gable roof. All windows had been blown out of their frames, thumb-sized machine gun rounds had pierced the outer walls. The whole right side was blasted open and had two man-sized openings. On the side, the house was apparently malformed; at least it was completely crooked and looked as if it would collapse at any moment. The Frenchman sobbed bitterly. Engelmann had to shout at him several times in German and French before he finally left the street.

The platoon vacated the small coastal village behind, the rest of the company followed close behind. Rosenkamp's command tank remained with the panzers, which formed the rearguard. The 9th Company, with Engelmann's 1st Platoon in the lead, moved towards the sandy dune landscape, which lay like a miniature version of the Sahara between the fertile French soil and the beach.

Dark bushes, light green grass and man-sized sea buckthorn, which had light red berries between narrow, pointed leaves, spread over the dunes. The ground was littered with silver grass tufts, seashells were sticking out of the sand. The air tasted salty; it smelled like fish, like sea... like cordite.

Engelmann heard the noise of fighting and the thunder of guns from all over the place. In front of his tank a steep dune stretched out. The lieutenant had to throw his head back to look up to the top of the dune.

"Be careful not to get stuck on the soft ground," he shouted into his throat microphone, while Quasimodo's tracks dug themselves into the sand. Despite dozens of hours of training and testing, the lieutenant was still not quite sure what these Russian treads were capable of.

"You know, I've driven a tank before," Münster returned

venomously.

"Are we getting cocky again?" Engelmann packed a good portion of threats into his voice; with it he kept his sometimes rebellious driver in check, who in the end did not dare to break out of the strict hierarchy of the Wehrmacht – of that Engelmann was sure.

"No, Leutnant," Münster immediately returned in a subdued voice.

Via Stendal, Engelmann ordered the platoon to stop and form a skirmish line. Quickly the 2nd and 3rd Platoon caught up. Captain Rosenkamp stayed behind with the tanks of Leader Group.

"Give me the company frequency," Engelmann demanded. Moments later there was a crack in his headphones.

"Drive up to the top of the dune, there observation stop. Reports to me," Rosenkamp's voice went through the ether.

Observation stop again? Engelmann touched his forehead.

The tanks of the company drove up, struggled through the soft sand of the dunes, pushing bushes and branches into the ground. The tracks burrowed grimly through the terrain. Slowly they advanced; slowly but steadily. In a wide spread out line they made their way up the dune, finally reaching the top. Immediately a tank of the 2nd Platoon was torn apart, then another one. Next Anna 2 got a hit and the engine died. Smoke leaked out through all the slots and openings, then the hatches were unclosed and coughing tankers climbed out of the hull. Engelmann was relieved to see that Nitz was among them.

"Shermans ahead!"

"30 enemy tanks!"

"Two down!"

"Thrown Track!"

The reports on the company frequency followed in quick succession, only Rosenkamp remained silent. The tanks of the 9th Company had run head-on into an ambush of the Canadians. The Shermans with the strange rings around their hulls had taken advantageous firing positions down on the beach. Partly, only their turrets peeked out from between the hilly dunes, which now gave a decent fire. Sand whirled up between the tanks of the 9th Company; a massive wall of dust and dirt built up. The Germans also fired, but their Panzer III and captured tanks with Panzer III turrets had to come closer to cause damage.

The firefight took place at a distance of about 700 meters. The 9th Company tank men landed several hits, but they only scratched the Canadians. More Panzers III went up in flames. The panzers of the 9th dropped like flies. Münster cursed furiously.

"Hold position... ahem... fire... return fire!" Rosenkamp's voice was fragile.

"Damn it, Rita, we got to get out of here!" Engelmann yelled into the throat microphone. Through his observation slit he noticed the obvious: a strong enemy superiority, which dismantled his company by every trick in the book.

"Hold position!" Rosenkamp ranted.

Engelmann cursed obscenely.

"What's happening over there?" the captain then asked. His command tank stood at the foot of the dune in the shadow of the other tanks and did not move. Reports of the platoon leaders about enemy strength and own losses mixed with each other.

"Take us back," Engelmann demanded one more time. Rosenkamp's answer came timidly: "We must... fire... return."

Engelmann punched the steel of the copula with his fist so hard that a terrible pain stroke through his wrist. He bit his teeth together, then Anna 3 was suddenly enveloped in a huge ball of flame. The turret jumped out of its basket and flew, spinning on its own axis, through the air for meters. No one could have survived that. Anna 2 also received another hit in the right tread. The track shattered, single parts whirled around.

"Report... report the situation again," Rosenkamp stuttered. In the meantime, the captain had climbed out of the turret of his command tank and spread a map over it. Wildly gesticulating, he looked alternately at the map and up to his panzers, of which over a fifth had already been

183

destroyed.

"I... I..." Rosenkamp stuttered.

"Himmel, Arsch und Zwirn!" Engelmann roared and pressed the headphones against his ears. The Shermans were still shooting on all cylinders. A burning Panzer III wreck rolled backwards down the dune while hectic men jumped out of the hatches. The flames were licking at them, but the tankers were already burning.

"Anna to all!" Engelmann suddenly hammered into the company frequency. "We have to get out of the ambush immediately!" The lieutenant snorted. "Berta, discharge smoke grenades and keep an eye on the enemy! Claudia, reverse immediately! Reverse slope position. Rita 1, break out to the left, but stay in cover behind the crest of the dune. Prepare for flanking attack on the left!"

"What...?" Rosenkamp shouted, then he stopped himself. After that the radio circuit was spared his voice. The captain disappeared in his tank and closed the hatch. The other platoon leaders, on the other hand, confirmed Engelmann's instructions and immediately set to work.

The smoke grenade dischargers of the tanks of the 2nd Platoon, which were mounted in racks on the turret sides, fired, spitting white smoke. Within seconds the panzers were completely wrapped in a white, opaque cloud. At the same time Engelmann let his platoon as well as the 3rd back down the dune. The tanks jerked and disappeared from the crest of the dune, thus disappearing from the Shermans' field of fire. AP rounds chased after the German tanks, detonated on the dune or hissed over it. Fountains of sand splashed. Meanwhile, the tanks of Rita 1 started moving. Only Rosenkamp's tank remained motionless behind the dune. Rita 1 went to the left and lay in wait at a distance of 300 meters from the rest of the company.

The panzers of Engelmann's platoon and 3rd Platoon came to a halt at the foot of the dune. Engelmann stared intently at the top of the dune in front of him. The company's position behind the slope was ideal.

The tank men held their breath, all eyes were on the dune's crest. The tension in the air was like a blanket

184

covering the Germans – it seemed sensible, touchable. Engelmann's heart was beating in his throat. Would the Canadians step into the trap or would they not? That was what mattered now, because they couldn't defeat the superior Shermans any other way than by such a ruse. Engelmann, however, was confident that there were young soldiers in the Canadian tanks, whose first combat mission was this one, and who would therefore roll straight into any ambush with waving flags.

Indeed, Engelmann thought he could hear the squeaking of moving tracks through the roar of distant fighting. Still the sound was more a hunch which the wind carried over the dune. Engelmann opened the lid of his hatch, stretched out of the copula and listened. Sounds of tracks, indeed! They came closer.

The lieutenant looked up to the top of the dune to the right, where 2nd Platoon was still embedded in a hood of white smoke.

"Berta, it's Anna," he whispered into his microphone in a strained voice.

"Listening," Kranz's voice returned.

"You too, now back behind the hilltop in reverse slope position. One of you stay with the enemy, play dead!"

"Reverse slope position; dead man. Copy that!"

Dead man was a dangerous undertaking: The tankers shut down engine and electronics and ceased to give a sign of life. This way the tank men sometimes managed to make the enemy think their tin can had been shot. Not every destroyed tank burned or burst apart, sometimes only a hole the size of a fist could be seen on the outside of a bullet with armor-piercing ammunition, while inside the hit had made a mess.

Two of the three remaining Berta tanks rolled backwards down the slope in the lifting smoke.

Perfect timing, Engelmann was pleased. The enemy should think the Germans have retreated.

When the smoke had completely disappeared, only the commander's tank of Berta was left behind, lying like dead on the crest of the dune, next to two burning tanks.

185

Engelmann nodded approvingly at the single combat vehicle. So Kranz had taken over the dead man affair himself.

Minutes went by. The sounds of the enemy tanks' tracks were unmistakable. They were close! All of the German panzer cannons were aimed at the top of the dune. Suddenly Berta 1 broke the radio silence: "They're here!" Kranz whispered. "All of them."

Twelve steely bodies, gleaming in the sunshine, pushed themselves nearly simultaneously over the top of the dune. Engelmann commanded to shoot. The surprise fire of the company came like out of one barrel and destroyed all twelve enemy Shermans. The Anti-tank rounds cut through their hulls, blew up their turrets; turned them into hell-hot flaming cauldrons. Burning, the wrecks slid down the dune.

"Enemy stops," Berta 1 reported, before its engine started up again. Immediately the tank aligned its barrel and fired, but Engelmann couldn't see whether Kranz's gunner had hit. The lieutenant tapped against the throat microphone, then hissed: "Rita 1, now! Flank on the left! Rest of you wait for my signal."

The platoon leaders confirmed, at the same time the panzers of Rita 1 started pushing forward. Mechanically groaning they struggled up the dune, reached the top and disappeared behind it. Immediately, cannon fire started thundering. Even Berta 1, around which sand fountains were rising, roared away.

"They're after us," the company sergeant major squeaked over the radio.

"We're coming!" Engelmann assured and gave the order to attack to all sub-units.

"Fire at will!"

The panzers of Anna, Berta and Claudia let their engines roar. The heavy machines pulled themselves up the dune; the tracks were rattling horribly under the effort. The tanks reached the top of the dune, rushed beyond it and crashed into the sloping sand behind it. Engelmann stretched himself out of the commander's hatch. He froze briefly at the sight of the enemy's gigantic fleet, which seemed to occupy the entire English Channel. Up to the horizon, to all sides the water was covered with ships of all sizes and shapes. Now it was necessary to interlock with the enemy, to ask him for a close-quarters dance and not to let go of him. Only in this way they could escape the deadly naval guns.

Engelmann spotted several Sherman's that had been eliminated. Rita 1 had apparently caught the enemy on the wrong foot. The rest of the Canadian tanks had fallen into the trap immediately afterwards: They had aligned their front ends with Rita 1 and were engaged in a fierce firefight with the four German panzers. The tank of the company sergeant major was already lying there with a thrown track. Engelmann and his tank front, on the other hand, rushed directly into the enemy's vulnerable flank, which is why the subsequent tank battle was only of short duration.

In the end the 9th Company had destroyed the enemy down to the last tank. 30 times Canadian scrap metal lined the dunes in this section. Grenadiers, who followed Engelmann on his push through the dunes, collected two dozen Canadians who had surrendered and led them away.

The way to the beach was thus free; the way to the enemy landing crafts. Engelmann didn't allow himself and the men a break. They had to move on! Concentrations of troops standing around were deadly in view of the enemy air superiority. And now that they were already on the coast, the invasion troops had to be crushed before more could go ashore. So move on!

After all: Engelmann had imagined the enemy air superiority to be worse. According to the reports of Africa veterans he had spoken to, he had imagined with shuddering horror that the sky would be darkened by countless fighter bombers that would attack anything that moved and displayed an Iron Cross. But so far the lieutenant had not spotted a single enemy aircraft.

Suddenly, propeller engines roared in the distance. Engelmann looked up into the sky with a petrified expression.

"Thank you, Lord," he whispered sarcastically. From the

East, four enemy fighter bombers approached at high speed. The fuselages of the planes were enclosed by two tail booms each, with a propeller rotating on each tip. White stars were visible on their flanks. In no time, the planes were in the airspace above the 9th Company, flying out to the sea and describing a long curve. They went on an attack course!

"They are double-tailed devils," Ludwig remarked in awe. African veterans told terrifying things about these things, which were used against air and ground targets and had inflicted terrible losses on the German Africa Corps.

Engelmann's body tensed up by itself. The planes had completed their curve, now they raced from the sea towards the panzers of 9th Company. The birds of steel lowered their beaks. They headed straight for Quasimodo.

"Shit," Münster murmured in a thin voice.

"Shit" was the perfect word to describe this situation. The entire company was in a state of shock. All eyes were on the approaching fighter bombers. Anticipating the very end, the tank men clenched themselves in the steel of their panzers, squeezed their eyes shut and gritted their teeth. The enemy strafers dashed inevitably towards them.

Suddenly a deafening bang swept across the beach. Several arrow-shaped objects hissed through the airspace. They were so fast that Engelmann couldn't tell how many were out there. They were faster than anything the lieutenant had ever seen – much faster. They flew through the air like lightning. The sound of ship's guns was heard. The American fighter bombers scattered, emitting billows of smoke and catching fire. The arrow machines shot off in the blink of an eye and disappeared. Only the deep rumble of their strange engines continued to fill the air. Four enemy fighter-bombers crashed into the sea in front of 9th Company.

"What was that?" Münster gasped for breath.

"If I only knew," Engelmann whispered and wiped his sweaty forehead. "But they seem to belong to us, which I appreciate a lot right now." The lieutenant struggled for a weak smile.

188

"Maybe one of those jet fighters, or whatever they're called?" Stendal pondered, not getting attention for his uttered thought.

Sparks flew over Quasimodo's steel skin. In front between the dunes muzzle flashes came up. Engelmann let himself fall back onto his seat and closed the hatch. The fight went on.

German infantry advanced under the protection of 9th Company against the enemy invasion troops who had entrenched themselves in the dunes. Another steel storm swept over the coast of Northern France, sawing up bodies, taking lives, making men scream like children.

For hours both sides fought over every sand hill, every hollow, every bush. The tanks attacked the approaching landing crafts with direct fire.

Slowly the British and Canadians, who had dug in here, had to give way; they retreated and soon had wet feet. On the unprotected beach they died by hundreds or surrendered. To the left of the 9th, Stollwerk's tanks had already reached the water, to the right the 10th was still stuck in the dunes, fighting for a few meters of land. The Abteilung had sent the 11th into battle as reinforcement. The invasion troops had no chance. I Abteilung, fully equipped with Panzer V Panther, sealed off the battlefield to the South.

At some point, Engelmann had the company move to the right. He was relieved to see that the enemy ship artillery still did not intervene in the fighting. Probably the Allies were afraid to fire on their own men, because they certainly did not have a complete picture of the situation after the first, hectic hours of the invasion. Nevertheless, Engelmann wanted to keep his panzers in motion and to retreat as quickly as possible to the cover of the hinterland after the work was done.

Again sparks flew over the steel of his tanks. The enemy had set up machine gun nests in the dunes, but Anti-tank shock troops were also lying in wait, which were very dangerous with their portable PIAT anti-tank weapons. Several projectiles of this AT-arm hissed just past the panzers of the 9th, one of them smashed the engine of a vehicle of 2nd Platoon. The British and Canadians, however, fought a losing battle. From all sides they were confronted by tanks and infantry. Meter by meter the Germans retook the dunes.

Engelmann had Quasimodo dash over a small hill. The tank worked its way up the slope, rumbled over the crest and surprised two Canadians who were crouched behind it in a hastily dug hole. Ludwig and Stendal's hands immediately reached for their submachine guns, but Münster stopped them from firing: "Let it be," he rejoiced. "Rolling is better than shooting!" With burning eyes, he stepped on the gas and headed for the Canadians' cover hole. Trembling, the men stood there, dropped their weapons and froze in the face of the strange tank. But Münster wasn't interested in that. Even before Engelmann could say anything, the staff sergeant placed the tank's hull over the hole. The two Canadians had ducked away at the last moment, but that was of no use to them; their last hour had come.

Münster made his tank rotate to the left and right in fast, jerky movements, so that the tracks poured a torrent of sand into the hole with every quarter turn. The men's cries sounded muffled through the steel hull.

"I'll bury those dogs alive," Münster proclaimed, tugging at his levers.

"Hans!" Engelmann ranted angrily. "Stop at once!"

"Oh, Sepp. Nobody's gonna miss them!" Münster hung on the levers full of hate.

"I order you to stop at once!" Engelmann yelled suddenly. Münster was startled and immediately backed away from the steering. He had seldom heard his commander like that.

"Go back," he hissed. "Release the men."

Münster obeyed with a pinched face. Creaking, Quasimodo pulled back, and released two shivering, totally disturbed Canadians, who were covered all over with sand. Engelmann opened the hatch, pulled out his pistol and aimed at the two soldiers whose home was 20,000 kilometers away from this beach. The Canadians raised

190

their hands. They trembled as if they had been connected to a high voltage battery. Engelmann lowered his gun – and the prisoners took a deep breath. Occasional fire and shouts still echoed over the dunes from everywhere, but the battle was over – at least here, on this small stretch of beach.

Bénouville, France, June 6th, 1944

During the afternoon, the forces of the 744 Infantry Regiment came into the area of the double bridges. Now there were considerable defensive forces: At the Canal Bridge, 4th Company, a machine gun unit, had established itself with 12 heavy MGs and six mortars, while the equivalent of this company in the form of the 12th had taken up position over at Ranville. Two other infantry companies, the 3rd and 5th of the regiment, were standing by just a few miles away.

Meanwhile the grenadiers of the crazy captain transported the wounded, the fallen, the POWs as well as the spoils of war to assembly points hastily set up by the division.

Schneider had gotten a rebuke from Fritze for his brisk pursuit against the English, as well as a lot of praise for his behavior. Fritze worked according to the doctrine "Success proves you right". And success proved Schneider right. Schneider had spent the rest of the day working with Huber on a new defense concept for the bridge, repositioning their weapons and making provisional repairs to their emplacements. Of course, the Brandenburgers also had to bring their dead to the trucks that were ready for transport. This had been the most difficult task of the day for everyone. Not to mention the fact that a fallen soldier in the war was not only motionless and cold, but also torn apart, ripped open and disfigured.

The sun had passed its zenith and sank back to the

191

horizon. A humid evening air filled the scenery. It was cool, with occasional drops falling from the clouds, but the weather on June 6th had remained much more stable and calm than the German Weather Service had predicted. This showed the disadvantageous circumstance that the Germans had no worldwide network of weather stations due to the war situation.

From the North, the noise of gunfire and impacts could be heard. Allied planes roared through the air as they pleased, but they left the German guards of the double bridges alone. The risk of damaging or even destroying one of the crossings seemed too great for the enemy.

Schneider had to swallow every time the sky above him seemed to scream from the roar of the bomber and fighter plane rotors. Not once he had spotted a German airman in the firmament. On this day the British and American bomber units had continuously flown into the hinterland. The German flak had continuously launched explosive rounds into the formations of the enemy planes, mostly without bringing anything down from the sky.

The British paratroopers had not been seen since last night, and now that German forces were at the bridges in battalion strength, they would have a hard time if they really should dare to attack again. No, Schneider was sure that the British would not try it again. Instead, they would probably head North to make their way through to the British landing zone. For Schneider, this seemed to be their only chance.

In the twilight the master sergeant strolled over the Canal Bridge to the Eastern bank, where there was still a lot of activity. The men of the machine gun company fortified their nests with sandbags and excavated soil. Landsers were running around, carrying ammunition, rations and tools. Higher ranks shouted orders. The men set up defense positions on the two outer banks – the West bank at Bénouville and the East bank at Ranville, while the Brandenburgers took over the inwardly facing sides of the river. Strictly speaking, only the division commander could order the Brandenburgers to change positions, but Fritze had approved the deployment in agreement with the regimental commander. Thus the much better trained Brandenburgers could be deployed as emergency forces at both crossings. Schneider nevertheless had an uneasy feeling in his stomach at the sight of the approaching grenadiers. All of them were elderly or men who would have been rejected as unfit according to the pre-war criteria. In addition, their level of training did not seem to be very high, and Schneider did not even want to think about combat experience. Some of them had served in the Great War, but the majority had not seen combat, at least not since the beginning of the 1920s.

"Hooray," he thought with an ironic undertone.

Schneider finally reached the West bank of the opening bridge. The road pointed to the West, where it ended up as a T-junction after a good kilometer. From there you could follow it North to the coast; or South to Caen. There were two multi-storey buildings to the left and right of the road, which the Germans had completely occupied. On the right side there was a large walled garden in front of the two houses, in which some deciduous trees offered protection against airplanes. Behind that garden a low house stood – now abandoned as well. The remaining three tanks of Czech design had taken up position in the garden and destroyed all vegetation with their tracks. Now one of the engines roared up, as the tank men were checking the readiness of their panzer. Shouts were heard. A tractor unit dragged the wrecked tank away.

Suddenly Schneider heard the shrill voice of the crazy captain who seemed to call him. He followed the sound and saw the captain standing over at his command post waving. The master sergeant started to move, while the officer put his pipe between his teeth.

"Ah, Feldwebel!" the captain snorted. Thanks to the pipe, he sounded as if he had a blanket in his mouth. "You're a windy little fellow, aren't you?"

Schneider did not know exactly what that meant. He nodded carefully.

"I have to show you something. I want to know what you

193

think."

"All right, Herr Hauptmann."

"Ha! Let's go to the map!" The captain lifted up his index finger, thinking for a moment. Then he turned on his heel and disappeared into the house.

"Come on, come on!" Schneider heard the voice of the captain. He followed him and wondered what would happen.

The captain trudged into one of the rear rooms, where several soldiers were busy with maps, radios and other command and control equipment. He snatched a large map of the situation from a master sergeant, who, according to Schneider's judgment, had not only taken part in the Great War, but also in the Franco-Prussian War... and in the battle against Napoleon. The captain immediately spread the map out on the ground. Already he squatted over the paper and pulled a pencil out of his field blouse.

"Come on, come on, Feldwebel!" The captain was happy like a little child and pulled Schneider down to him. "Crouching down and having fun! Ha! Reading the map on the floor. It's like in combat!" He smiled broadly. Schneider nodded and had his own thoughts on the matter. Suddenly the eyes of the officer became fixed, the captain seemed to have drifted off into a completely different world. "...as in battle..." he whispered before the officer shook himself. Suddenly his eyes sparkled. He looked at Schneider and dragged on his pipe. The smell of tobacco filled the room.

"Have I told you about the fourth battle of Flanders, Feldwebel?"

"Another time, please."

"Yes, you're right. The duty! Duty calls! Or: Call of Duty. That would be one splendid title for a book, wouldn't it? Or for a game?"

"A game, Sir?"

"Like a board game... argh, never mind! Take a look at my map."

And Schneider looked at the map that showed Northern France. The captain began to outline the enemy's areas of assembly while he was speaking: "Let us concentrate on the

194

English. They landed in three places – here – here – and here."

Three large circles framed the coastal area from North of Bénouville down to Bayeux. The first circle was located North and Northwest of the double bridges and covered a coastal strip of about eight kilometers from Saint-Aubin-sur-Mer to Ouistreham at the mouth of the Orne. The second circle intersected with the first at Saint-Aubin-sur-Mer and continued westward from there, where its line reached Courseulles-sur-Mer. The third circle followed directly from there and included the coastal village of Ver-sur-Mer in the West.

"I thought Canadians had landed at Ver-sur-Mer," Schneider remarked.

"They're just British people who speak French." The captain made a spinning movement with his hand, then he continued: "Just North of us, the Englishman has taken the beach and partly entered the hinterland."

The enemy was less than four kilometers from Bénouville.

"It seems that the landings of the island monkeys have failed, except at the mouth of the Orne. That's where the Englishman is biting. In addition, there are reports of enemy paratroopers just behind all landing sections, which now seem to move down towards the mouth of the Orne. And then this." The captain drew a big circle around the area East of the Orne, from Merville on the coast to Varaville in the East and Ranville on the Orne. Then, once again, he tapped with the pencil on the area just circled.

"In this area, it appears that an entire division of the British have descended. In addition, there are fights all over the place. The enemy is holding Merville and is making life difficult for our flak boys at Troarn."

Schneider had attentively followed the captain's presentation. Now he nodded slowly and frowned. So far he had made up his picture of the situation from single reports and rumors. Even Fritze had only given the platoon a quick briefing, perhaps he didn't know more himself. Schneider had assumed that the enemy landing had also taken place East of the Orne. That this was not the case was

195

a completely new insight for him. The captain looked up and stared at the master sergeant with his friendly eyes.

"Well? What do you think?" the officer asked. Schneider was not surprised that the captain seriously asked for his opinion. Instead he said: "Two things. First: The way I see it, the enemy paratroopers are trapped East of the Orne. I guess their plan was to take the double bridges here and then join with the landing troops and push to the East. Second: That inevitably means, things are going to get messy here soon."

"Aha!" the captain said with a sharp eye and dragged on his pipe. "I noticed that, Feldwebel! Go on."

"We have to assume that the Tommies on the beach and the paratroopers are in contact. Therefore, the paratroopers in the East probably know that the British landing in those sections is not quite working out."

"So they will try to break through," the captain concluded. He nodded with a serious expression.

"I think so. A division of elite fighters would certainly strengthen the British landing head sufficiently. And with each day that the enemy bites on the coast continuously, he can land more troops. In other words, with each passing day, it becomes less likely to throw the British back into the water. Not to mention the Yanks."

"Yes... the Yanks... they're more successful, I hear. They landed on the Cotentin. If the enemies get their claws into the North of France, then it will be exactly what old Rommel had always been warning about. Little Feldwebel, I'm going to tell you something that will upset you, but it's true: If the enemy invasion succeeds, we will have lost this war."

Schneider raised one eyebrow. Of course he was aware of this fact, but he was surprised how rationally the captain was sometimes able to judge a situation. "They won't be able to swim through the river with a whole division and probably heavy equipment," the officer continued to think, "especially since they would have to go through a river and a canal..."

"The crossings at Caen are also out of question. We have a

whole regiment of panzers there..." Schneider remarked.

"Which the island monkeys will certainly know, because their reconnaissance seems to be really excellent."

Schneider expressed the final thought that occupied both of them at that moment: "This leaves only one possible place for the breakthrough: our double bridges. Who will try the breakthrough? The forces on the beach to the North of us or the paratroopers division? Either way, we'll be in trouble here again." Schneider scratched his chin, when suddenly, as if inspired by a fresh spirit of life, the captain jumped up and raised his index finger. "Ha!" he shouted. "Let the Tommies try it! I have 81 good men here who were just waiting to beat the Englishman again!"

Anyway, Schneider thought, but then he realized that they had ignored one possibility: Perhaps the attack would happen simultaneously from both sides.

Bern, Switzerland, June 6th, 1944

The very last rays of the sunshine just made its way into the small bedroom. A fine tingling in Taylor's pelvis woke him up gently. The first thing he saw were Luise's wonderful eyes, deep and dark as the universe. He was naked, and so was she. He was laying on his back and she had her soft body over his. With light, rhythmic movements, she stimulated his penis, which she had taken inside of her.

Is there a better way to be awakened? Thomas mused. Their lips touched, their tongues entwined like lovers.

She bit her lower lip, squealed in delight. Her breathing picked up speed, as did the circling movement she made with her abdomen.

Thomas dug his fingers into the sheet. He didn't really want to yet; the act of love had caught him completely unprepared. He gritted his teeth, took Luise by both arms

197

and reared up when he reached the climax.

Immediately he sank back into the soft lap of the bed. Luise's abdomen now rested motionlessly on him. She wiped a wisp of hair from her face.

"Did you like that?" she asked bluntly.

"Yes," Thomas moaned reluctantly. He was embarrassed by his early orgasm.

Luise lifted herself from him and released his penis. Thomas noticed that she hadn't put a condom on him. He stared at his shiny penis, unsure what to think of it. Luise let herself fall into the sheets beside him. She wrapped her arms and legs around his body like a constrictor.

She had been more than happy since the news of the Allied invasion of France had reached Switzerland around noon. After the attack on Italy had not brought the success she had hoped for, she firmly believed that the military presence of the Western forces on French soil would finally break the Germans' neck.

"I liked it too," she whispered with her eyes closed.

Thomas grabbed for cigarettes and matches lying on the floor next to the bed and put two cigarettes in his mouth. He lit them both and gave her one of them. She had a deep drag. Spicy tobacco scent filled the bedroom.

Thomas' thoughts were racing. Bad presentiments tormented his mind. He also had to think incessantly about the enemy landing, which had been hovering over the German Reich like a sword of Damocles for months. And now the Allied troops were there – with brute force, as it could be heard in Switzerland.

Luise's voice ripped him from his thoughts, "You know what really pisses me off?"

"What is it?"

"My boss says I have a signature like a little kid... and laughs every time he gets his hands on something signed by me."

"Norton should shut the fuck up," Thomas whispered, dragging on his cigarette.

But Luise did not stop: "But I think he is right. My signature looks like a child's scrawl."

198

She got up and walked naked through the apartment. Thomas' gaze followed her attentively. Luise disappeared briefly in the kitchen, then she returned with a pencil and a piece of paper. "Of course, it's not the same with a crayon instead of a fountain pen," she murmured after sitting back on the bed. With a waving hand movement she put her signature on the paper and presented the result to Thomas.

Norton's right, he thought when he saw the writing. "No, not at all," he proclaimed. "I don't know what Norton means. Looks perfectly all right."

"You really think so?"

In disbelief she stared at her signature, a creation consisting of three scrawled lines.

"Let me see your signature," she finally asked, and gave him a pen and paper.

Thomas looked at her questioningly. *What women always have on their minds!*

When he saw in her eyes that she would not rest until he had signed on the paper, he took the writing utensils with a sigh and put his signature right under hers. With a bored look he put the paper in her hand.

Luise looked at it with a furrowed brow.

Suddenly an unrestrained heat flooded Thomas' body. Sweat was coming out of his pores. Within seconds his armpits were wet and sticky. Holding his breath, his eyes fluttering, he looked at the paper in Luise's hands.

"Thomas Taylor" he had scribbled on it clearly and legibly. Luise looked at the signature for a long time. Thomas did not dare to move. Very slowly she raised her head, turned to Thomas, looked at him with shivering eyes. Waiting, Thomas looked at her face, but couldn't read anything from it - didn't know what she felt at that moment.

Suddenly her mouth opened: "Your signature looks much more professional than mine!" She smiled softly and fluttered her eyes. "But it can't be deciphered."

Boldly she stuck out her tongue at him. Both grinned, but Thomas had to force himself to do it. His heart was pounding in his chest. Luise, on the other hand, stretched out yawning, stood up and dodged into the kitchen.

199

The tension fell off Thomas like a concrete-heavy skin. He sank back into the pillow, exhaled strongly and rubbed his face with both hands.

Lucky me, he moaned in his mind. *I was very lucky!*

He remained lying down for a moment, staring at the ceiling and taking the last drag from his cigarette. Then he rose halfway up and grabbed an ashtray that stood beside the bed on a small night table. Thomas pressed the cigarette butt against the bottom of the ashtray, where it bent in half, tore and the embers finally died. Satisfied, Thomas turned around – and froze!

"You lying bastard," Luise whispered in a broken voice. She stood in the door frame – naked – and had her left hand placed over her breasts. Her right had clenched into a fist that enclosed the pistol, which Thomas had kept hidden in the double-bottomed bag.

"Luise..." he pleaded.

"Shut up!" Screaming, she cut him short, pointing the gun threateningly at his chest. Tears were rolling down her cheeks.

Slowly Thomas raised his hands, made gestures of confusion and appeasement, but he saw in her eyes that there was nothing left to appease. Luise had uncovered him. In her face, anger, determination and fear were struggling together. Her mouth was moving like an earthquake. Her eyelids twitched.

"I have often wondered," her voice trembled, "and I found your gun a while ago." She cried. "But I did not want to believe it! I should have known better, stupid girl..."

"Luise, please..."

"Shut up!" She jerked her gun in a threatening move, then burst into tears. "Please tell me you're not German," she sobbed.

Thomas was silent – with this he seemed to tell her more than with every word on this earth. He looked at her. He felt his heart burst in his chest. A whirlwind ripped through his intestines. An infinite pain, worse than a thousand bullets could have produced, chased through his body and made him feel like vomiting. But he remained steadfast. He had realized that his time with Luise was over now.

Carefully he sat up in bed.

"What now, Luise?" he asked in a clear voice. "Are you going to shoot me?"

Streams of tears swept down her cheeks like a flood. She bared her breasts and held her hand over her mouth instead, but she could not hide her emotional involvement. Her features flickered like a flame in the wind. She held the gun tightly, her index finger resting on the trigger, but she did not answer his question. Thomas realized that his P08 was unlocked; and it was loaded too, because he had always kept it loaded. But he now also realized that Luise was very uncertain. Attacking him with the gun seemed to be an absolute kneejerk reaction. Luise's eyeballs flew from right to left in search of a way out. Taylor realized he had to take the offensive. This was his only chance.

He got out of bed.

"Stay where you are!" she yelled at him. But Taylor ignored her order. With gentle steps he approached her. His bare feet made slapping noises on the tiled floor.

"Luise, listen to me," he said to her, "put the gun down before something bad happens." He spoke calmly, in a subdued voice, like a father worried about his child. Luise screamed in between, cried, howled, waved the gun around in front of him. She took a step back and slammed the back of her head against the wood of the door frame. But it was too late anyway, Taylor had worked his way up to her at arm's length.

With a careful movement he put his hand on the arm that held the pistol.

"Luise, look at me," he whispered. She did. Her water blue eyes, flooded with tears, reflected all her fear. Longing lay in them – longing for peace, for calm, for fearlessness. Her eyes became soft, her tense muscles loosened a little. Taylor's hand gently stroked her arm. He smiled slightly and nodded at her. She nodded back with her mouth open.

"Give me the gun," he whispered. She nodded again. Thick teardrops rolled down her cheeks. Slowly, Taylor's hand slid down her arm, passing her wrist. He could feel her pulse for a split second. It was fast and strong like a pneumatic hammer. Then Taylor's fingers reached the cold steel of the Pistole Parabellum and stroked the round knob of the knee joint slide.

His hand reached for the gun.

"No!" she suddenly screamed, as if awakened from a trance. She retreated and stumbled halfway into the kitchen. Taylor rushed after her. His hand was stuck to the gun. She tugged at the gun. So did he. They struggled for the piece of metal inside of which eight deadly messengers waited for their release. She screamed like a banshee, tugged the gun back and forth. He never let go of the piece. Louder and more insistent, he talked to her. But his words bounced off her. Finally, his hand gripped the entire weapon, including her fingers between them. That was the moment! Taylor grabbed with all his might. She screamed out in pain as he drew the gun towards him. Once again she struggled desperately against him, but Taylor was too strong.

When the shot went off, the bullet shattered out of the barrel with a drum-crackling noise. Taylor's hearing turned into a single, painful ringing. Moments later, he noticed the second pain spreading through his body. The bullet had gone clean through his shoulder. Dark, thick blood came out of a tiny hole. Behind Taylor, fine splashes of blood covered the floor. A torn and cracked wound gaped in his upper body. His face distorted into a silent scream as he threatened to lose his footing. With both hands he clung to the door frame. Luise's eyes were opened, her whole body went into shock. The P08 hit the tiles with a rattling sound. Taylor quickly recovered and bounced back to a firm footing. His right hand automatically clenched to his fist before he smashed Luise's face with it. Her delicate nasal bone burst like a vase under the force of the impact. Blood came out and splashed over her cheeks and against Taylor. She went down screaming and grabbed her face with both hands.

"Fucking Jewish bitch!" Taylor hissed, then froze. Their eyes met.

202

What did I just say? he asked himself, shocked at his own words. Well, many years of education in the Third Reich made it possible!

But Taylor had no more time to think about it. He had to go! He grabbed the gun off the floor, grabbed his clothes and was out of the door in seconds. He had to run. Get out of Switzerland!

West of Courseulles-sur-Mer, France, June 6th, 1944

According to first information from captured soldiers, the Western forces had given aliases to the relevant beach sections. At the entrance to the Cotentin peninsula, between Pouppeville and Quinéville, the Americans had landed at the so-called Utah section – and had been able to form a large landing head. There the situation was most dangerous, and the Germans had to push quickly into the occupied territories before the enemy could land people and material on a larger scale. If the Allied superiority were to sweep onto the mainland, it would be over.

Southeast of it, near Colleville-sur-Mer, was another American section, which they called Omaha. The situation in this area seemed to be under control and the landing could be considered a failure. The GIs were trapped on the beach in German defensive fire, nailed to the sand and unable to move forward or backward. East of Omaha, near Caen and to the West of it, were the British-Canadian landing sites called Gold, Juno and Sword. The Panzer Regiment 2 had driven a razor-thin wedge into the British-Canadian troops at Juno. Now the regiment stood in the dunes West of Courseulles-sur-Mer and behind Banville. Engelmann had opened his hatch and looked out over the sea, which was sloshing back and forth like drunk. Long rays of the sinking sun broke on the Channel swaying in the

203

current. Sunken landing crafts protruded from the shallow water at the shore, shot-up boats were stuck in the sand. Floating tanks, which were now scrap metal, lined the shores and dunes. Some landsers carried the corpses together into large heaps, while two officers of the local defense forces of the emplacements 29-31 searched the killed officers for useful command resources. Engelmann had to think of Nitz, but the old master sergeant proved to be a tough bastard. He had come to the military hospital with minor injuries, but had promised Engelmann to be back soon; even though the lieutenant did not want to hear about it. He insisted that Nitz should finally recover properly. The master sergeant would not listen to him after all.

The enemy had moved away on both sides, had set off to the East and West, where he probably tried to reach the nearest landing zones. At Gold, in the West of Engelmann's position, as well as at Sword in the East, things looked much darker for the Wehrmacht. There the enemy had conquered the beach, had eliminated the German resistance nests and threatened to move into the hinterland. In the Gold section, the enemy troops had pushed directly into the border between the 716th Infantry Division and the 5th Jäger Division. The soldiers of both units had to give way after fierce fighting, often because in the combined fire of the enemy fighter-bombers and naval guns no position could be held anymore.

The 16th Panzer Division, however, was nothing to sneeze at; their units started to march. While the focus of their counterattack against the enemy forces was led just North of Caen, the regiment was to move westward to begin the pursuit of the escaping British and Canadians.

Hurry up, Engelmann raved in his mind and looked at his watch. The company had been standing still between the dunes for 30 minutes; meanwhile the other units had long since started moving. Speed was the only way the Germans could still ensure their survival. If Rommel had already ordered the 16th Panzer Division defenseless to the coast, only steady movement could help them to avoid enemy air

204

and artillery attacks.

Once again Engelmann looked at his watch. Another minute had already passed.

What is Rosenkamp doing? The lieutenant seethed. *How can that guy leave us standing here in the dunes?* The platoons of 9th Company had already received their orders. All platoon leaders, all commanders were briefed and waited for the marching orders.

What's this guy waiting for? Engelmann exhaled scornfully, while his heart was beating.

The narrow-faced driver of the captain fought his way through the dunes on the double. Gasping, he reached Quasimodo.

"Herr Leutnant?"

Engelmann sighed, "Yes?"

"Herr Hauptmann sent me. He sent word that he's out of action and wants you to take over the company." The private looked up at the lieutenant with his eyes narrowed.

"Out of action? How?"

"Herr Hauptmann is not feeling well."

"He isn't feeling well? HE..." Engelmann swallowed his anger before it could burst out of him. After all, the private was not to blame.

"Understood." Engelmann lowered himself into his tank and sat on the commander's seat.

"Stendal?" he said into his throat microphone.

"Yes?"

"Put the company on my ear."

Stendal operated switches and knobs, then he knocked Engelmann against the boot. The lieutenant rearranged his throat microphone and gave his instructions to the company: "Anna to all."

"Berta here."

"Claudia here."

"Rita 1 listening." The company sergeant major officially had taken over Rita 1.

"Anna here. Rita down. Repeat: Rita down. I'm taking over. Company will march off immediately according to orders. I'm taking the lead."

The tanks of the 9th started to move. Their destination was the enemy, who at that very second was rushing into the French mainland. He had to be defeated; here, on this day, on the beach, before he could find all his strength. Otherwise the German Reich would lose the war. While Münster revved up the tank engine, which filled the tin can with the light vibrations so familiar to the tankers, Engelmann thought for a split second of Elly's letter, which he still carried unopened in his pocket.

To Lieutenant Josef Engelmann, May 18th, 1944
F.P. 34444

My Sepp!

We miss you very much, but we're fine. Gudrun runs around all day that it's exhausting to keep up! And she laughs a lot and repeats things parrot-fashion. It's great how well she's doing! And I think that everything else is also slowly taking a turn for the better. I have been reading the Deutsche Allgemeine Zeitung every day since you left, so that I don't miss anything, if something happens. But it doesn't! In the East the war has come to a standstill, in Italy our front is standing solid, in the West the Americans apparently don't want to come any more either. The day before yesterday there was an article about the current situation in the newspaper, which made me feel very confident, because I am very worried about you and Gudrun, that something will happen because of the bombs. So I am glad to hear something positive. The article said that the war could be over soon, because the Russians don't want to go on and don't see any success in the East, and the Americans don't want to go on either. In Italy, we really gave them a hard time, so that they are now thinking about staying out of it completely, which I very much hope they will. Then England would be the only country in the world that wants to continue the war. But without Russia and the USA they can't do that. At least that's what the article said.

It also said that the invasion in France will not happen at all, because we have too many soldiers in France now. That's probably why all the plans have been cancelled and that's probably why the USA doesn't want anymore. Oh, Sepp, now I'm already talking politics, stupid girl, that's what happened! But wouldn't it be nice if I was right? If the war would just stop and all soldiers could go home? I wish it would turn out that way. Maybe you'll be home by Christmas, and I won't have to worry about you having to leave again!

In love
Elly

Berlin, Germany, June 7th, 1944

Reich Chancellor Erwin von Witzleben, whose face was marked by deep exhaustion, sat at the wide wooden table in his office together with his guest, the Japanese Ambassador Ōshima Hiroshi. From a white porcelain pot, placed over a tea light, rippling steam rose. The juicy, woody smell of green tea was in the air. Ōshima had always brought the tea that had been prepared according to the Ryokucha method to the increasingly frequent meetings with the Chancellor. Only in the summer of 1943 and in February of this year the ambassador had to go without the gift; the difficult supply situation made such luxury goods rare, even for the elite. Then the two gentlemen had had to make do with black tea and coffee, but that was fine, too. After all, they did not meet for green tea, but to find a common answer to the difficult situation of the Japanese and the German Empire. Von Witzleben was convinced from the beginning of his term of office that this war could only be won together with the Japanese. For this reason, he had been intensively engaged with the Eastern allies since the end of 1942 and

207

had already achieved some results together with Ōshima, a fervent supporter of the war. However, the negotiations were difficult and were additionally affected by the overall situation.

Germany and Japan were not exactly neighbors; there were about 20,000 kilometers of land and water between the two nations in enemy hands. Moreover, the Allies were excellent at spying, and the German Reich was only slowly catching up in this respect. Under Hitler, many reports of the Abwehr had not even made it through to the Führer for fear that they might upset him. But von Witzleben always had an open ear for Canaris' intelligence agency. In addition, the Chancellor had provided the Abwehr with extensive resources and competencies, which were primarily made available through the integration of the Reich Main Security Office of the SS into the Abwehr. The first results of such efforts have already been achieved: Thus, through the efforts of the secret service, the German navy learned that the Enigma code had been cracked by the enemy. They also learned about the American practice of reading Ōshimas dispatches. Von Witzleben was aware that only the tip of the iceberg of enemy spying activities had been uncovered, but the results could already be worked with – and above all it enabled the Japanese and the Germans to launch deceptions. The Chancellor tried to wipe away the fatigue that had struck him and made thinking difficult.

Ōshima, a chubby Japanese man in his mid-50s, brought the cup to his mouth and took a sip of tea. Von Witzleben looked nervously at his watch.

"I must point out once again that we can continue our conversation on another day, my good friend," Ōshima began in reasonable German. "It would not be a disgrace to postpone a diplomatic appointment in these difficult hours until the situation in France returns to normal." The ambassador looked at his opposite with a serious look, but the Chancellor smiled gently and replied: "My dear Hiroshi, I have generals who care about the war. Believe me, our meetings are too important to be delayed."

Ōshima seemed to agree with that. He lowered his head, took another sip from the cup and whispered, "Hai."

"So, my friend, how are the preparations going?" von Witzleben got straight to the point.

"The attack will proceed as planned."

"This is good news." But von Witzleben looked a little bit distressed, which did not go unnoticed by Ōshima.

"What is the matter with you, my friend?" he immediately asked.

"Oh Hiroshi, it's just the heavy burden of these days resting on my shoulders. Now, we urge you to fight again as your situation is difficult enough already."

Immediately Ōshima replied: "Erwin, that your thoughts are with my people, honors you and fills my chest with pride." Respectfully he lowered his head before continuing: "But do not burden your mind with such thoughts. These are difficult times for both of our people. We are surrounded by our enemies and they seek to destroy us."

In von Witzleben's mind the thought flashed up that it had been the Germans and Japanese who had brought war upon foreign peoples – who had done cruel things. But that no longer played a role. The Chancellor could not afford to look to the past, his attention was only on the future.

"The Emperor is very happy that your government is so open and trusting. Herr Adolf Hitler, I must say, unfortunately did not understand how cooperation can work, or he did not want it. I also think he did not trust my people. You, however, have proved to us that we have your trust. At your instigation, Heisenberg and his team went to Tokyo to work with our scientists on the new weapon. The Emperor sees this as an immense leap of faith, because in doing so the German Empire is giving away all the possibilities of this new technology from its hands and entrusting it to my people. In addition, you are letting the Japanese Empire share your rocket technology; the jet aircraft – you have given us your most powerful weapons for license construction. The Japanese Empire is deeply in debt to Germany, which the Emperor is trying to settle."

Von Witzleben had to think about this crazy uranium

project. Scientists going on and on about super weapons. This had nothing to do with reality, so it was easy for him to hand over this project to his ally.

"Believe me, Hiroshi, the technology transfer project was preceded by some struggles within my government. The idea of giving our most advanced technology to other countries is not appealing to many. But I see no other way to get through these difficult times – and I couldn't imagine it in better hands."

Von Witzleben trusted Ōshima, sometimes more than his own people. It seemed to him that he alone understood that Germany could not win this war on its own.

"Which you may be right about." Ōshima nodded and emptied his cup.

"Nevertheless, technology transfer is one thing. An additional war is something completely different," von Witzleben mused.

"True, but the Japanese people are willing to make this necessary sacrifice. You see, Erwin, one way or another it'll come to a war between us and them. Furthermore, the general staff has never given up on the dream of Siberia."

Von Witzleben agreed with dark eyes. He focused on his counterpart and spoke with puckered lips: "The sacrifice of your people against the Americans is already unparalleled. But this new war will cost the Japanese Empire just as dearly in human lives." The Chancellor sensed that he was about to talk himself into trouble in front of the ambassador, but the trust in his friend prevailed over diplomatic concerns.

"Then it will be that way," Ōshima declared soberly. When it came to battle and death, the Japanese had a completely different attitude than the Europeans. Von Witzleben also experienced this again and again in his conversations with Ōshima. "The Americans have inflicted bitter losses on us, I admit that. They have destroyed our fleets and destroyed our planes. The American arms industry is one devil's work when you consider how many battleships, how many planes and how many weapons it is able to spit out. Enough to serve two theaters of war

210

properly! This is why the fight against the Americans must be fought together. The Japanese Empire did well to change the focus of its armament from ships to tanks, because no matter how many boats we launch, the Americans have more and are crushing our fleets before they can go into open water. Therefore there can only be one remedy against these bastards: Entrenching in every strip of land we own and fighting to the last bullet. The English bootlickers want their colonies back? Then they will pay for every foot of it with lots of blood!" At times Ōshima talked himself into a rage. "We may have to bury our expansion plans for the time being, but we will not give way! We will bind the enemy in the Pacific for as long as it takes. Five years. Ten years! Three generations if we have to!"

Von Witzleben flinched. *Hopefully it will not take that long*, he prayed in his mind, but nevertheless he knew that the Japanese were tough guys, and he believed them capable of fighting this battle for so long.

"Doku kuwaba, sara made," Ōshima said in a grim mood.

"What does that mean?"

"If they shall take poison, then the whole plate." Ōshima grinned wildly.

"Very well," von Witzleben concluded, folding his hands in front of his face with a distorted smile. He had to remember that the armament of the Japanese tanks with German support had been an intelligent move. Germany's navy was not worth mentioning, and Japan's fleet had not recovered from the Battle of Midway. The enemy ruled the oceans, an undeniable fact. Therefore, the decisive battles had to be fought on land. In addition, Germany and Japan ran out of raw materials. The shortage of molybdenum already caused German tanks, which left the factories these days, to have only weakened armor. The lack of tungsten meant that new and very effective armor-piercing ammunition could not be produced. With the Japanese it was mainly the fuel that ran out. Also from this perspective, the planned attack was therefore an absolute necessity. Without Asia's large oil fields, the Imperial Japanese Army would soon be condemned to a standstill – as would the

211

Wehrmacht. The question was how much time was left for Japan. The American troops jumped from island to island. On many Pacific islands the US flag was already waving, others were cut off from supplies until the Japanese soldiers starved to death. The Allied war machinery approached the main Japanese islands almost inexorably. Month after month it gained ground. Time was running out for Japan.

"Always remember," Ōshima warned, "if one falls, all others stumble."

Von Witzleben's eyes narrowed. "It goes both ways," he remarked in a thin voice.

"Hai."

Aftermath

Roebuck's unit had taken up position in the dunes overlooking Utah Beach. They were preparing to march towards Sainte-Mère-Église.

"Body count!" the gunny yelled, and the Marines started counting. But Roebuck's gaze was glued to the edge of the beach. And what he saw there he liked extraordinarily well. What he saw was literally screaming, "We're going to kick the fuckin' Jerries' ass!"

A gigantic fleet lay in the catchment area of the beach. Tethered balloons hovered over hundreds of transport ships, which were stuck in the mudflats with open hatches. Tanks rolled out of them. Tanks as far as the eye could see! Hundreds, thousands were landing within the hour. Jeeps drove in between, guides shouted orders. Endless rows of soldiers marched into the hinterland. The liberation of Europe had begun. Germany had just lost the war.

Note from Tom Zola

Dear readers,

while the book itself was edited by some true English experts, I wrote this small note myself. Since English is not my mother tongue, this note contains some weird Germanized grammar and sentences for sure. I suggest you read it in a strong German accent ☺

I would like to take the chance to thank you for buying our book. The EK-2 Publishing Team put a lot of effort into the PANZERS series, especially was the translation one hell of a job. As said, we are glad to have real English experts on board (at this point I would like to gratefully thank Martina Wehr and Jill Marc Münstermann for their marvelous efforts and commitment!!!) Even for native speakers it is one heck of a task to work on a text that is full of technical terms and detailed military descriptions.

On the one hand you have ranks, German trivia and other national or regional specialties. Should we translate German nicknames like *Stuka* for the Junkers Ju 87 or should we leave it in its German form in the text? Almost from line to line we struggled with this very question and had to find a new answer to it each time.

When it comes to ranks, we did translate them to obtain a better reading experience, although in direct speech we sometimes kept original German or Russian ranks – that depends on the overall paragraph and how it would influence readability.

On the other hand, in the original text there are a lot of references to typical German trivia, which gave all of us a hard time translating them. Things like the military function of a "Kompanietruppführer" only exists in the German Army. There is no translation, no comparable function in other armed forces, and it even is very difficult to explain its meaning without a deep understanding of the functioning of the German military. So, what should we do

213

with such things? How should we translate the text in a way that its originality does not get lost, but that it is at the same time fully understandable in English? Believe me, finding that balance is no easy task! I hope we have gotten most things right!

Our overall goal was to provide a very unique reading experience for English readers. This text is written by a former German soldier (me), it focuses on a German perspective and is very technical in its details. I often find posts and articles on the Internet that are about Germany or the German Army, written by foreigners in English, hilariously mistaking our very special little German idiosyncrasies (no accusation meant, I would struggle similarly trying to understand a culture I am a total stranger to). Thus, I hope it is interesting for you to read something from Germany that really tries to translate these idiosyncrasies correctly into English. Nevertheless we tried everything to preserve a special German touch. That is why we sometimes left a German word or phrase in the text. At the same time, we tried to ensure that English readers can understand everything without using a dictionary or Wehrmacht textbook from time to time and that the whole thing stays readable.

Another thing we did in order to manage this balancing act is that we separated German words for better readability and understanding although they are not separated originally. We Germans are infamous for our very long words like Bundeswehrstrukturanpassungsgesetz or Donau-Dampfschifffahrtsgesellschaft. In English words are separated way more often to keep them short. Germans say Armeekorps, English folks say army group. So for example we made Panzer Korps out of Panzerkorps in the text hoping that this will help you to read the book without stumbling too often.

The PANZERS series consists of 12 books, and I promise in book 12 I provide a satisfying ending. No cliffhangers!

Additionally, EK-2 Publishing holds a bunch of other German military literature licenses that we really would love to introduce to English readers. So, stay tuned for more to come! And please give us feedback on what you think about this book, our project and the EK-2 Publishing idea of bringing military literature from the motherland of military to English readers. Also let us know how we can improve the reading experience for you and how we managed the thin red line between readability and originality of the text.

We love to hear from you!!

info@ek2-publishing.com

(I am connected to this email address and will personally read and answer your mails!)

In the following I provide some additional information: a glossary of all words and specialist terms you may have stumbled upon while reading, an overview of Wehrmacht ranks, German military formation sizes and abbreviations. Since I wrote those glossaries myself, too, I recommend you keep the German accent …

Glossary

76-millimeters divisional gun M1942: Soviet field gun that produced a unique sound while firing, which consisted of some kind of hissing, followed by the detonation boom. Therefore the Germans Wehrmacht soldiers called it "Ratsch Bumm".

Abwehr: German Military Intelligence Service

Acht-Acht: German infamous 8.8 centimeter Flak anti-aircraft and anti-tank gun. Acht-Acht is German meaning nothing less than eight-eight.

215

Afrika Korps: German expeditionary force in North Africa; it was sent to Libya to support the Italian Armed Forces in 1941, since the Italians were not able to defend what they had conquered from the British and desperately needed some backing. Hitler's favorite general Rommel was the Afrika Korps' commander. Over the years he gained some remarkable victories over the British, but after two years of fierce fighting ... two years, in which the Axis' capabilities to move supplies and reinforcements over the Mediterranean Sea constantly decreased due to an allied air superiority that grew stronger by the day, Rommel no longer stood a chance against his opponents. Finally the U.S.A. entered the war and invaded North Africa in November 1942. Hitler prohibited the Afrika Korps to retreat back to Europe or even to shorten the front line by conducting tactical retreats. Because of that nearly 300 000 Axis' soldiers became POWs, with thousands of tons of important war supplies and weapons getting lost as well when the Afrika Korps surrendered in May 1943, just months after the 6th Army had surrendered in Stalingrad.

In the PANZERS series von Witzleben allows the Afrika Korps to retreat just in time. Axis' forces abandon North Africa by the end of 1942, saving hundreds of thousands of soldiers and important war material.

Ami: German word for US-Americans (short form for Amerikaner = American; plural Amis). It is not always meant as a derogatory term, but can also be meant in a neutral or even positive way. It very much depends on who uses this term in which context.

AOK: Short for Armeeoberkommando, meaning Army Higher Command. In this case army stands for the formation of an army, not the military branch

Arabic numerals vs. Roman numerals in German military formation names: I decided to keep Arabic as well as Roman numerals in the translation, therefore you will find a 1st Squad, but an II Abteilung. Normally all battalions and corpses have Roman numerals, the rest Arabic ones.

Armee Abteilung: More or less equivalent to an army. The Germans of WW2 really had confusing manners to organize and name their military formations.

Assault Gun: Fighting Vehicle intended to accompany and support infantry formations. Assault guns were equipped with a tank-like main gun in order to combat enemy strongholds or fortified positions to clear the way for the infantry. An assault gun had no rotatable turret, but a casemate. This made them very interesting especially for Germany, because they could be produced faster and at lower material costs than proper combat tanks.

Assistant machine gunner: In the Wehrmacht you usually had three soldiers to handle one MG: a gunner and two assistants. The first assistant carried the spare barrel as well as some small tools for cleaning and maintaining the weapon plus extra belted ammunition in boxes. The second assistant carried even more ammunition around. In German the three guys are called: MG-1, MG-2 and MG-3.

Ausführung: German word for variant. Panzer IV Ausführung F means that it is the F variant of that very tank. The Wehrmacht improved their tanks continuously, and gave each major improvement a new letter.

Avanti: German slur name for Italians.

Babushka: Russian word for "grandmother" or "elderly woman"

Balkenkreuz: Well-known black cross on white background that has been used by every all-German armed force ever since and also before the first German unification by the Prussian military.

Battle of Stalingrad: The battle of Stalingrad is often seen as the crucial turning point of the war between the Third Reich and the Soviet Union. For the first time the Wehrmacht suffered an overwhelming defeat, when the 6th Army was encircled in the city of Stalingrad and had to surrender after it had withstood numerous Soviet attacks, a bitterly cold Russian winter and a lack of supplies and food due to the encirclement. Hitler was obsessed with the desire to conquer the city with the name of his opponent on it – Stalin – and thus didn't listen to his generals, who thought of Stalingrad as a place without great strategic use.

In reality the battle took place between August 1942 and February 1943. The encirclement of the Axis' forces was completed by the end of November 1942. The Axis' powers lost around 300 000 men. After surrendering 108 000 members of the 6th Army became POWs, of which only 6 000 survivors returned to Germany after the war.

In the PANZERS series von Witzleben listens to his generals and withdraws all troops from the city of Stalingrad in time. Thus the encirclement never happens.

Beck Doctrines: A set of orders issued by President of the Reich Ludwig Beck that demands a human treatment of POWs and civilians in occupied territories. The doctrines are an invention of me, neither did they exist in reality, nor was Beck ever President of the Reich (but the main protagonists of the 20 July plot, of whom Beck was one, wanted him for that very position).

Bohemian Private: In German it is "Böhmischer Gefreiter", a mocking nickname for Hitler, which was used by German officers to highlight that Hitler never got promoted beyond the rank of private in World War I. Besides basic training Hitler never attended any kind of military education. It is said that president Hindenburg first came up with this nickname. He did not like Hitler and wrongfully believed he was from the Braunau district in Bohemia, not Braunau am Inn in Austria.

Brandenburgers: German military special force (first assigned to Abwehr, on 1st April 1943 alleged to the Wehrmacht) that consists of many foreign soldiers in order to conduct covert operations behind enemy lines. The name "Brandenburgers" refers to their garrison in Brandenburg an der Havel (near Berlin).

Büchsenlicht: Büchse = tin can (also archaic for a rifle); Licht = light; having Büchsenlicht means that there is enough daylight for aiming and shooting.

Churchill tank: Heavy British infantry tank, with about 40 tons it was one of the heaviest allied tanks of the war. Through the Lend-Lease policy it saw action on the Russian side, too. Its full name is Tank, Infantry, Mk IV (A22) Churchill.

Clubfoot: Refers to Joseph Goebbels, a high-ranking Nazi politician, one of Hitler's most important companions and Reich Minister of Propaganda (Secretary of Propaganda). He coined names like "Vergeltungswaffe" (= weapon of revenge) for the A4 ballistic missile and glorified a total war, meaning all Germans – men, women, elderly and children alike – had to contribute to "final victory". He is one of the reasons why German children, wounded and old men had to fight at the front lines during the last years of the Third Reich. "Clubfoot" refers to the fact that Goebbels suffered from a deformed right foot.

Commissar Order: An order issued by the Wehrmacht's high command before the start of the invasion of the USSR that demanded to shoot any Soviet political commissar, who had been captured. In May 1942 the order was canceled after multiple complaints from officers, many of them pointing out that it made the enemy fight until last man standing instead of surrendering to German troops. In the Nuremberg Trials the Commissar Order was used as evidence for the barbaric nature of the German war campaign.

Comrade: This was a hard one for us. In the German military the term "Kamerad" is commonly used to address fellow soldiers, at the same time communists and social democrats call themselves "Genosse" in German. In English there only is this one word "comrade", and it often has a communistic touch. I guess an US-soldier would not call his fellow soldiers "comrade"? Since the word "Kamerad" is very, very common in the German military we decided to translate it with "comrade", but do not intend a communistic meaning in a German military context.

Comrade Lace-up: A nickname German soldiers invented for Austrian soldiers during World War 1 ("Kamerad Schnürrschuh")

Danke: Thank you in German

Deutsche Allgemeine Zeitung: German newspaper that was de jure independent but de facto had to apply the standards defined by the Reich Ministry of Public Enlightenment and Propaganda

East-Battalions: Units that consisted of voluntaries from German-occupied regions of the Soviet Union and soviet POWs

Eastern Front Medal: Awarded to all axis soldiers who served in the winter campaign of 1941/1942.

Edi: Eduard Born's nickname

Einheits-PKW: A family of 3 types of military vehicles (light, medium and heavy) that featured all-wheel drive and were supposed to replace civilian cars the Reichswehr had procured before. The name translates to Standard Passenger Car.

Eiserner Gustav: German nickname for Iljushin Il-2 "Shturmovik" (= iron Gustav). Gustav is a German male first name.

EK 1: See Iron Cross

Elfriede: Nickname, Engelmann gave his Panzer IV. Elfriede was a common German female given name during that time.

Endsieg: Refers to the final victory over all enemies.

Éxgüsee: Swiss German for "sorry". By the way German dialects can be very peculiar. Bavarian, Austrian, Low German or other variations of German are hard to understand even for Germans, who are not from that particular region. Especially Swiss German is one not easy to understand variation of German, so often when a Swiss is interviewed on German TV subtitles are added. For interregional communication matters most Germans stick to High German, which is understood in all German-speaking areas.

E-series tanks: Series of German tank designs, which should replace the tanks in use. Among those concepts was yet another super heavy tank (E-100) that was developed parallelly to the Maus tank.

Fat Pig: Refers to Hermann Göring, one of Nazi Germany's most influential party members. As the commander of the Luftwaffe he was responsible for a series of failures. He also was infamous for being drug-addicted and generally out of touch with reality. Moreover he coveted military decorations and therefore made sure that he was awarded with every medal available despite the fact that he did not do anything to earn it. Göring was the highest-ranking Nazi leader living long enough to testify in the Nuremberg Trials. He committed suicide to avoid being executed by the Allies.

Faustpatrone ordnance device: See Knocker

Ferdinand: Massive German tank destroyer that later was improved and renamed to "Elefant" (= Elephant, while Ferdinand is a German given name – to be precise, it is Ferdinand Porsches given name, founder of Porsche and one of the design engineers of this steely monster). Today the Porsche AG is known for building sports cars.

Like many other very progressive German weaponry developed during the war, the Ferdinand suffered from Hitler personally intervening to alter design and production details. Hitler always thought to be cleverer than his engineers and experts. E.g. he forced the Aircraft constructor Messerschmitt to equip its jet-powered fighter aircraft Me 262 as a dive bomber, while it was constructed to be a fighter and while the Luftwaffe already had lost air superiority at all theaters of war (so you need fighters to regain air superiority before you can even think about bombers). Same story with the Ferdinand: Hitler desperately wanted the Ferdinand to take part in the battle of Kursk, so he demanded its mass production on the basis of prototypes that hadn't been tested at all. German soldiers had to catch up on those tests during live action! Despite its enormous fire power, the Ferdinand proofed to be full of mechanical flaws, which led to lots of total losses. Due to a lack of any secondary weapon and its nearly non-movable main gun the Ferdinand was a death trap for its crew in close combat. Another problem was the Ferdinand's weight of around 65 tons. A lot of bridges and streets were to weak or narrow to survive one of these monsters passing by, let alone a whole battalion if them.

Nevertheless the heavy tank destroyer proofed to be a proper defense weapon that could kill a T-34 frontally at a distance of more than two miles.

Its full name is Panzerjäger Tiger (P) "Ferdinand" (or "Elefant") Sd.Kfz. 184. Sd.Kfz stands for "Sonderkraftfahrzeug" meaning "special purpose vehicle".

Flak: German for AA-gun

Frau: Mrs.

Front: May refer to a Soviet military formation equal to an army group

Führer: Do I really have to lose any word about the most infamous German Austrian? (By the way, it is "Führer", not "Fuhrer". If you cannot find the "ü" on your keyboard, you can use "ue" as replacement).

Gestapo: Acronym for "Geheime Staatspolizei" (= Secret State Police), a police force that mainly pursued political enemies of the state.

Gröfaz: Mocking nickname for Adolf Hitler. It is an acronym for "greatest commander of all times" (= größter Feldherr aller Zeiten) and was involuntarily coined by Field Marshal Keitel. During the battle of France Keitel, who was known for being servile towards Hitler, hailed him by saying: "My Führer, you are the greatest commander of all times!" It quickly became a winged word among German soldiers – and finally the acronym was born.

Grüessech: Swiss salute

Grüss Gott: Salute that one often hears in southern Germany and Austria. It literally means "Greetings to the Lord".

Guten Abend: Good evening

Heeresgruppe: Army group. The Wehrmacht wasn't very consistent in naming their army groups. Sometime letters were used, sometimes names of locations or cardinal directions. To continue the madness high command frequently renamed their army groups. In this book "Heeresgruppe Mitte" refers to the center of the Eastern

Front (= Army Group Center), "Heeresgruppe Süd" refers to the southern section (= Army Group South).

Heimat: A less patriotic, more dreamy word than Vaterland (= fatherland) to address one's home country.

Heinkel He 177 Greif: German long-range heavy bomber. "Greif" means griffin. The Germans soon coined the nickname "Fliegendes Reichsfeuerzeug" (= flying Reich lighter) due to the fact that the He 177's engines tended to catch fire while the bomber was in the air.

Henschel Hs 127: German ground-attack aircraft designed and produced mainly by Henschel. Due to its capabilities to destroy tanks German soldiers coined the nickname "can opener".

Herein: German word for "come in". Hey, by the end of this book you will be a real German expert!

Herr: Mister (German soldiers address sex AND rank, meaning they would say "Mister sergeant" instead of "sergeant")

Herr General: In the German military, it does not matter which of the general ranks a general inhabits, he is always addressed by "Herr General". It is the same in the US military I guess.

Himmel, Arsch und Zwirn: German curse. Literally it means: Sky, ass and yarn.

Hiwi: Abbreviation of the German word "Hilfswilliger", which literally means "someone who is willing to help". The term describes (mostly) Russian volunteers who served as auxiliary forces for the Third Reich. As many military terms from the two world wars also "Hiwi" has deeply embedded itself into the German language. A lot of Germans use this word today to describe unskilled workers without even knowing anything about its origin.

HQ platoon leader: In German "Kompanietruppführer" refers to a special NCO, who exists in every company. The HQ platoon leader is best described as being the company commander's right hand.

IIs, IIIs, IVs: In German you sometimes would say "Zweier" (= a twoer), when talking about a Panzer II for example. We tried our best to transfer this mannerism into English.

Iljushin Il-2 "Shturmovik": Very effective Russian dive bomber, high in numbers on the Eastern Front and a very dangerous tank hunter. There are reports of groups of Shturmoviks having destroyed numerous panzers within minutes. Stalin loved this very aircraft and personally supervised its production. The German nickname is "Eiserner Gustav" (= iron Gustav). Gustav is a German male given name.

Iron Cross: German war decoration restored by Hitler in 1939. It had been issued by Prussia during earlier military conflicts but in WW2 it was available to all German soldiers. There were three different tiers: Iron Cross (= Eisernes Kreuz) – 2nd class and 1st class –, Knight's Cross of the Iron Cross (= Ritterkreuz des Eisernen Kreuzes) – Knight's Cross without any features, Knight's Cross with Oak Leaves, Knight's Cross with Oak Leaves and Swords, Knight's Cross with Oak Leaves, Swords and Diamond and Knight's Cross with Golden Oak Leaves, Swords and Diamond –, and Grand Cross of the Iron Cross (= Großkreuz des Eisernen Kreuzes) – one without additional features and one called Star of the Grand Cross. By the way the German abbreviation for the Iron Cross 2nd class is EK2, alright?

Island monkeys: German slur for the British (= Inselaffen)

Itaka: German slur word for Italian soldier. It is an abbreviation for "Italienischer Kamerad" meaning Italian comrade.

Ivan: As English people give us Germans nicknames like "Fritz", "Kraut" or "Jerry", we also come up with nicknames for most nationalities. Ivan (actually it is "Iwan" in German) was a commonly used nickname for Russians during both World Wars.

Jawohl: A submissive substitute for "yes" (= "ja"), which is widely used in the German military, but also in daily life

Jäger: German military term that historically refers to light infantry but is of much boarder usage today. In the Bundeswehr for example the term Jäger has more or less replaced the term infantry. Jäger is also a rank in some military specializations.

K98k: Also Mauser 98k or Gewehr 98k (Gewehr = rifle). The K98k was the German standard infantry weapon during World War 2. The second k stands for "kurz", meaning it is a shorter version of the original rifle that already had been used in World War 1. Since it is a short version, it is correctly called carbine instead of rifle -- the first k stands for "Karabiner", which is the German word for carbine.

Kama: Refers to the Kama tank school, a secret training facility for German tank crews in the Soviet Union. After World War 1 the German Armed Forces (then called "Reichswehr") were restricted to 100 000 men because of the treaty of Versailles. Also no tanks and other heavy weaponry was permitted. The Germans sought for other ways to build up an own tank force, so they came to an agreement with the Soviet Union over secretly training German tankers at Kama. The German-Soviet cooperation ended with the rise of the Nazis to power in Germany.

Kampfgruppe: Combat formation that often was set up temporarily. Kampfgruppen had no defined size, some were of the size of a company, others were as big as a corps.

Kaputt: German word for "broken"; at one Point in the story Pappendorf uses this word describing a dead soldier. This means that he reduces the dead man to an object, since "kaputt" is only used for objects.

Katyusha: Soviet multiple rocket launcher. The Katyushas were feared by all German soldiers for its highly destructive salvos. Because of the piercing firing sound, the Germans coined the nickname "Stalin's organ" (= Stalinorgel).

Kinon glas: Special bulletproof glass produced by German manufacturer Glas- und Spiegelmanufaktur N. Kinon that was used for German panzer's eye slits. The well-known Tiger scene in the movie Saving Private Ryan would not have happened this way in reality, because one could not just stick one's firearm into the eye slit of a German panzer in order to kill its crew.

Knight's Cross: See Iron Cross

Knocker: German nickname for the Faustpatrone ordance device, the ancestor of the well-known Panzerfaust. German soldiers coined the nickname due to the bad penetrating power of this weapon. Often it just knocked at an enemy tank instead of penetrating its armor because its warhead simply bounced off instead of exploding.

Kolkhoz: Also collective farm; alleged cooperatively organized farming firm. Kolkhozes were one important component of the Soviet farming sector. In the eyes of the Soviet ideology they were a counter-concept to private family farms as well as to feudal serfdom. In reality kolkhozes were pools of slavery and inequality.

Kubelwagen: German military light vehicle (in German it is Kübelwagen)

KV-2: Specs: Armor plating of up to 110-millimeters thickness, a 152-millimeters howitzer as main gun; ate Tiger tanks for breakfast … if its crew managed to move that heavy son of a bitch into a firing position in the first place.

Lager: Short for "Konzentrationslager" = concentration camp

Landser: German slang for a grunt

Larisch embroidery: Old Prussian embroidery forming a certain pattern that was used for collar patches of generals

Leopard: German light tank project that was abandoned in 1943. The full name is VK1602 Leopard.

Luftwaffe: German Air Force

Marder II: German tank destroyer based on a Panzer II chassis

Maus tank: Very heavy German tank that never left development phase. It weighed 188 tons and was armed with a 128-millimeter Pak cannon. Maximum speed was around 20 Kilometers per hour on a street and far less in terrain. By the end of the war two prototypes were build. The correct name is Panzerkampfwagen VIII Maus (= "tank combat vehicle VIII Mouse").

Meat Mount: This is my try of translating the German colloquial military term "Fleischlafette", which means that one soldier functions as a mount for an MG by putting it on his shoulder while a second one fires the weapon.

MG 34: German machine gun that was used by the infantry as well as by tankers as a secondary armament.

And have you ever noticed that some stormtroopers in the original Star Wars movie from 1977 carry nearly unmodified MG 34s around?

MG 42: German machine gun that features an incredible rate of fire of up to 1 500 rounds per minute (that's 25 per second!). It is also called "Hitler's buzzsaw", because a fire burst literally could cut someone in two halves. Its successor, the MG 3, is still in use in nowadays German Armed Forces (Bundeswehr).

Millimeter/centimeter/meter/kilometer: Since Germans make use of the metric system you will find some of those measuring units within direct speeches. Within the text we mostly transferred distance information into yards, miles or feet.

Modi: Swiss-German word for girl

Moin: Means: good morning. "Moin" or "Moin, Moin" are part of several dialects found in Northern Germany. Pay this region a visit and you will hear these greetings very often and actually at EVERY time of the day.

MP 40: German submachine gun, in service from 1938 to 1945

NCO corps: This was a hard one to translate, since we did not find any similar concept in any English armed force. The NCO corps (= Unteroffizierskorps) refers to the entity of German noncommissioned officers. It is nor organized not powerful by any means, but more of an abstract concept of thought.

Officer corps: Same thing as in NCO corps. The officer corps (= Offizierkorps) refers to the entity of German officers. It is nor organized not powerful by any means, but more of an abstract concept of thought.

Pak: German word for anti-tank gun (= abbreviation for "Panzerabwehrkanone")

Panje Wagon: Small-framed two-axle buck car, which was pulled one-piece by a horse. Typical vehicle for eastern European and Soviet agronomies.

Panther: Many experts consider the Panther to be the best German WW2 tank. Why, you may ask, when the Wehrmacht also had steel beasts like the Tiger II or the Ferdinand at hand? Well, firepower is not everything. One also should consider mobility, production costs and how difficult it is to operate the tank as well as maintain and repair it on the battlefield. While the hugest German tanks like the Tiger II suffered from technical shortcomings, the Panther was a well-balanced mix of many important variables. Also it featured a sloped armor shape that could withstand direct hits very well. Since the Panther tank development was rushed and Hitler personally demanded some nonsensical changes the tank finally also suffered from some minor shortcomings, nevertheless it proofed to be an effective combat vehicle after all.

Panzer 38(t): Or Panzerkampfwagen 38(t) was a small Czechoslovak tank adopted by the Wehrmacht after it occupied Czechoslovakia. The 38(t) was no match for Russian medium tanks like the T-34 and was only adopted, because the German Armed Forces desperately needed anything with an engine in order to increase the degree of motorization of their troops.

Whenever you find a letter in brackets within the name of a German tank, it is a hint at its foreign origin. For example, French tanks were given an (f), Czechoslovak tanks an (t). Since the 38(t) was riveted instead of welded, each hit endangered the crew, even if the round did not penetrate the armor. Often the rivets sprung out because of the energy set free by the hit. They then became lethal projectiles to the tankers.

Panzer II: Although being a small and by the end of the 1930s outdated tank, the Panzer II was the backbone of the German Army during the first years of the war due to a lack of heavier tanks in sufficient numbers. With its two-Centimeter cannon it only could knock at Russian tanks like the T-34, but never penetrate their armor. The full name is Panzerkampfwagen II (= tank combat vehicle II).

Panzer III: Medium German tank. Actually the correct name is Panzerkampfwagen III (= tank combat vehicle III). Production was stopped in 1943 due to the fact that the Panzer III then was totally outdated. Even in 1941, when the invasion of Russia started, this panzer wasn't a real match for most medium Soviet tanks anymore.

Panzer IV: Very common German medium tank. Actually the correct name is Panzerkampfwagen IV (= tank combat vehicle IV). I know, I know … in video games and movies it is all about the Tiger tank, but in reality an Allied or Russian soldier rather saw a Panzer IV than a Tiger. Just compare the numbers: Germany produced around 8 500 Panzer IVs of all variants, but only 1350 Tiger tanks.

Panzergrenadier: Motorized/mechanized infantry (don't mess with these guys!)

Panzerjäger I: First German tank destroyer. It featured an 4.7-centimeters gun. The name literally translates with "Tank Hunter 1".

Papa: Daddy

Penalty area: Soccer term for that rectangular area directly in front of each soccer goal. When a rival striker enters your team's penalty area, he or she impends to score a goal against you. By the way, soccer is an enhanced, more civilized version of that weird game called "American Football" – just in case you wondered ;)

Piefke: Austrian nickname for Germans, often meant in a denigrating manner

Plan Wahlen: A plan that was developed by Swiss Federal Council Wahlen in order to ensure food supplies for the Swiss population in case of an embargo or even an attack of the Axis powers. Since Hitler had started to occupy all neighboring nations he considered to be German anyway, a German attack on Switzerland felt very real for the Swiss. Because of the war they suffered supply shortages and mobilized their army. They even suffered casualties from dogfights with misled German and Allied bombers, because Swiss fighter planes attacked each and every military aircraft that entered their airspace (later they often "overlooked" airspace violations by allied planes though). Switzerland also captured and imprisoned a good number of German and Allied pilots, who crash-landed on their soil.

Since the war raging in most parts of Europe influenced the Swiss, too, they finally came up with the Plan Wahlen in 1940 in order to increase Swiss sustenance. Therefore every piece of land was used as farmland, e.g. crops were cultivated on football fields and in public parks.

I think, the situation of Switzerland during the war is a very interesting and yet quiet unknown aspect of the war. I therefore used the Taylor episode to explore it.

Potato Masher: Nickname for German stick hand grenades which look alike a potato masher a lot

Order of Michael the Brave: Highest Rumanian military decoration that was rewarded to some German soldiers, since Rumania was one of Germany's allies until August 1944.

Ratte tank: 1 000 tons tank concept, called land cruiser or landship. Ratte should feature more than ten guns of different calibers and a crew of over 40 men. The project never saw prototype status. Ratte means rat.

Reichsbahn: German national railway (Deutsche Reichsbahn)

Reichsheini: Mocking nickname for Heinrich Himmler (refers to his function as "Reichsführer SS" (= Reich Leader SS) in combination with an alteration of his first name. At the same time "Heini" is a German offensive term used for stupid people.

Reichskanzler: Chancellor of the German Reich

SA: Short form for "Sturmabteilung" (literally: storm detachment); it had been the Nazi Party's original paramilitary organization until it was disempowered by the SS in 1934.

Scheisse: German for "Crap". Actually it is spelled "Scheiße" with an "ß", but since this letter is unknown in the English language and since it is pronounced very much like "ss", we altered it this way so that you do not mistake it for a "b".
Same thing holds true for the characters Claasen and Weiss. In the original German text both are written with an "ß".

Scho-Ka-Kola: Bitter-sweet chocolate with a lot of caffeine in it

Sd.Kfz. 234: Family of German armored cars

Sepp: Short form of Josef, nickname for Engelmann

Sherman Tank (M4): Medium US-tank that was produced in very large numbers (nearly 50 000 were built between 1942 and 1945) and was used by most allied forces. Through the Lend-Lease program the tank also saw action on the Eastern Front. Its big advantage over all German panzers was its main gun stabilizer, which allowed for precise shooting while driving. German tankers were not allowed to shoot while driving due to Wehrmacht regulations. Because of the missing stabilizers it would have been a waste of ammunition anyway. The name of this US-tank refers to American Civil War general William Tecumseh Sherman.

Let's compare the dimensions: The Third Reich's overall tank production added up to around 50 000 between the pre-war phase and 1945 (all models and their variants like the 38 (t) Hetzer together, so: Panzer Is, IIs, IIIs, IVs, Panthers, Tigers, 38(t)s, Tiger IIs and Ferdinands/Elefants combined)!

Sicherheitsdienst: Intelligence service of the SS

Sir: Obviously Germans do not say "Sir", but that was the closest thing we could do to substitute a polite form that exists in the German language. There is no match for that in the English language: In German parts of a sentence changes when using the polite form. If one asks for a light in German, one would say "Hast du Feuer?" to a friend, but "Haben Sie Feuer?" to a stranger or any person one have not agreed with to leave away the polite form yet. During the Second World War the German polite form was commonly spread, in very conservative families children had to use the polite form to address their parents and even some couples used it among themselves. Today the polite form slowly is vanishing. Some companies like Ikea even addresses customers informally in the first place – something that was an absolute no-go 50 years ago.

In this one scene where the Colonel argues with First Lieutenant Haus he gets upset, because Haus does not say "Sir" (once more: difficult to translate). In the Wehrmacht a superior was addressed with "Herr" plus his rank, in the Waffen SS the "Herr" was left out; a soldier was addressed only by his rank like it is common in armed forces of English-speaking countries. Also one would leave the "Herr" out when one wants to disparage the one addressed, like Papendorf often does when calling Berning "Unteroffizier" instead of "Herr Unteroffizier".

SS: Abbreviation of "Schutzstaffel" (= Protection Squadron). The SS was a paramilitary Nazi-organization, led by Heinrich Himmler. Since the SS operated the death camps, had the Gestapo under their roof as well as had their own military force (Waffen SS) that competed with the Wehrmacht it is not easy to outline their primary task during the era of the Third Reich. Maybe the SS is best described as some sort of general Nazi instrument of terror against all inner and outer enemies.

Stavka: High command of the Red Army

Struwwelpeter: Infamous German bedtime kid's book that features ten very violent stories of people, who suffer under the disastrous consequences of their misbehavior. Need an Example? One story features a boy, who sucks his thumbs until a tailor appears cutting the boy's thumbs off with a huge scissor. The book definitely promises fun for the whole family!
(Nowadays it is not read out to kids anymore, but even I, who grew up in the 90s, had to listen to that crap). In the U.S.A. the book is also known under the title "Slovenly Peter".

Stahlhelm: German helmet with its distinctive coal scuttle shape, as Wikipedia puts it. The literal translation would be steel helmet.

Stuka: An acronym for a dive bomber in general (= "Sturzkampfbomber"), but often refers to that one German dive bomber you may know: the Junkers Ju 87.

Sturm: Among other things Sturm is an Austrian vocabulary for a Federweisser, which is a wine-like beverage made from grape must.

Sturmgeschütz: German term for assault gun

Tank killer: Tanks specifically designed to combat enemy tanks. Often tank destroyers rely on massive firepower and capable armor (the latter is achieved by a non-rotatable turret that allows for thicker frontal armor). Also called tank hunter or tank destroyer. The German term is "Jagdpanzer", which literally means hunting tank.

T-34: Medium Russian tank that really frightened German tankers when it first showed up in 1941. First the T-34 was superior to all existing German tanks (with the exception of Panzer IV variant F that was equipped with a longer cannon and thicker armor). The T-34 was also available in huge numbers really quick. During the war the Soviet Union produced more than 35 000 T-34 plus more than 29 000 of the enhanced T-34/85 model! Remember the Sherman tank? So the production of only these two tanks outnumbered the overall German combat tank production by a factor of more than two!

T-34/85: Enhanced T-34 with a better main gun (85-millimeters cannon) and better armor. It also featured a fifth crew member, thus the tank commander could concentrate on commanding his vehicle rather than have to aim and shoot at the same time.

T-70: Light Soviet tank that weighted less than 10 tons. Although it was a small tank that featured a 45-millimeters main gun, one should not underestimate the T-70. There are reports of them destroying Panthers and other medium or heavy German panzers.

Tiger tank: Heavy German combat tank, also known as Tiger I that featured a variant of the accurate and high-powered 88-millimeters anti-aircraft cannon "Acht-Acht". The correct name is Panzerkampfwagen VI Tiger (= tank combat vehicle VI Tiger).

Tin can: During World War 2 some German soldiers called tanks tin can (= Büchse), so we thought it would be nice to keep that expression in the translation as well.

SU-122: Soviet assault gun that carried a 122-millimeters main gun, which was capable of destroying even heavy German tanks from a fair distance.

Vaterland: Fatherland

VK4502(P): Heavy tank project by Porsche that never got beyond drawing board status despite some turrets, which were produced by Krupp and later mounted on Tiger II tanks.

Volksempfänger: Range of radio receivers developed on the request of Propaganda Minister Goebbels to make us of the new medium in order to spread his propaganda. It literally translates with "people's receiver" and was an affordable device for most Germans.

Völkischer Beobachter: Newspaper of the NSDAP that was full of propaganda and agitation against minorities and enemy warring parties

Waffen SS: Waffen = arms; it was the armed wing of the Nazi Party's SS organization, which was a paramilitary organization itself.

Waidmannsheil: German hunters use this call to wish good luck ("Waidmann" is an antique German word for hunter, "Heil" means well-being). As many hunting terms, Waidmannsheil made its way into German military language.

Wound Badge: German decoration for wounded soldiers or those, who suffered frostbites. The wound badge was awarded in three stages: black for being wounded once or

twice, silver for the third and fourth wound, gold thereafter.
US equivalent: Purple Heart.

Zampolit: Political commissar; an officer responsible for political indoctrination in the Red Army

Wehrmacht ranks (Army)

All military branches have their own ranks, even the medical service.

Rank	US equivalent
Anwärter	Candidate (NCO or officer)
Soldat (or Schütze, Kanonier, Pionier, Funker, Reiter, Jäger, Grenadier … depends on the branch of service)	Private
Obersoldat (Oberschütze, Oberkanonier …)	Private First Class
Gefreiter	Lance Corporal
Obergefreiter	Senior Lance Corporal
Stabsgefreiter	Corporal
Unteroffizier	Sergeant
Fahnenjunker	Ensign
Unterfeldwebel/ Unterwachtmeister (Wachtmeister only in cavalry and artillery)	Staff Sergeant
Feldwebel/ Wachtmeister	Master Sergeant
Oberfeldwebel/ Oberwachtmeister	Master Sergeant
Oberfähnrich	Ensign First Class
Stabsfeldwebel/ Stabswachtmeister	Sergeant Major
Hauptfeldwebel	This is not a rank, but an NCO function

	responsible for personnel and order within a company
Leutnant	Second Lieutenant
Oberleutnant	First Lieutenant
Hauptmann/Rittmeister (Rittmeister only in cavalry and artillery)	Captain
Major	Major
Oberstleutnant	Lieutenant Colonel
Oberst	Colonel
Generalmajor	Major General
Generalleutnant	Lieutenant General
General der ... (depends on the branch of service: - Infanterie (Infantry) - Kavallerie (Cavalry) - Artillerie (Artillery) - Panzertruppe (Tank troops) - Pioniere (Engineers) - Gebirgstruppe (Mountain Troops) - Nachrichtentruppe (Signal Troops)	General (four-star)
Generaloberst	Colonel General
Generalfeldmarschall	Field Marshal

Check out this German military fiction book

At the beginning of November 1944, the 28th US Infantry Division attacks the village of Schmidt in the Hurtgen Forest with three regiments. What follows is one of the bloodiest battles of the Western Front.

German veteran and military fiction author Stefan Köhler depicts the battles for Schmidt from a German as well as an American perspective and shows how close friendship and enmity lie together in the madness of drumfire. He catapults the reader right into the bitter struggle for a few ruins, while tank tracks grind and the wounded roar.

"Brotherly Battle in the Hurtgen Forest" is thrilling from the first to the last page, leaving the reader with a thick lump in his throat - guaranteed!

Published by EK-2 Publishing GmbH
Friedensstraße 12
47228 Duisburg
Germany
Registry court: Duisburg, Germany
Registry court ID: HRB 30321
Chief Executive Officer: Monika Münstermann

E-Mail: info@ek2-publishing.com

Cover art: Peter Ashford
Author: Tom Zola
Translated from German by Martina Wehr
English translation edited by Jill Marc Münstermann
Proofreading: Jill marc Münstermann
German Editor: Lanz Martell
Innerbook: Jill Marc Münstermann

Paperback ISBN: 978-3-96403-093-1
Kindle ISBN: 978-3-96403-094-8
2nd Edition, December 2020